THE SECRETS WE KEEP

J. Lipsky

Thank you to Kaylee for her unwavering love and support for this project. To Kimbie, thanks for taking a chance with your photo.

A special thanks to Paul and Rhys, my happy place, and to Gavin, a wonderful son who pushed me to finish what I started.

CONTENTS

PROLOGUE

Grayson

SECRETS. They may be abstract in nature, but we treat them as tangible possessions, holding them, trading them, and often guarding them as though priceless, and as treasured as the Arc of the Covenant. Most people aren't very good at keeping them - not in a true or complete sense. They tend to reveal small parts of it, like peeling the skin from a piece of fruit, allowing a glimpse of the flesh beneath, but leaving the core a mystery. Me? I'm a master of keeping secrets - from my family, my friends, and well.....everyone. I don't always like it, but it's an occupational hazard.

But more impressive than my ability to keep secrets is my talent in getting others to reveal theirs. At the risk of sounding immodest, it's a gift. Really. There are any number of skills and characteristics one must possess in order to do this well - knowledge in psychology and reading body language, intelligence, charm, charisma, salesmanship, and sometimes when necessary, the physicality to exert intimidation and brute force. Though force is used as a last resort, since that type of interrogation only leads to disclosure of useless information. Whatever tool is needed, I have it in my arsenal. I've revealed a substantial amount of flesh and quite a few cores. That's why I've been a successful operative with the CIA.

And that's what makes this situation all the more embarrassing. For all the confidence I have in my ability to do my job well, I failed to uncover the secrets of the one person I thought I knew best - well if not the best, than the most intimately at least.

Another skill is the ability to reassess a situation and regroup in a moment's notice. Changing the game plan mid-stride takes experience and skill, but must be accompanied by the ability to execute quickly. Yet somehow, I currently find my feet rooted to the ground, looking and feeling completely dumbstruck.

I'll set the scene. Picture a rundown wedding chapel off the Vegas strip. It's much like you'd expect in Vegas – dull, white walls enclose a small room about half the size of my apartment. There are two rows of worn and scratched wood pews on either side of a center aisle marked with a faded red carpet, showing stains from the shoes of the no doubt thousands of feet that scurried across anxious to tie the knot, often in a drunken and impulsive haze. The minister presiding over the ceremony is at least solemn and dignified in black trousers, white dress shirt and gray tie, a preferable choice to the Elvis impersonator who luckily wasn't available anyway. His wife, a stout and pleasant woman wearing a purple muumuu and a big smile, stands off to the side, an obvious expert in multi-tasking.

While waiting for the ceremony to begin, she explained. Pointing to the pen tucked into her massive cleavage, her job as witness was to sign the marriage certificate. What wedding would be complete without the requisite wedding march? She proudly labeled herself music coordinator, motioning to the CD player sitting on the stool to her left. Sitting beside the CD player was a bowel of rice, which required no explanation but clearly designated her as a happy guest at the ready to throw said rice at the conclusion. She also explained that she would be maid of honor by holding the complimentary bouquet of half-wilted flowers during the ring exchange, though she referred to it as the lovely floral arrangement. Thank god I opted for the deluxe upgrade, otherwise who knows what the flowers would have looked like.

Now, I'm not the most romantic guy, but this venue wasn't my first choice. And even though I knew the woman I was marrying didn't put a lot of stock into romance, this setting should have made her cringe knowing that the memory of her wedding day would forever be linked with this cheesy setting. But there she stood, seemingly oblivious to her surroundings, her beautiful eyes locked onto mine. Her beige silk dress hung gently around her soft curves, stopping at mid-thigh and exposing her long, smooth legs and delicate feet encased in simple tan heels. Her long, dark hair was pulled back gently into a gold clip at the back of her head, those beautiful tresses flowing in gentle waves down her back, while wisps of loose hair delicately framed her soft face. She was, quite simply, stunning. Which is probably why I heard almost nothing of the minister's ramblings about love and commitment, fidelity and honesty, choosing instead to imagine my future waking up every morning next to this extraordinary woman.

I should've paid more attention to the minister. I only snapped back to the moment when I was asked to repeat those familiar vows. I held the hands, noting a slight tremble, of my bride-to-be, and began to speak the promises that, until that moment, I had only thought of as a formality since my heart had already taken the plunge from the moment we met.

As I vowed to take this woman as my lawfully wedded wife, a deep baritone voice from the back of the chapel rang out in a mocking tone, "That bitch in front of you may be who you agree to take, buddy, but that sure as hell *ain't* who you're getting." The sudden interruption caused my head to whip around toward the entrance to the chapel, only to catch a brief glimpse of a man in tattered jeans and black t-shirt, tattoos in intricate patterns adorning the length of both arms. I could barely make out the features of his face, partially obscured by shaggy, long blond hair as he turned and exited quickly.

Instinctively sensing no immediate danger, I turned back around to see the fallen face of the woman I had hoped to spend my life with, a single tear leaving a wet path along her now pale cheek, as she lowered her eyes and whispered in a barely audible voice, "I'm so sorry."

Well, fuck.

CHAPTER 1

Grayson - Three Months Ago

I sat in the last booth in the back of a grimy diner that I suspected the Health Department would have shut down years ago had they been able to find it. It was located in the middle of nowhere, and though it didn't make the list of most dangerous places I've been, it was clearly a hazard to my health. My career put me in more precarious situations, but the bacteria living on the top of this table would certainly give that list a run for its money.

Despite the dingy gray walls, muted lighting that would make Quasimodo look good, and sticky floors that would caution against wearing nice shoes, I understood the appeal of this place. It was far enough removed from Langley that the likelihood of running into someone I knew was minimal, and both patrons and employees in this kind of joint tend to be intentionally unobservant.

As was habit, I scanned the layout of the diner, and observed the other patrons and employees. I had already familiarized himself with the surrounding area before entering and had an idea of the number and kind of vehicles in the parking lot. Being on medical leave for a leg injury did nothing to lessen the instinct to always have a situational awareness of my surroundings.

The front door opened and I watched as Jared Trainor, a long time friend and a brilliant analyst, entered, headed in my direction, and slid into the seat across from me. Jared, in his late-fifties, was showing strains of his job that gave him the appearance of being much older. His full head of once brown hair was now almost entirely gray. The thick, black rim of his glasses did nothing to conceal the lines on his forehead and around his eyes that appeared more pronounced since the last time I saw him.

Normally one to cut to the chase when I have nothing to gain from a meeting, I usually tried to get to the point then leave as quickly as possible. But on this occasion, I hesitated, as Jared is a friend, and despite this meeting seeming odd and out of character for him, I decided to keep the mood light until circumstances dictated otherwise.

"How they hanging, Jared?" I greeted him with a muted smile.

Jared's face remained stoic and unreadable. This was not all that unusual, but given the cryptic nature of the message Jared had left to set up this meeting, his blank expression ticked the needle up a few notches on my *'Oh Shit'* meter.

"Look," Jared started. *Crap.* Nothing good ever came after a sentence that started that way. But before I could speak, Jared continued. "Sorry about the whole cloak and dagger routine, Gray, but I wasn't sure about getting you involved in this thing." *Danger, Will Robinson*, I thought as I mentally timed the distance to the front door.

So much for keeping the mood light. I needed to get to the point quickly. "Whoa. You said you needed a favor. I thought you wanted to borrow my Porsche for a date or something. This is starting to feel more like an *'I-need-you-to-give-me-one-of-your-kidneys'* -kind of favor. What's going on?"

Jared started to shift in his seat. Not a good sign. He paused for a moment and I realized this was going to be serious, so I allowed him the time to gather his thoughts before pushing him to continue. When Jared started, his voice had an unsteadiness I normally wouldn't associate with someone whose job required calm and rational analysis. "I need you to look into something for me. But it has to be done outside official channels and quietly. I know this is asking a lot, and I wouldn't, except you're one of the few people I know I can trust and the timing works out with you being on medical leave. It won't raise any questions if you leave D.C. for a while. You know, for R & R."

"Leave D.C.? Where am I going exactly?"

"I need to tell you a story first," Jared said with the even and measured quality returning to his tone. I sat back, shook my head and raised my eyebrows at the approaching waitress, stopping Jared from saying anything further for a moment.

"What can I get you boys?" the buxom, red-headed woman greeted. She barely registered our presence as she stared at her order pad with pencil in hand.

6

"Just coffee," Jared ordered.

"Same for me, but I'll also have a slice of apple pie."

"Sure thing, sugar," the waitress said as she turned and headed toward the counter. We waited in silence until the waitress brought over two cups of coffee and a slice of apple pie. As soon as she left the table, Jared sighed deeply then resumed his story.

"Do you remember me telling your stories about Col. Marshall Westfield?"

I nodded. "Yeah, I remember. Though it's not like the guy would be a mystery otherwise. He had quite a reputation. From what I heard, he spent his early years in Special Ops then went on to train the next generation. He was known as a real hard ass – in and out of uniform. What about him?"

"He and I go way back. We were from the same shit-hole town in Idaho. We stayed in touch over the years and we'd go out for a beer whenever he was in Washington." The corner of Jared's mouth turned up slightly as he looked into his coffee, as if recalling a pleasant memory. But almost as soon as I noticed his expression, it was quickly replaced with a frown as he continued.

"A little over two years ago, he started getting in touch with me more often than usual, calling or sending messages. Sometimes, it was real cryptic. It felt to me like he was...... almost like he was losing it a little. You know, getting slightly paranoid. The last time I saw him, we met at a dive bar outside Fairfax. Not our usual stomping ground. He told me he had suspicions about something to do with military weapons research. He was gathering information, but couldn't turn it over 'cause he didn't know what he had and wasn't sure who to trust. He said he would be in touch and was hoping I could help when the time came."

I hadn't known what to expect, but this certainly was about as far removed from anything I could have guessed. "Shit. Did you believe him?"

"Yes and no," Jared hedged. "He was always a little high strung, but this? Even for him it seemed a little over the top. I let it go, thinking if he ever found anything tangible, I'd look over whatever he had, not really expecting he would. Then, a couple months after that meeting, he was dead."

7

"Yeah. I heard he was in a car crash that killed him and his wife." I started to suspect I wouldn't like where this conversation was going.

"Well.....," Jared hesitated. He seemed unsure about continuing. Finally, he took a heavy breath and resumed the story. "The State Troopers ruled it an accident, so I left it alone. Then I found out his house was cleared out by a bunch of black suits. It seemed a little fishy, but I wasn't concerned until I learned that his daughter took off the day they put the bodies in the ground. She fell off the radar completely for almost two years."

"He had a kid? Didn't know that." I was genuinely surprised and just a bit more curious. I had heard stories about Marshall Westfield, particularly because he was rumored to have unique skills in covert operations though having never actually served in any intelligence branch – that I knew of. It was common knowledge that he had a wife, but there was never any mention of a child.

"Her name is Tallulah Jane, but she goes by 'Lou'". She was adopted by Marshall and his wife when she was nine. She's twenty-six now. Anyway, like I said, she was in the wind for almost two years. No *U.S.* bank accounts, credit cards, job history, nothing. I did as thorough of a background as I could, but nothing came up that would help me locate her, so I put it all on hold about eight months ago. Then last week, I find out she's been in Colorado for at least the last few months."

"How did you find her?"

"I didn't find her, exactly. She just started appearing on paper again, and she used her real name to get licensed."

"Licensed? To do what?"

"Fugitive recovery. She's a bounty hunter." Jared flashed a smile for the first time since sitting down.

WTF? I was trained in keeping a neutral expression on my face and never giving a hint as to what I was thinking, but I was sure the look I was sporting now clearly said that I was surprised. This story was beginning to sound like the makings of a Hollywood movie script, but I didn't know where I fit into this plot. "What do you want me to do?"

Jared took a sip of coffee then started rubbing his forehead. When he looked up, I saw deep concern etched into his face. "After she disappeared, I ran a quick scan through all the usual databases just to see if her name would pop. Nothing ever did. When her name came up last week, I started digging more into trying to find her and discovered I'm not the only one who's looking."

I tried to process what Jared was saying. Who else would concern themselves with Marshall Westfield's daughter, and why?

"I tried to back-trace the inquiries, but came up empty. Whoever's looking knows how to cover their tracks. The odd thing is, while I can't nail down the source, I can tell you that whoever it is, wasn't actively watching those records. They were monitoring to see if anyone else was looking." Jared looked down and started rubbing his forehead again. When his eyes met mine, he appeared to have aged several years in the few minutes we'd been sitting there. "It appears as though an alert or trigger of some kind was placed in a few key databases. An electronic trip wire of sorts. When my last search turned up results..."

"You tripped the alert," I guessed.

Through his haggard look, Jared continued. "Yeah, I did. After that, I had a buddy with the California State Troopers pull the old accident file from Marshall's crash. The official report concludes Marshall was speeding, lost control of the car and slammed into a tree. But the on-site accident investigator's notes shows paint scrapings from a different car on the driver's side and rear bumper of his car, like someone forced him off the road. And the airbags never deployed. Those facts never made it into the official report which subsequently got swept under the rug. I'm starting to think Marshall wasn't so paranoid after all. I think he was worried someone was on to him, so he reached out to me, only he died before he could let me in on whatever he was investigating. Lou went underground for a reason. She may have surfaced, thinking that no one is still looking for her, but if so, she's wrong. I need to talk to her, but even if I could find her, it would be a mistake to approach her. Someone else knows I'm looking for her and I don't know who or why." Jared raised an eyebrow clearly indicating this was where I was going to come in.

Only now I was confused about his last statement. "What do you mean, 'if you can find her'? I thought you said she was in Colorado?"

"She is." Jared's voice held a hint of frustration. "But the information on her is sketchy and my ability to get more intel is limited from behind a desk. All I know about her current situation is that she only takes fugitive recovery jobs contracted through some slimy bail bondsman in Denver. He's the only one that can get in touch with her." Jared pulled a thick file from his briefcase and handed it to me. "This is everything I have on her since I first started looking. I need to you find her, make sure she's okay and find out if she knows anything about what Marshall was looking into." It wasn't a question, but I saw my friend's request through his cautious but hopeful eyes.

I grabbed the file and stared at the seemingly non-threatening brown cover, a deception not unlike the Stonefish; innocently camouflaged in the rocks at the bottom of the sea, yet also the most poisonous in the world. As I tried to process some of the information Jared just imparted, an image came to my mind of a little girl with pigtails and braces and immediately dismissed the idea that she could have any information about the Colonel's investigation. "From what I know about Marshall, it seems unlikely he'd involve his daughter in anything dangerous. I doubt she'd know anything." At least I hoped so.

"You're probably right about that. But if others are looking into her, she could be in danger and not even know it's coming her way. Marshall could be a tyrant and a real asshole sometimes, but he was a friend. He trusted me and I just need to look into it, even if there's nothing to it."

We stared at each other a moment not saying anything. The look in Jared's eyes seemed to be asking for understanding, but he remained silent. I contemplated the story and my friend before making a decision, somehow already knowing it was one I'd regret.

"Okay. I've got two more weeks before the doc will give me clearance to go back in the field. I'll look over what you have and figure out how to find her. It probably is nothing, but on the off chance his daughter has information and others are looking, it's better if you and I aren't communicating until I get back. I'll contact you only if I need anything. Otherwise, let's keep this between us for now."

Jared released a deep breath in a long sigh and relaxed his shoulders. "I really appreciate this, man. I wouldn't ask, but I need help. I'm an analyst, not a field agent. I wouldn't know how to do this and I just need to know she's okay."

"No sweat. It'll turn out to be nothing at all and years from now, we'll chuckle about how we overreacted like a couple of little old ladies," I said, trying out what I hoped was a reassuring smile.

"You've got some reading to do, so why don't you head out. I'll get the check. I'm just going to sit here and finish my coffee." Jared's demeanor seemed to lighten considerably. "Hey, you didn't touch your pie. May I?" I looked down at the untouched plate and full cup of coffee in front of me.

"Be my guest, though I wouldn't recommend it. That pie looks almost as old as you are."

As I stood to leave, Jared looked up and smiled. "Bet you're wishing all I wanted was a kidney."

I sat on the couch and looked at the closed file sitting on the coffee table. Admittedly, I was bored being on medical leave, and while doing this for Jared was a sure-fire cure for boredom, it could also prove to be more drama than I needed right now.

Nevertheless, Jared was not only my friend, but a smart guy. One of the smartest I knew. He wasn't prone to exaggeration and was careful not to jump to any conclusions; lives often rested upon the information he gathered and analyzed. Jared would not have asked for my help if he didn't feel there was some validity to his concerns.

I popped open a beer and took a long swig before opening the file in front of me. My attention was immediately drawn to a black and white photo of Tallulah Jane Westfield stapled to the top left side of the file. *Holy shit!* What struck me was the way her eyes appeared almost translucent in the picture. They appeared to be gazing right at me and I was instantly mesmerized by the image. This woman possessed an ethereal beauty I had never seen before. The skin on her oval face and high cheekbones appeared flawless. She had full lips and a straight nose, but it was those eyes that left me unable to look at anything else in the file for a good ten minutes. Even in a black and white photo, those eyes were bewitching. Her hair appeared to be dark, but pulled back in a ponytail.

I proceeded to read through the thick file. Despite its completeness, it held surprisingly little information and only raised more questions. She was born Tallulah Jane Roberts; her biological father unknown. Her biological mother, Diana Roberts, was a homeless drifter until her death from a drug overdose when Tallulah was only 8. *Jesus.* Shortly after her mother's death, Tallulah was adopted by Col. Marshall Westfield and his wife, Laura. There was a notation that her original file from the Department of Children and Family Services could not be located.

There was a transcript from a recorded interview with Laura Westfield's sister, Eileen, who apparently didn't think much of the Colonel. She described him as a bully that ran his household as he would a platoon. He barked orders and expected nothing less than complete and blind obedience. She claimed Tallulah was raised by the Colonel as if she were a son, and that he taught her to fight, shoot guns and hunt. She described Tallulah as shy and withdrawn, though she'd only seen her a few times. She implied - without directly accusing - that the Colonel smacked his wife and daughter around and assumed it was why Tallulah had been home-schooled and allowed little or no contact outside the Colonel and his wife.

Jared highlighted the portion of the interview where Eileen had expressed surprise that Marshall and Laura had adopted Tallulah, saying that neither had voiced a desire to have children and the appearance of Tallulah in their lives was very sudden and unexpected. A few months after that first interview, Jared had additional questions he wanted to ask, so he attempted to contact Eileen again, but learned she had passed from cancer. The Westfields appeared to have no other family.

When Tallulah turned 14, the Colonel was stationed in Germany for a couple of years. The only evidence that she was also in Germany appeared in the form of a medical report from the base hospital that showed that at age 15, she was treated for a sprained wrist and bruises and abrasions on her hand and knuckles, almost as if she had been in a fist fight. The interesting part of that incident was a similar report at the same base hospital that said three drunken soldiers returning from leave were admitted at the same time as Tallulah, suffering from injuries ranging from a broken nose and cut lip, to bruised ribs and a fractured jaw. The kicker was that while all three had been brought to the hospital by military police, they were treated and released, and no other incident or arrest report had been filed. There had to be a story there and Tallulah was in the middle of it, I was sure.

She was apparently a smart girl. Although home-schooled, her aptitude tests were extraordinarily high and her SAT scores were perfect. At age 17, the family had returned to the States and Tallulah gained admission to MIT where she earned her undergraduate degree in Computer Engineering and a graduate degree in Mathematics. She had just completed her Ph.D. in Applied Mathematics from CalTech when the Colonel and his wife were killed in a car crash.

This woman held a Ph.D. and was working as a bounty hunter? She also held copyrights on several computer programs and phone apps she designed in college that were still paying royalties, but the proceeds were, by contract, paid to a Colorado corporation whose registered agent was a law firm in Denver. While the corporation filed returns and paid taxes, no individual was paid dividends or drew a salary from its income. Other than minimal administrative expenses, the corporation seemed to exist only as a depository for the royalties paid.

The photocopy of her driver's license showed the same picture as the one stapled in the file. The license said she was 5'8", 125 lbs. with brown hair and blue eyes. It was issued only a few months ago. Her application for a bail enforcement license included fingerprints, the same photo from the front of the file and a questionnaire that provided little information about her past. The mandatory background check was unremarkable, and she had a number of registered guns, as well as a conceal/carry permit. The interesting thing was, all of it was applied for and issued in the last six months. There was no information for the two year period following her adopted parents' death. There were also no other photos that Jared could find.

Her residence was listed in Denver, but there were satellite images that Jared had pulled showing that the home address was located smack-dab in the middle of an impoverished, gang-controlled area of the city. *What the hell?* Surveillance in that neighborhood would be impossible. The property was owned by a holding company and rented to a Cora Mae Brookes. Tallulah's name wasn't on the lease, but she received mail at that address.

She had a surprisingly high rate of success in her short tenure as a bounty hunter and her only contact was through a bail bondsman named Charlie Brodsky. That's where I'd have to start.

I didn't have any reliable contacts in Denver, and not knowing what to expect, I decided to pack for different contingencies and drive to Colorado, rather than fly. I gathered up the necessary equipment and loaded up my Jeep. It was a day and a half drive with short stops, but it was a safer way to travel without alerting anyone to my activities.

I spent the next day gathering additional equipment I would need. I went to see Morgan, the biggest nerd and techno geek I knew, but who also subcontracted with the Agency and had access to some cool surveillance and communication equipment that didn't require filling out requisition forms to borrow. Morgan owed me several favors after I had cleaned up a few of his messes, one in particular, following his illegal surveillance of a sexy neighbor that went sour.

Early the next morning, I hit the road, headed to Colorado in search of this intriguing and mysterious woman.

CHAPTER 2

Tallulah

I sat across the desk from Charlie Brodsky at his shabby office on Broadway. I normally didn't meet at his office, but he still owed me money from my last recovery and his "check's in the mail" routine had lost all humor. It's not like I really needed the money, but I couldn't let Charlie take advantage of me, and it would seem odd to him if I wasn't asking about my fee. Besides, he had asked me to stop by and I didn't feel like I could refuse.

I owed Charlie for getting me started in the business and pulling strings to get my applications and paperwork pushed through. Though he had a gruff exterior, was slovenly dressed and his long, salt and pepper hair looked like it was styled with a tub of Crisco, I knew deep down, he was a good guy. Well, not so much good, but not bad in that *I'm-pretty-sure-he's-not-a-serial-killer* sort of way. He agreed to handle all contact for the jobs I took and never asked any questions about my past. He was all business and usually got right to the point. Qualities I greatly appreciated.

"So that Daniels guy you picked up for me a month ago. You know, the possession charge in Englewood? He pled out, got released three days ago, and got popped last night on a DUI. That fucker had the nerve to call me again. You believe that?" Charlie tried to feign an incredulous look on his face, but the truth was, all his clients were dirt bags and we both knew it. Charlie's uncharacteristic foray into shop talk raised my hackles and the need to get out of there quickly.

"Cut the shit, Charlie," I said with a hard tone. "Just give me my check and I'll get out of your hair." Charlie's unusually chatty disposition this morning was particularly unwanted. I had just spent all night chasing down a lead on a fugitive, only to learn the cops had arrested him earlier in the day following a routine traffic stop. I was tired, hungry and in no mood for idle chit-chat.

Charlie pulled a check out of the top drawer and held it across his desk to me. Before I was able to grab it, he pulled it back. "Just one more thing."

I rolled my eyes and stood, my patience running thin. "Unless you want that thing to be you kissing the business end of the baseball bat you have stashed behind the filing cabinet, I suggest you just hand over my check."

"Hey, don't be a bitch. I just wanted to ask if you were interested in another job. It's not one of mine. I got a call this morning from Joe Sendak at Midnight Bail Bonds. He's got a new guy working with him. The guy is green and the jumper's a real wily fucker with a pension for B&E. He likes strippers and hookers and Joe thought you could get close enough to snag him. Interested? Thirty G bond with the usual fee." Charlie had a hopeful look on his face.

I relaxed a little knowing what was behind this meeting. Charlie was motivated by collecting two things: money and favors. Farming me out to help Joe Sendak with a tricky recovery garnered him both.

"And you get your usual cut for the referral, right? Where's the file?" I sat back down in the chair and crossed my arms. I really had another computer program I needed to work on, and though I hesitated to deal with anyone other than Charlie, it wouldn't hurt to have another source of work, as long as the job came through him.

"I haven't got it. Joe is sending it with the new guy and said he would meet you to hand it over this afternoon."

The hairs on the back of my neck stood on end. Normally other bail bondsmen would fax the paperwork to Charlie's office. "Fuck that. You know the drill. I only deal with you." I was nothing if not cautious, and had learned to trust my instincts. And right now, they were telling me to walk out.

"Yeah, well Joe said there was some info you should have going in. The new guy has the deets, so he set up the hand-off." Charlie grinned. *Jeez.* That smile would terrify zombies.

"I don't like it." *I barely like you.*

"This would be good for both of us. Having Joe owe me a favor would benefit you, too." That statement suddenly left me with a need to take a hot shower and scrub my skin with a Brillo pad, but Charlie went on. "Besides, I've never asked you for a favor, and you owe me, so I'm calling it in."

"Jeez, Charlie. Your sales pitch went from used car salesman to Vito Corleone in two seconds flat. Why is this so important?" Charlie never pushed hard on anything without an ulterior motive.

Charlie folded his hands that were clearly in need of soap and rested them on his desk over my check. He looked up at me as if assessing whether or not to let me in on classified secrets. After a moment, he looked resigned and said, "Joe's thinking about retiring. His kid doesn't want the business, so he's planning on closing up shop. That means he'll be selling his building on 25th Avenue and I want first dibs on buying it. That location is a big step up from here."

"A motel room that rents by the hour is a step up from this dump," I said dryly. Charlie sneered at me. *Ah, shit.* "Okay. I get it. You want to lower your budget for roach traps and tetanus shots. But why me? Can't Snake chase this guy?" Snake was another bounty hunter Charlie used. He was big and mean with a snake tattoo that wrapped around his left bicep.

"Didn't you hear me say that the jumper's into strippers and hookers? Snake wouldn't get within a mile of this guy."

"Oh, I don't know. Snake isn't *cute*, cute, but he's got a nice ass."

The scowl on Charlie's face got bigger, as did his frustration. I didn't like the situation and despite my instincts telling me to leave, the bottom line was, I did owe Charlie a lot. "Okay, fine. But just this once. Where and what time?"

Charlie grabbed a note tucked under a paperweight on his desk and handed it to me. "It's a diner south of downtown. Here's the address. Three o'clock. I don't know what the guy looks like, but Joe said he'll find you."

I grabbed the note, stood up and stared down at him with a raised eyebrow.

"What?" Charlie asked looking genuinely perplexed.

17

"My check." Charlie handed it over and I started to head out. Just as I placed my hand on the door, I said without looking back, "You better hope I don't regret this, or you will, too."

It had been a few months since I emerged from my self-imposed exile. I knew I now had a paper trail that could potentially bring unwanted attention to my door. So far, nothing out of the ordinary appeared in my life, but I wasn't about to let down my guard. I never knew when or if someone would come looking for me, and old habits die hard. The main problem was I didn't know what or whom I was on the look-out for. The only thing I knew for certain was that my life was filled with too many secrets, and not all of them my own.

Two and a half years ago, when I suspected others wanted in on those secrets, I felt my only option was to run. Only now, I often questioned the wisdom of that decision. Was fleeing an overreaction brought on by the Colonel's paranoia in the months before his death? In the time since I went silent, I never caught sight of anything in my life that would suggest anyone was looking for me. I'd never know if that was because I was just that good at laying low, or if no one was actually looking. Still, there was enough suspicion to warrant that I err on the side of caution. Though only partially out in the open now, I still maintained as much anonymity that I could while trying to build a life that resembled something normal. Now if I could just figure out what normal was. I was pretty sure normal didn't entail arriving at the diner fifteen minutes early to scope out the area. Baby steps. It might take a few years before I felt comfortable enough to enter a grocery store without first casing the neighborhood, but better safe than sorry.

I studied the streets leading away from the location and road down the alley behind the diner to check for other entrances to the small restaurant. I took note of the surrounding buildings and rooftops. Nothing seemed out of the ordinary.

The entire front of the diner had windows that started at table height and went up to the ceiling. There were also large windows on the south side closest to the entrance that looked into the small parking lot. Since the alley was clear and the kitchen staff left the delivery door cracked open, it made sense that any surprise would come through the back, so I settled on parking my bike on the street right in front.

I walked in and saw the restaurant was fairly empty; only two patrons at the counter and an older couple in a booth in the larger dining area. I slid into a booth against the front window that allowed unobstructed views of the front door, parking lot and kitchen access. It was two minutes to three.

CHAPTER 3

Grayson

I stared out the window of the laundry mat a few doors down and across the street from the diner. Luckily, I had connections that knew Joe Sendak, owner of Midnight Bail Bonds, who was more than willing to set up the meeting with Tallulah for a generous fee.

Joe even suggested the site for a meeting I didn't plan on attending. The laundry mat was the perfect place to watch her come and go and the large front windows of the diner provided an excellent view inside. The diner's parking lot sat to the south, and depending on where she sat, could not be completely seen from inside.

My plan was simple. I would draw her out with the lure of a job, then track her movements. Give her a wide berth and plenty of distance so I could determine if anyone else was watching. Once I determined whether anyone else had eyes on her, I could decide on my next move. But I knew approaching her immediately would be a mistake.

At five minutes to three, a Suzuki V-Strom 650 motorcycle pulled in front of the diner and parked on the street near the front entrance, the same motorcycle that earlier had circled the block. I was entranced by the way the rider dismounted the bike and carefully lowered it on the kickstand. I saw a long dark braid emerging from beneath a dark blue helmet, and knew it was her. As she slowly removed the helmet, I could tell that she was casually canvassing the area around the diner. Despite her boyish attire that included a denim jacket over a light blue shirt, jeans and Chucks, the ease of her movements as she headed toward the diner's entrance revealed a feline grace and a distinctly feminine sway in her hips. Each movement, while deceptively casual, was deliberate and calculated, as if prepared for any danger that may lurk. The slight bulge under the left shoulder of her jacket signaled she was armed. She took a seat in a booth with the widest view of the inside and her bike in plain sight out the window. She was alert and obviously cautious. Unfortunately, that meant I could scrap my plan for planting a tracker. At least the license plate was visible. I pulled out the secure satphone Morgan had loaned me, dialed his number and took the rifle scope from my jacket pocket and trained it on the bike.

"If any of my equipment is damaged, I swear you will never-" Morgan was never big on traditional greetings or small talk.

I cut him off. "Don't get your panties in a twist. The stuff is fine. I just need you to run a license plate for me. Colorado State. Sierra, golf, tango, 7-4-5. Got it?"

"I got it." He sounded like a whiney child being told to clean his room. "Just for the record, though, I've paid all my favors and then some. The chits are now racking up on my side of the ledger."

I had to smile. The guy had balls. "Just run the plate, and I'll consider not shooting you when I get back."

"You're a real prince. I'm on it."

I returned my attention to the young woman sitting in the diner. Using the scope, I was able to get up close and personal from across the street. Her picture didn't do her justice. Her dark hair was loosely braided down her back and loose strands of hair fell around her face. And what a face. I could now see her eyes were a cool, ice blue. The lightness of her eyes in the photo paled in comparison to the shocking effect of the glacial appearance only a real-time observation could capture. Even with no make-up on, she was beautiful. The waitress filled the coffee cup at her table and moved away quickly. While Tallulah's head remained stationary, her eyes seemed to be on a constant scan of her surroundings. She raised a cup of coffee to her full lips then glanced at her watch.

I considered my options. With her unobstructed line of sight to the bike, there was no chance for getting a tracking device planted before she left. Trying to tail her from the restaurant could be a problem as well. I was skilled in the technique, but she'd been invisible for two years, which means she is careful, paranoid or both, a fact further confirmed by her movements since arriving at the diner. If she's watching for a tail and suspects she's being followed, it might spook her and send her back underground. No. Better to take my time and analyze the situation for all possible angles.

At exactly 3:10 p.m., she stood up, dropped a few bills on the table, and headed to the door. I watched as she walked outside, put her helmet and sunglasses on and pulled out heading south, but not before taking a careful inventory of everything around her. As I continued to stand near the window of the laundry mat, the image of her face played over in my mind. Only the sudden vibration of the phone jolted me back to the moment and I started getting anxious. My need to know about this woman grew with every piece of information I uncovered.

"Tell me something," I answered, knowing Morgan was on the other end of the line. I waited for Morgan to respond as I walked out of the laundry mat and headed toward my Jeep parked a block away.
"Kind of strange, really," Morgan started. "That plate is registered to a foreign corporation, Sterces, Inc. It's some kind of holding company, domesticated in Colorado, but I can't pin down the country of origin or any of the principals without more time. It's buried pretty deep and runs through several layers. Don't know how long it'll take me to untangle."

I thought for a moment. This woman surfaced after two years, but was still making it hard for anyone to find or learn anything about her. "Who's the registered agent in Colorado?"

"Service of papers would go to a receiving agent, but they get forwarded to an attorney in Denver named Preston Claypool. He's a partner at Cooper, Daniels & Claypool. They have offices in California, Illinois, Colorado and the District, and Claypool is licensed in all four."

"I've seen his name somewhere before. I need to check it out. Anything else?"

"Yeah." Morgan waited a beat before continuing and I knew he was only doing it for the effect. What a drama queen.

"Well?"

"Well. Brilliant guy that I am, I looked into other vehicles registered to this Sterces company, but got nothing. You know, most people don't realize this, but when you search ownership of vehicles, you won't get boats and RVs; they're registered in a different database."

"Just tell me you found something." I was getting annoyed, but trying to be patient since Morgan was doing me a favor.

"I found an RV registered to the same company, but it's kind of strange."

"How so?" I asked, trying to remain calm.

"It's registered as an RV, but the vehicle description says it's a Sprinter van. You know, those high-top commercial cargo vans. No GPS, so I can't get a fix on it. Want me to keep digging into Sterces?"

"Yeah, see what you can find and tread lightly, but first send me a list of all trailer parks and campsites in the area. Keep it in a 50 mile radius of downtown Denver."

"I'll email you a list. Though, if she's stealth camping in the city, you'll never find her until she comes up for air."

"I know, but I'm counting on her having to drag a trailer for the bike, making stealth camping not only difficult, but unwise if you have to leave it parked."

I know I shouldn't ask, but-"

"Then don't!" I cut him off and ended the call. Morgan was a great source of equipment and information, but he could really get on a guy's nerves.

I reached the Jeep and decided I needed to regroup. I headed back to the motel I was staying at so I could think. I chose a motel of the pay-in-cash-no-questions-asked variety, meaning room service was non-existent, so I grabbed a burger on the way. I knew the name of that attorney sounded familiar, and I needed to know why.

As soon as I entered my room, I went straight for the file Jared had given me and started to go through it again. *Well, well, well.* Preston Claypool had a connection to the attorney who handled Tallulah's adoption by Col. and Mrs. Westfield, though it seemed Jared was the only one who looked hard or deep enough to find it. The adoption attorney, Nicholas Dalchimsky, was a California attorney with a small practice just outside Sacramento. A couple years after he facilitated the Westfield adoption, he agreed to open a new firm with a partner named Preston Claypool.

Unfortunately, Dalchimsky died from a heart attack just after moving into the new office space, and Preston Claypool went on to join a well-established, multi-state firm, taking Dalchimsky's files with him. Although that seemed to answer my question about the familiarity of his name, I was still bothered by the feeling that I knew him for other reasons. When it hit me, I got on the phone right away. One call to a buddy of mine in the FBI was all it took to confirm what I had remembered.

Claypool's expansion in the years following Dalchimsky's death went from obscurity as a sole practitioner to respected law firm partner. He was rumored to have questionable scruples in his practice and client selection. Over the course of his career, law enforcement began to suspect that he was becoming the go-to guy for laundering money for arms dealers, art thieves and forgers. As principles go, he drew the line at drug dealers, but he was still a slime. Despite what seemed to be common knowledge about his extracurricular activities, the Feds never seemed to have enough to arrest him, let alone get a conviction. In business and legal circles, he was known as a smart and savvy corporate attorney while hiding the fact that he worked with some very dangerous characters.

I didn't want to judge Tallulah for using this shyster for her own business dealings, but I understood the need. Often times, operatives had to recruit assets that had less than stellar reputations, especially if that asset had skills or information that was mission critical. If Tallulah was trying to stay off the grid for her own safety, then utilizing a guy like Claypool, however distasteful, was a necessary evil.

I had to think. I couldn't use Claypool to get to Tallulah since he was likely as careful, if not more so, than she was – for him, an occupational necessity. I needed more time, intel and a plan.

I got up to grab a beer, when I got call from Morgan advising me to check an email account he had set up for me. Sure enough there was an email with attachment. It was a list of RV and mobile home parks that was fairly long, but I decided to go through each location as if I were Tallulah.

I made a mental list, trying to think like someone who was trying to keep a low profile. She would want somewhere easily accessible to fast routes out of town, and far enough off the beaten path to avoid attracting attention. She'd want a site that was low key and allowed her to come and go easily. Privacy would be essential, but when she needed to take a job hunting a fugitive, she wouldn't want to be too far away from home base. Scanning the list and marking each location on a map I had pinned to the wall of my motel room, I decided to narrow the search to three possible sites that fit the bill. Evening had fallen, so I would have to start the search in the morning.

As I dug into the burger, I stared at Tallulah's picture. From the angle of the photo, it appeared as though she were staring right at me. The image haunted me long into the night.

CHAPTER 4

Tallulah

The ride home from the diner was a little unnerving. I kept watching the rear view mirror, thinking someone would be following me. Everything about this felt wrong, and though I never caught sight of a tail, I decided to take several detours and double back twice on the way home, just in case. No one had shown up at that meeting, and that got my anger directed at Charlie.

As soon as I walked into the van I now referred to as "home", I dialed Charlie's number.

"Brodsky Bail Bonds." Charlie answered abruptly, seeming more irritated than usual.

"What the hell, Charlie?" I was equally irritated, and since we never exchanged pleasantries on the best of days, saying hello was just a waste of words.

"Be more specific, and pull out whatever crawled up your ass and died before you answer me." Clearly, he was in a bad mood, and for Charlie, that wasn't always easy to distinguish from his default personality.

"Joe's guy didn't show. I wasted a trip and time I could have spent doing other things. Call Joe and tell him, favor or not, he can take his job and stuff it."

Charlie was silent for a moment, then dared to ask, "so how long did you wait?"

My simmering irritation and anger was now boiling over. "He wasn't there at three. Once you're late, *how* late is irrelevant! I'm not waiting around to find out." I was practically yelling, but Charlie didn't let up.

"How long?" Charlie wanted a favor from Joe, so he wasn't about to let it go.

"I left at ten after." Wait for it – –

"Goddammit!!" Aaaaand there it is. "You're killing me here, Lou. The guy may have gotten a little hung up and you bail after ten minutes?" Big sigh. "I'll call Joe and straighten this out, but I still want you to do this job."

"And I want cheese whiz to come in a bigger can. Guess we'll both have to learn to live with disappointment." I hung up and paced the floor. There would be no working on programming now. I was too pissed off.

The anger quickly morphed into panic as the ire directed toward Charlie faded. I tried to calmly assess the situation. Charlie's motive for setting up the meet was pretty transparent. Joe's? - not so much. Was there even a job? I could call Joe, but if he had already talked to Charlie, he could cover by saying his guy arrived after I left. If Joe were setting me up, he'd never cop to it unless he knew I had him cold, but what was his end game? It was also possible that Joe was being played.

It suddenly hit me and I started to laugh. I was becoming as paranoid as the Colonel. Sure, the meeting was a little suspicious, but nothing so ominous as to warrant this level of panic. It was time to calm down and maybe try to get some rest. Sleep deprivation was never helpful when trying to think things through, so I kicked off my shoes, laid on my bed and closed my eyes. Only sleep wouldn't come. I couldn't settle my mind.

I thought about the circumstances that caused me to act with such caution and my mind began to spin. I had always suspected that whatever the Colonel had left behind had value – at least in his mind - but I would never know unless I retrieved all of it. I had found some of his hidden treasures, mostly cash and guns, but I knew this last thing would probably be the most valuable to him, and I wanted nothing to do with it. He may have been an asshole, but his tyrannical ways pounded some very valuable skills into my brain, so while he may have seemed a little crazy in the months before he died, I had no doubt that whatever he felt compelled to burden me with, it was securely hidden where no one else would ever find it. Up till now, I was sure it was best left that way.

My thoughts drifted to the years I spent as the adopted daughter of Col. Marshall and Laura Westfield. I never referred to them as my parents and only addressed Laura by her first name. I know that hurt her at times. The Colonel only answered to his title or "sir." I thought about all the time I spent learning skills I never figured to have any practical application in my life. Why would I need to shoot a gun, or hunt and fish, or survive in the wilderness? What possible good could come from understanding explosives? Even the lessons I referred to as "spy stuff" was so far out on the fringe as to be useful. Sure, the hand-to-hand thing and battlefield first aid proved to come in handy more than once, but being able to dismantle and reassemble a variety of firearms while blindfolded wasn't a recognized talent for a game show, much less real life. Little did I know.

Laura, on the other hand, felt the need to balance the Colonel's "training" with other, more practical pursuits. I learned in my time with her that she had once been a high school science teacher. Unfortunately, the constant moving was part of the Colonel's career and made her a less than appealing candidate for permanent employment in most school districts, so she was instead left in charge of my traditional education. Despite the Colonel's strict instruction and limitations on Laura's educational influence, she managed to sneak in lessons on cooking, sewing and social etiquette. She even managed to teach me a few basic ballroom dance steps. Though I grew to love Laura and appreciated her tutelage, there was always a distance between us that neither of us made any effort to close. That was my one regret where she was concerned.

My belief that my time with my adoptive parents was difficult paled in comparison to the years that followed their deaths. Being alone and wrapped in a fear of unknown forces made me grateful for all the Colonel had taught me, though those skills endeared me to a less than reputable crowd. But now, having emerged from that darker time in my life, I was grateful for the things I learned along the way, but ready to move on. I had to stop being afraid of things I couldn't see and hopefully start a new phase in my crazy life. I continued to employ some of the security measures instilled in me by the Colonel, particularly the practice of compartmentalizing different aspects of my life. It helped protect the people who were in my life, as well as reveal any betrayals by knowing which people were privy to information about me or my past.

With my mind beginning to settle but sleep still out of reach, I decided to get up and work on a problem that was plaguing my current programming project. Alpha testing of the software I designed to analyze specific kinds of statistical data had failed miserably. That was the first time that had happened since I started programming in college. Well, back to the drawing board. I spent the rest of the night reworking different lines of code. It was tedious work but successfully kept my mind from over-analyzing the events from earlier that day.

By 1:00 a.m., my eyes could no longer distinguish one line of characters from the next, so I threw in the towel and headed to bed. Despite the drain of the previous day, I awoke at 5:30 a.m., as usual. I found that no matter the circumstance, my body seemed programmed to hop-to before the crack of dawn. Another benefit of the Colonel's training.

I headed to a local gym I used for a workout and shower, then stopped at the farmer's market for some fruit. I had to work on a few more issues with my program, but I really needed to get out today for something other than a job, so I settled on working in the morning and spending the afternoon at the zoo. That always seemed to relax me, so once I put in a sufficient amount of time on work, I packed a small cooler with bottles of water, a turkey sandwich and some carrot sticks, and headed out in an attempt to decompress from my stresses of late.

I was right - the zoo was a great place to hang out and ease the tension in my body. As I headed home after a nice relaxing afternoon, I felt rejuvenated enough to now focus on the tasks I had planned for myself over the next few days. As I approached my van, my heart fell into my stomach as I realized that what I saw destroyed all my plans and confirmed the fears I had convinced myself were simply an over-reaction. A mistake I won't be making again.

CHAPTER 5

Grayson

I spent the better part of the morning driving through two RV parks looking for any sign of Tallulah. I had plate numbers, a general description of the van from registration records and knew she tooled around on a motorcycle. So far, I had struck out. The third location seemed promising. While close to the city, the landscaping throughout provided privacy between spaces, had more than one access point, and appeared very low key. And with cool fall weather approaching, the park was almost deserted.

As I drove around a corner, I spotted a black van that fit the description Morgan had provided. It was pulled back further into its space than the other RVs and as I approached, my heart picked up the pace as I spotted a motorcycle parked beside it. It was her Suzuki.

I made a mental note of the surrounding area then headed for the park's office just off the main road. I reserved the space that was across from Tallulah, and close enough that, with strategic parking, would offer a view of the sliding side door to her van.

On the ride back to the motel, I called Morgan. "I need you to rent me an RV, small and low key."

Morgan laughed. "Yeah, when you asked about RV parks, I figured that might be where you were going with whatever this is. I already called my buddy, Slide-rule. The guy's a genius and used to be a programmer for Millennium Games. He hit the jackpot with one of his game designs and retired to Estes Park. He still designs first-person shooter games, but he's real low key. He's got an RV he takes to gaming conventions. Just your luck he's not using it right now. He said he'd drop it off at your motel, probably within the hour."

"He'll just loan out his RV to some stranger?" Even a favor of this magnitude was beyond what I expected Morgan could pull off.

"Let's just say he owes me – big time. Also, this guy is serious about his equipment, and his RV is tricked out. Just make sure you return it in the same condition you get it in."

"Wow." I said, genuinely shocked. "I guess we are even now."

Twenty minutes later a small Winnebago pulled into the motel parking lot, followed by a blue Ford sedan. One man exited from each vehicle, both of whom looked like the kind of guys you'd meet at Comic Con. I assumed the guy who was in the Winnebago must be Morgan's friend, Slide-rule. I approached him with my hand extended.

Slide-rule ignored the gesture and gave me an examining look as if to assess whether I was worthy of borrowing his RV. "You're Morgan's friend," he finally spoke after looking me over a couple of times.

"Yeah. I'm-"

Slide-rule cut me off. "Don't need to know. Don't care. Call Morgan when you're done and let him know where I can pick it up. There are a few things you need to know. Follow me."

His voice was almost as robotic as his appearance, and even his gait as he walked back toward the RV reminded me of some kind of android from *Star Wars*. It didn't escape my notice that Slide-rule was obviously unhappy about this arrangement, but this was important and the urgency I was feeling to find out what I could about Tallulah trumped any doubts I had about using up my pool of favors.

Slide-rule spent the next 15 minutes giving me a tour of the amenities and special little quirks I needed to pay attention to when hooking up to campsite utilities. When he dropped the keys in my hand, he stared at me with the same robotic expression he maintained throughout, then turned abruptly and headed toward the other vehicle and the guy who, with a similar expression, stood next to his vehicle and watched silently. Both men climbed in the sedan and drove off.

I immediately began packing up the motel room and moving the contents to the RV. The interior, while not particularly roomy, had everything I would need. The bed in the rear seemed comfortable, though the tiny shower would prove to be a challenge. The fridge had a nice capacity, but was empty, so I needed to pick up supplies. I decided to leave the Jeep in the motel parking lot. Satisfied that I had everything cleared out, I went to the motel office and paid for an additional week for the room, just in case I needed a temporary safe house.

When I arrived at the park, I noticed Tallulah's motorcycle was gone. Just as well. It was better for me to get set up without being seen. I found that while the back end of my RV would remain out of sight, the tiny windows from the bunk above the cab provided a perfect vantage point for viewing the entrance to Tallulah's van and the side where she had an outdoor table and chairs set up. The layout of the spaces in this park, coupled with the landscaping would allow for discreet perimeter checks without being detected. I set cameras in position and made a comfortable spot to lie in while I watched her movements.

Once set up was complete, I called the park office to find out about transportation options. It turned out a city bus stopped not far from the park and two transfers later, would have me within two blocks of the motel. I set off, taking note of the fact that Tallulah had not yet returned home.

By the time I returned to the park in my Jeep after picking up supplies, it was almost 4 p.m. I found some empty parking spaces near one entrance to the park where I could leave my Jeep. After parking it, I did a walk through the park to familiarize myself with the layout, then headed back to my borrowed Winnebago. I noticed her Suzuki was still gone.

I heard her bike pull up about 20 minutes later, and watched as she parked and hopped in her van without looking around. Odd, given her normal cautiousness.

I turned on a small light in the back, but left all the other lights off and climbed into the bunk above the cab. I looked through the lens of the camera that had already been set up and took a careful look. After a few hours, I set the specialized motion sensors Morgan had outfitted on the cameras and climbed down to try and get some rest in the more comfortable bed in back. Unfortunately, with thoughts of Tallulah and an unending list of questions, sleep would elude me - again.

CHAPTER 6

Tallulah

The next morning, I lay in my bed staring blankly at the ceiling. This was not good, not good at all. I had spent a relaxing afternoon at the zoo, only to return home to find a new neighbor had taken up residence in the space near mine.

What concerned me was that the Jeep parked near the south entrance was the same one that was parked near the diner where my meeting was supposed to have taken place only yesterday. *Coincidence? I think not.* Other things caught my attention that set off internal alarms. I was sure I hadn't been followed when I left the diner, but my unease about the situation was justified by this turn of events. Just as I was about to pick up the phone to make a call, I glanced out the window and saw a man exit the Winnebago.

He looked to be a little over six feet tall and his broad, muscular build was evident through a thin, white t-shirt. There was a slight waviness to his brown hair and stubble on his face. There was too much distance to see his eyes, but he appeared handsome.

He emerged barefoot and walked to the back of his rig, then just as quickly, returned inside. Genuine concern morphed into morbid curiosity regarding this mystery man, with his solid build and rugged features. I pushed away thoughts that were starting to boarder on lust so I could focus and figure out how to find out what he was up to.

But how to do that was the real question. I could spend days watching him watch me, but that may not get any more answers than I had now. I could wait until he made some kind of move, but that held too much risk without knowing his end game. I needed to be proactive, and maybe throw him off balance. I spent too much time in hiding and I didn't want to go back to that. I was building a new life, and I wasn't as easily intimidated as I once was. I needed to be smart. Since the day of my adopted parents' funeral, I suspected that someone might come looking for me. Two and a half years of being prepared for it, did little to lessen the apprehension of actually being faced with it now. Giving myself a mental shake, I sat down and outlined a plan.

I knew he back door of my van was not visible from the space my new neighbor occupied. I caught a few hours of sleep then slipped out undetected around 5 a.m. I exited at the rear, snuck through the brush that bordered the back side of my space, slipped through the hole in the fence and walked through the wooded area behind the RV park. By my calculation, a brisk walk would bring me to the small strip mall a few miles away by 6:00 a.m., just in time for *The Coffee Bean* to open. It was a small shop that served pretty good coffee and a variety of pastries.

The café door was being unlocked just as I arrived. Before entering, I called a local cab company, then entered and ordered two large coffees, a croissant, a bear claw and a couple of donuts. I waited outside and quickly got in the cab that arrived a few minutes later.

I instructed the driver to pull up right next to the new guy's space and walked right up to his door. I knocked loudly and waited. Sounds of someone fumbling around and a few choice curse words came from inside. The door flung open and our mutually shocked expressions faced each other.
My jaw was nearly hitting the ground because the face of the man who answered the door was not what I was expecting. Not only did he have a ruggedly handsome face, but new guy came to the door in nothing but a pair of low slung jeans with the top button undone. His tanned torso was muscular and well defined with toned abs narrowing to the sexy V that pointed right at his... HELLO! *Oh God, look up!* My eyes shot up to his face. *Shit, not helping.* The sunlight seemed to reflect gold specks in his light brown eyes that were surrounded by thick lashes. The intensity of his gaze froze me in my tracks and momentarily stunned me into silence.

I recovered, and noted that his eyes were doing a similar perusal of my body, but seemed to linger at my chest a little longer than would be considered appropriate. That was enough to snap me back to attention. I pointed two fingers at my chest and slowly moved them up to my eyes. "Dude, my eyes are up here," I smirked.

New guy finally broke his gaze away from my body and shook his head as if he needed to clear the cobwebs. "Uh, can I help you?" His voice was deep and gruff with sleep.

I kept my eyes focused on his. "Hi. I'm Lou. I'm in the space over there," I indicated by lifting my chin in the direction of my space. "But you already know that, don't you."'

"Excuse me?" New guy appeared momentarily confused, but he, too, seemed to have the ability to recover quickly. "What do you want?"

"I thought we should talk. I even bought breakfast." I held up the coffee in the cardboard drink carrier and the paper bag. "I'll be sitting at my table over there. Why don't you put on a shirt and join me?" I turned and walked away, then called over my shoulder, "You should hurry so your coffee doesn't get cold."

I was hoping this would work. I had to be logical about my assessment, and instinct aside, I didn't think he was there to do me harm. Had he wanted to, he would not have taken up residence so close that I could make him so quickly. He would have surveilled from a better vantage point without tipping me to his presence, then make his move before I knew what hit me. No. He was definitely just trying to get a lay of the land.

My gun was tucked in the shoulder holster under my jacket, but I hoped the meeting wouldn't go that way. I took the chair facing his door and waited. And waited. I sipped black coffee and was just about to give up and go inside to pack up when his door opened. He emerged wearing jeans, and a flannel button down open over a white t-shirt. He wore black hiking boots and it seemed as though he hadn't done anything to bring his unruly hair under control, nor did he shave. As he walked toward me, I noticed a slight limp in his left leg, though he appeared to be trying to hide it.

When he reached the table, I gestured for him to take a seat across from me and handed him a coffee. "It's just black. There's cream and sugar in the bag, if you need it." I took a sip and watched him eye the large cup before removing the plastic lid. He took the coffee, but remained standing.

"Thanks. Black is fine." He seemed tentative, but gave a slight smile. "What else is in the bag?"

"Breakfast. Help yourself. And please sit." I pulled out a donut, placed it on a napkin in front of me and slid the bag across to him. The seat across from me would have put his back facing his own space. Instead, he carefully moved to my left and sat in the adjacent seat with his back to my van.

"Trying to get close?" I asked.

"I just prefer my back to a wall," he replied, as his eyes did a sweep of the area around him.

"Then you'll love talking to me," I mumbled.

The corner of his mouth turned up slightly, but he didn't move or respond. When I said nothing else, he looked directly into my eyes as if hoping to discover some secret hidden there and spoke in a quiet tone. "What did you want to talk about?"

"Why don't we start with your name and go from there."

"It's Grayson." Aaaaaand..... nothing else.

That's it? Jeez, I've met mimes that talk more than this guy. So he was playing this slow and easy. Waiting to see what I knew and trying to throw me off. The way his eyes bore into mine was so intense, I was beginning to question the wisdom of this plan, but clearly that ship sailed, so I pressed on. "Okay. So we're done with pleasantries then. Why don't you start by telling me why you're here."

"Why do you think I'm here?" He opened the bag, pulled out a donut and took a bite.

Concern, coupled with slight Irritation, set in. "Are you going to answer my question?"

"Are you going to ask so many?" He flashed a cocky smirk.

"You need to work on your conversational ability."

"Most of my interactions with women don't usually require that skill. Besides this feels more like an interrogation."

"You sound like a guy whose been hanging around the wrong women."

"And you sound like you're trying to channel my mother."

I decided to throw in the towel. "Okay, we're done!"

"Now you sound like the last girl I was with after she had her fourth orgas-"

I lifted my hand in a clear indication for him to stop. "Don't finish that thought," I said. His answering smile spread wider across his face and I immediately regretted starting this conversation.

His smile appeared genuine and his eyes suddenly seemed warm. His intense gaze softened and his posture appeared more relaxed. I knew the point of this ridiculous conversation was to try and get some answers, but the train had veered so far off the track that I momentarily lost sight of my objective. Starting this conversation opened a door and there was no going back. I would either learn what he wanted from me, be forced to pack up and leave, or I'd have to shoot him. I didn't want to exercise option two or three, but as always has been the case in my life, I had few options and none of them all that appealing.

The strange thing was that I knew I was the reason for his sudden appearance, but somehow, I didn't feel threatened exactly. I was feeling fear, but not of him, just maybe because of him. If his intention was to hurt me, he certainly had a few opportunities before now. No, he was watching me, but why? I sensed I already knew the answer, but I didn't want to acknowledge it. I had decided a long time ago not to go down that path. As it turned out, living in denial didn't eliminate the problem. It just prolonged the inevitable.

CHAPTER 7

Grayson

*S*hit! I couldn't believe what was happening. Not only did she catch me off guard, but I openly gawked at her, and I did it while sporting the morning wood I had barely tamed that resulted from the near wet dream I was having about her only moments before she knocked on my door. *Christ.* I needed to get a grip, and fast. Though that might prove to be easier said than done now that I saw her up close. God, she was beautiful.

I couldn't imagine why she thought calling me out after less than a day was a good idea, but sitting here with her, verbally sparring, she appeared to be regretting that decision.

I had managed to at least pull myself together enough to step out of the RV with my confidence restored, but not before checking on a few things.

I quickly checked the footage from the night before and found nothing had been captured since I fell asleep around 3:45 a.m. until she appeared at my door. She obviously decided to slip out the back and catch me off guard. Mission accomplished, but I regroup quickly so that tactic had little effect. I was more thrown by simply staring into her eyes than I was by anything she had done intentionally.

The bigger problem was what to do. I'd been made. She was obviously smart and figuratively speaking, had quite the set of balls. I underestimated her. She couldn't have learned much about me in the short time I was there, yet, she was attacking the situation head on. There was only one way to play this. Let her take the lead and try to feel her up....uh, out. Feel her out. *Shit.* I hadn't observed her long enough to detect whether or not anyone else was watching, but there was nothing I could do about that now. My brief observations both here and at the diner yesterday, led me to believe that I alone had taken up surveillance of Tallulah, but less than 24 hours into it, I could only hope I hadn't missed any obvious signs.

I did my best to pull myself together and ran a hand through my hair. As I approached her, I tried to take in as much about her as I could. Her delicate face held a slight smile, but her relaxed posture was alarmingly deceptive. I could tell by the position of her legs and the right hand resting lightly on her stomach that she was prepared for any potential trouble. I had no doubt she could leap from her seat or draw her weapon within a second of sensing danger. I needed to keep her calm and assure her I wasn't a threat without revealing too much too soon.

I was clearly enjoying the banter, but noticing her body position never changed, I silently acknowledged that this was a dangerous woman, and I had to be careful not to let my guard down. She flashed me a look that would equate to the kind of predatory glare one might see on a jungle cat right before she unsheathed her deadly claws to tear into flesh. I immediately became alarmed when I saw her right hand move ever so slightly, from her stomach to just inside her jacket. *Shit.* Messing with her was probably a bad strategy.

She must have sensed my concern because her smile, what seemed to be a real genuine smile, widened and she slowly let her right hand slide back to her stomach. I also realized I had unconsciously shifted my body position so my hand could reach behind to the small of my back where my gun was tucked. A small giggle escaped her lips and within a few seconds morphed into full blown laughter. As pleasant a sound as it was, I was sure that somehow it was at my expense.

"Do I amuse you?" I asked, a little worried about her answer.

"Yeah." She finally answered when her laughter died down. She wiped a few tears from her eyes and stared at me thoughtfully. "You three-letter-agency guys are a hoot. Don't worry, I wasn't planning on shooting you........yet."

I realized she noticed my movement and found humor in that acute observation. This woman was fascinating. Beautiful, smart, tough, had an oddly similar sense of humor to mine, and based on her magical appearance this morning, quite stealthy. I instantly had a burning desire to know everything about her - favorite foods, favorite books, bra size? Yeah, I'm a boob man, so sue me. I knew my thoughts were veering off course, but at the moment, I didn't care. At least not until I actually contemplated her words. "You think I work for some three-letter-agency?"

"Quit pussyfooting around and just tell me what you want. I really don't have the energy or inclination to play games anymore." Her posture remained on alert, but her eyes seemed to signal resignation. They looked tired - not physically, but mentally and emotionally, for sure.

Still I wasn't prepared to reveal all just yet. "How do you know I'm not just passing through?"

She rolled her eyes and glared at me. "Because sadly for you, the pathway between my eyes and my brain actually work."

When I said nothing, she knew I wasn't going to give up anything soon. There was a look of despondency in her expression that gutted me. It dawned on me then that the fatigue she was showing was not the result of a lack of sleep but the kind of emotional exhaustion that sets in over time. The way agents in the field get burned out after years on the job, she was sporting the same kind of look. She'd been in hiding for over two years and it would seem she was tired of it. I could also sense that the next few minutes would determine if she would decide to run again. I didn't want her to. Something made me want to keep her close.

She took a deep breath. "You're not passing through because the Jeep you parked in the south lot has Virginia plates, but your RV belongs to Eugene Harmon, also known as Slide-rule. He's pretty well known in the tech world. It's also a well known fact that he flunked kindergarten because he doesn't like to share. I'm guessing you're a Fed and are probably holding something over him to get him to give up his geek-mobile. Hackers tend to make it onto a lot of government shit lists." I should have known. She was as much of a tech geek as Morgan and Slide-rule. Figures she would know this guy. Before I could come up with some smart retort, she continued on.

"I figure you're the guy who was supposed to meet me at the diner yesterday. Joe Sendak at Midnight Bail Bonds is known for bailing out dipshits that turn into law enforcement snitches, so it wouldn't be hard for a Fed to have connections to him as well. He could have set up that meeting for you. Your Jeep was parked near the diner, so I'm guessing you were staked out in the laundry mat."

I opened my mouth to speak, but she held up her hand to stop me. "You also made it obvious that you wanted eyes on my van. There's a good ten feet of space that you didn't back into and the connections to your water and power supply are stretched pretty taut. Your RV isn't very long but pulling it all the way back would lose your line of site to my door behind those trees. You're obviously watching me. So just tell me, what do you want?"

Wow. Just wow. I sat there and stared at her for what seemed like a very long time. Her knack for observation, reasoning and deduction would rival Sherlock Holmes. But I needed to set aside my admiration and apply some reasoning of my own. Tallulah was about to be spooked and the only way to keep her from running again would be to gain her trust, though I knew that, given what I'd read about her and observed thus far, that would be unlikely. Still, I had to try.

I considered telling her the truth, but that might spook her even further. She obviously trusted no one, and especially any no ones who worked for the government. She did pretty well to stay away from the prying eyes of Big Brother for two years.

But something told me that I needed to be honest with her. She was alone and vulnerable and may have no clue that anyone has been trying to find her. I found myself wanting to help her. Not because Jared had asked me to find her, but something about her brought out a protectiveness I didn't realize I possessed. The instinct to keep her safe surprised me because of how counter-intuitive it was to my usual mission objectives. Revealing secrets was one part of my job, but more than that was the ability to take that information and manipulate an asset into doing what I wanted, sometimes knowing that doing so would put them in jeopardy. Setting those thoughts aside for now, I tried to formulate an approach that was the least likely to have her running in the opposite direction. Or shooting me.

"Okay. Here it is. I was asked to find you by a friend of your father's, Jared Trainor. He knew your father very well and he's been worried about you since you took off over two years ago. When he heard you resurfaced, he wanted me to reach out to you." At first she seemed confused by this, but then I realized why when she clarified, "You mean the Colonel."

She apparently didn't refer to the Colonel as her father. I waited for some kind of reaction to the rest of what I said. Anything to let me know whether the honest approach had been a mistake. Admittedly, I was omitting quite a bit, but I didn't see the point in overwhelming her all at once.

She sat back slightly and studied me carefully, as if I were a germ under a microscope, her brow lifting slightly as she considered my words. When she finally spoke, her expression was blank, showing no hint of what she was thinking. "Why didn't he contact me himself?"

I had to consider how much to tell her regarding others who may be looking for her. I decided I needed to ease into everything slowly. "Jared is in D.C. and couldn't get away right now. Also, it's not like your number is published in the yellow pages. You may have come out of hiding, but you don't make it easy to find you. I'm sure he would have tried to 'friend' you on Facebook, if it were that easy. He just wants to know you're okay."

"Who said I was hiding? And why'd he send you? You pull the short straw among his Fed buddies? And don't give me that 'I'm not a Fed' routine. You may not be FBI, but you're definitely ex-military or law enforcement, possibly a spook."

There was no sense in arguing. "Right now I'm on leave from work, so I was available to help out Jared, who is a good friend. This is personal."

"Medical leave? For your leg injury? I noticed a limp. You hide it well." There was that smile again. I felt like kissing it right off her face.

When I didn't answer, she pressed on. "So, gunshot, stab wound, trying to leap tall buildings in a single bound?" She was clearly deflecting the conversation away from her. She waited a beat then raised one eyebrow.

"What does it matter?" I asked, a little irritated. I was usually good at directing conversation the way I wanted, but I was obviously distracted by her hypnotizing smile and the beautiful blue eyes staring at me from across the table, because this isn't how it was supposed to be going.

"It doesn't matter........yet. I was just curious." She was starting to make me a little crazy. I seemed to have the upper hand when the banter started, but now something about her was getting to me. I paused for a moment and regained my control. When I continued, I was determined to stay on track and not waiver, no matter how enchanting those gorgeous eyes were.

"Why did you leave so abruptly after your parents' funeral?" Back to business.

She seemed to consider the question carefully. I didn't think her hesitation was so that she could fabricate an answer, but more that she was weighing how much information she would share.

"School was done and my family was dead. There wasn't much holding me in place, so I took off." I knew there was more to it than that, but I needed to proceed carefully.

"And you didn't think to let Jared or anyone else know how to contact you?"

"First of all," her voice started to rise slightly, but she caught herself before her control slipped and continued slowly. "Jared was a friend of the Colonel's. I met him a few years ago and only saw him a few times after that. The last time was at the funeral. Hardly a close family friend. And how do you know if I told anyone else?"

"Because Jared has been looking for you for a while."

She frowned then pierced me with a cold gaze. "Is he the only one?"

Her response caught me by surprise. "Who else would be looking?" I asked as if the thought of anyone else being curious was quite the revelation.

Anger flared in her face, and she immediately shot to her feet. The sudden movement caused me to stand as well. "What? What's wrong?" I'd obviously hit a nerve.

She slammed both hands down and leaned across the table. With a glare that nearly burned me, and the tone of her voice dropping a few octaves, she said, "Speak to me again like you think I'm a moron and this conversation is over."

I frowned then softened my voice and expression, hoping to calm her down. "I don't think you're a moron."

Her tightly raised shoulders relaxed a bit and she took a calming breath. "I'm sorry. I didn't mean to overreact, but if you want me to trust what you're telling me, you're doing a piss poor job. I don't know if Mr. Trainor sent you or if you even know the man. You accuse me of hiding but act surprised that I suspect someone else might be looking for me. You say he asked you to reach out to me, yet you spent time watching me instead of knocking on my door. How long were you going to observe before you approached, or were you even planning on speaking to me at all?"

Her look of frustration made me feel as though I kicked a puppy. I knew that living underground came at a stiff cost and one was only as successful as she had been by doing it alone. She obviously had some inkling that people would come looking for her but I started to doubt that she completely understood the reasons behind it. Stress of unknown hazards would weigh down even the strongest wills and the effect on Tallulah was likely taking its toll. I needed her to trust me, and I couldn't see another way. I knew what I had to do. *Fine.*

"You're right. You have no reason to trust me," I said slowly. She looked up at me with a defeated expression, but I had to keep trying. "I don't know how to convince you, but Jared is the one who asked me to find you. All I can tell you is he has ways of getting information. He gathered as much of it on you as he could, going back as far as he could. He was hoping it would help him find you. Last week he tried running your name through a few databases again and found out someone else has been looking for you, too, only he hasn't been able to find out who, though he has suspicions as to why. It concerned him enough to ask for my help."

"Explain the why."

"Before he died, the Colonel told Jared he was investigating something. I can't say what, but when you took off after the funeral and he learned that your house was cleared out the same day, he got worried. He suspects that the Colonel had something somebody wants but no one's found yet."

"And he thinks I have it."

"Possibly."

"And he wants it."

"If only to protect you," I said softly.

Her expression morphed into one of disgust. "Yeah," she said calmly, "I call bullshit."

"Come again?"

Tallulah started walking toward the door to her van. She reached up and grabbed the handle, then turned her head back toward me. She spoke in my direction, but didn't meet my eyes. "I still don't know if anything you said is true, but if Jared did send you, go back and tell him 'mission accomplished.' You found me, I'm fine, and the only thing I have that belonged to the Colonel is a beat-up, old Swiss army knife." She reached into her front pocket, pulled out the knife and tossed it in my direction. "Give it to him with my regards, and tell him to leave me alone. I can take care of myself." She walked inside and closed the door.

FUCK. She's going to run.

CHAPTER 8

Tallulah

I walked inside and locked the door behind me. I was angry at this turn of events, but more than that, upset with myself. Upset because I couldn't figure out if I was mad that I may have to run again, or that this handsome stranger's presence was motivated only by what he thought I could give him - the Colonel's secrets. There was really no other reason for someone from the Colonel's past to try and find me, yet some twisted part of me wanted there to be something else. That I would have met this fascinating and very handsome stranger under different circumstances. There would always be concern when new people came into my life, and no one I knew or met would ever really know who I was. As solitary as that made me feel, I had always accepted it and distracted myself with activities and tasks that would keep me occupied so as to have no time for wallowing in self-pity. Unexpectedly, the overwhelming sense of loneliness that I managed to keep at bay suddenly wrapped itself around me after one ten minute conversation with a complete stranger. It hit me at the same time that I came to the realization that I would probably always be on the move, never putting down roots.

I stood and looked around the interior of my van. Even though it came on wheels, it was the first place in a long time I thought of as home. I looked at the table where my computer and notepads sat, and noticed the salt and pepper shakers I had bought just a couple of weeks ago. As silly as it sounded, buying those had meant something special to me. Being constantly on the move meant carrying only those items essential to my survival. I hated being on the run and those shakers were a symbol that my life could be different. As with all of the possessions I had hoped to keep from my past, these, too, would have to be hastily abandoned.

As I looked around, I glanced out the window and saw Grayson retreating toward his, or rather Slide-rule's RV. I needed to consider what he said and decide what, if any part of it, might be true. Nothing he told me revealed any insight as to why he was there, unless he was telling the truth, and I wasn't willing to believe that - yet.

I thought back to one of my last conversations with the Colonel. In the six months before his death, each time I was home from school for a visit, he relayed two things in his conversations with me. First, a new method he would use to secretly communicate with me in the event of an emergency; a method in which he needed to point me in a specific direction without anyone else being able to decipher its meaning. Second was the location of another slick, or in plain speak, a secret place where something was hidden. In this particular conversation, though, trust was the topic of the day.

"If anything happens and you can't get to me, don't trust anyone." We were sitting in the back booth of the local Pizza Hut. While I imagined that most girls my age came home from school to visit with friends and family, to hear and tell the latest goings on, my visits were always filled with "lessons" or "training." What was masked as a sweet father-daughter lunch, was the Colonel's way of imparting information without raising suspicion, though just once, I would have liked to have heard him simply say he missed my company and was proud of my accomplishments. Instead he continued on in his usual tone, voice lowered in caution, unaware or uncaring that, not only had I developed another program that a major software company was interested in buying, but I was only a few months away from earning my Ph.D.

"You need to be able to handle anything that happens on your own. Jared Trainor is someone I trust, but not absolutely. If you need help, he's someone you can ask, but don't ever give him any more information than is necessary to help him get you out of a jam." He suddenly turned quiet and contemplative. Unusual for the Colonel, since he gave of his time sparingly and used every minute to serve some purpose. All thought would have been analyzed long before he sat down to lunch. When he continued, his expression turned to one of regret. I almost didn't recognize it, since until that moment, I don't think I ever saw it cross his face. "Remember what I said about compartmentalizing different aspects of your life. Don't ever let anyone see the whole picture. It's for everyone's protection."

He looked at me with tired eyes and said, "I know you haven't traveled the easiest of roads in this life, but everything Laura and I did has been to keep you safe. You know that, right?"

I couldn't help feel a pang of regret that we had never tried to break through the rigid boundaries of our relationship, but I knew this conversation was about as close as I would ever get to a show of emotion from this man. "Yeah, I know that."

I found it strange that everyone around us assumed that the Colonel was abusive toward me and Laura, though oddly, never thought to do anything about it. Rumors circulated at every base he was stationed at that he was a hard-assed prick that smacked us around. I never sought to correct the record because the Colonel never seemed to care what anyone thought. It also worked in our favor in that no one would try to get close to our family, because doing so would mean having to acknowledge there was a problem and being forced to do something or be accused of culpability in allowing it to continue. Most people prefer to keep their heads in the sand, never having to make difficult choices or offer help to others who may need it. As I learned from the Colonel, when you have secrets to keep, isolating yourself is one technique for keeping curiosity at bay.

"If you need to reach Jared, use the email address I gave you before, but don't identify yourself. Just sign off as 'Honey R' and he'll know."

Though the Colonel didn't have much of a sense of humor, I knew name was a referenced to a James Bond character. I found funny the idea that he occasionally enjoyed reading the novels of Ian Fleming.

I sat at the table and picked up the salt shaker. I stared at it as if it held all the answers I needed. Sadly, it did not. But the realization was, I needed to face everything I had hoped was buried with the Colonel. It meant that every hope I had that the Colonel was paranoid or just plain crazy faded each time I looked out the window at the space across the way. Whatever the Colonel had hidden away, despite my hope that it was nothing of value, needed to be retrieved. I didn't know what it was but I knew how to find it. And until I did, I couldn't move on with my life.

Before first, I needed to shake Grayson loose. I knew I had to get away, but that didn't stop my girly parts from being disappointed. He was, after all, quite a fine specimen of a man, but whatever his motivation, he was an X-factor that needed to be removed from this equation.

Curiosity, however, started to get the better part of me. I couldn't deny that I was attracted to him, but I convinced myself that contacting Jared for information would help with my plan to escape Grayson's surveillance and not for any other reason. I sat down at my computer and hesitated for only a moment before I sent an email to

Jared, routing it through several servers across the globe to hide its origin. The message was simple.

Are you looking for Honey R?

While I waited for a response, I started pulling together the things I would take and making plans for the disposal of everything else.

CHAPTER 9

Grayson

W alking away from Tallulah was difficult, but I knew this was not the time to push her. I had bigger problems anyway. I was fucking this up and had no idea how to fix it. This fact was so far outside my comfort zone, given I always had back up plans ready to initiate in case things went wrong and built in redundancies to avoid mistakes. Right now, I had nothing. I had counted on having at least a few days to get the lay of the land and determine who, if anyone else, had found Tallulah. I knew she was getting ready to run, and I was helpless to stop it. Short of tying her to the bed, I wasn't sure how to prevent her from bolting. Although the idea of tying her to the bed..... *No. Not now.*

As I entered the RV I had borrowed, which as it turned out was a stupid idea, one that Morgan would surely pay for the next time I saw him, I let out a string of curses that would make a sailor blush. I needed to talk to Jared and let him know what was happening. He'd be relieved that Tallulah was okay, but pissed as hell that she would likely run again and that it was entirely my fault. I hadn't been careful enough and was stupid in assuming that her being intelligent on paper didn't equate to street-wise smarts, which as it happens, she actually possessed in spades.

I grabbed the satphone and dialed the number for Jared's secure cell phone. He picked up after one ring. "Trainor. This better be good."

"Jared, it's me." I paused for a moment considering what to start with. As far as picking from the good-news-bad-news pile, I was always a good-news-first kind of guy. "I found her and she's okay. Look -"

Jared cut me off before I could tell him she was about to run. "Listen, Gray, we've got big problems. Your Section Chief called me up to his office and I just took a twenty-minute ass chewing about sending you off half-cocked to find Lou. He's been trying to reach you, but you're not answering your cell and he is PISSED!"

Shit! "How the FUCK does he know about Tallulah?" *This is bad, bad, bad.*

"Not a stinking clue! He was ranting about you abandoning protocol and how your ass is grass and he's the lawnmower. I'm assuming one of my searches traced back to me, and when you went MIA, he must have figured I sent you out there to look for her. I got the impression that Lou wasn't on his radar until my searches came to his attention, then she suddenly became a hot commodity with the higher-ups. He's flying out to Denver tonight. He says he is taking charge of this unsanctioned op to bring Lou in and he's getting it done tomorrow. He didn't come right out and say it, but from the way he was carrying on, he knows all about her and suspects she has information about the Colonel."

"That's not gonna happen." I wasn't sure if that was because I wouldn't allow her to be exposed to danger or that she would simply be gone by then. "I need more time. I had a plan and it went to shit. I've already had contact with her, but it didn't go well, and I think she's going to bolt. And before you lay into me, yes, I fucked up. She's smarter than I gave her credit for and I got made. I told her you sent me to check on her, but -"

"Hang on," Jared cut me off. There was a moment of silence then I heard the distinct sounds of a computer keyboard clicking away. After an unbearable minute, I heard a loud sigh, then, "unbelievable."

"What??"

"I just got an encrypted email. She wants to contact me."

"Huh?" I was wrestling with panic and confusion.

"She sent me an email. The Colonel set up a way for her to contact me - never mind, that's not important. I can't let her contact me. I shouldn't even be talking to you, except I'm supposed to be setting up a meet. I'll try and relay a message to her that'll get her to talk to you, but there's no guarantee." I heard him pounding a short message on his keyboard. When he was done, he said, "and one more thing. I still haven't I.D.'d the other party looking for Lou. I don't know if the Section Chief had anything to do with setting up the trip wire, but at this moment, I wouldn't trust anyone."

This situation was turning into a major clusterfuck. My Section Chief, Ed Dombrowski, was an asshole on a good day, and extremely smart. He had also proved that he placed procuring actionable intel above all else, even at the expense of his operatives. It always bothered me that during one particular operation, he chose to secure highly sensitive information over the life of an agent. I couldn't hold that against him since that was his job. And the reality was that it's the job we all signed up for and we knew the risks, but watching it happen was never easy. In the end, I knew that if Dombrowski thought Tallulah had any information of value, he would do whatever it took to secure it - even if it meant putting her in danger. That thought haunted me as I heard Jared continue on.

"I sent her the message in a pre-designated chat room. Let's just hope this works. In the meantime, turn your damn cell phone on. Dombrowski will be trying to call you to confirm a meeting and he's expecting you to bring Lou in."

"No way." Without knowing enough about the situation, it was too dangerous. I had shut off my phone and removed the battery, knowing that would prevent anyone from tracking me. "I can't risk turning it on just yet. Can you get a secure message to him?"

"Yeah."

I gave him the address of the diner I was supposed to have met Tallulah at yesterday. "Tell him be there at 9:00 tomorrow morning and to come alone."

"He'll probably have that snot-nose weasel with him." Jared was referring to Eli Parsons, Dombrowski's aide, who despite being qualified for field duty, preferred the politics of the administrative side of things. He was a real douche bag and seemed to be joined at Dombrowski's hip. I never liked or trusted him, but they were a package deal.

"Just set it up. I'll deal with the rest." Something suddenly occurred to me. "How does he know Tallulah is in Denver?" There was a long pause signaling I already knew the answer.

"I told him." Jared didn't sound as if he was regretting the decision. I learned why when he pressed on. "Look, pal, I know we were trying to keep this quiet, but maybe we can use this to our advantage. If Tallulah does have or know anything, bringing her in will keep her safe. Even if she doesn't know anything, the act of bringing her in could make anyone else lose interest. And I'd feel better knowing you were with her when she meets with Dombrowski. I don't think he's the one who's been looking for her. He discovered my searches when I used my security access and codes to run through government databases. A quick investigation would have revealed who I was looking for and a quick background check would have explained why. That's why he called me out. If he was the one who'd been looking all along, he would have already known he'd find her in Denver and would have had a head start getting there."

When I didn't say anything, Jared made my decision. "Gray, we need to end this call. Go and talk to Lou and tell her your name is James, a licensed troubleshooter. That's how she'll know we're connected. See if you can talk her into coming in and clearing all this up. This isn't what we talked about but it's what's best for her and the only way I can think of to keep her safe. Too many people would have gotten wind by now that she's surfaced. This little mission of ours is no longer covert." With that, he hung up.

Son of a bitch! Assuming she would even talk to me again, I wasn't sure what I would ask of her. Without knowing if anyone else had eyes on her, bringing her to the meeting might be dangerous. On the other hand, not bringing her would mean she would have plenty of opportunity to leave undetected and it could be weeks or months before I found her again. Maybe never. I supposed much of that decision would be hers since she didn't strike me as the type of person who was easily influenced by others. She's proved that she's tough and definitely forges her own path. I needed to assess the situation on the fly. Not my preferred strategy, but I was short on information and time.

I headed out the door and started walking toward her van.

CHAPTER 10

Tallulah

I pulled my duffle out and started gathering up my clothes. As usual, I had limited space, so I had to be practical. Those really cool leather boots would have to be abandoned in favor of hiking boots and my chucks. I opened my underwear drawer and frowned. I had a dozen pair of cotton panties and bras. Sure they came in a variety of colors, but they were first and foremost comfortable and practical. But what caused my frown wasn't those sensible under things, rather the red lace panty and bra set I picked up at Victoria's Secret. I remember the day when I first settled into this van. I had been living between cheap motels and camping in the mountains. I was buying a few things in the hopes of getting myself in a positive state of mind. I bought a frying pan, coffee press, and a soft pillow. I was about to leave the department store when I saw Victoria's Secret across the mall. After living so long feeling like my life resembled one of a soldier, I had longed for something that would make me feel feminine. On an impulse, I strolled in and bought the sexiest bra and panty in the raciest color I could find. I spent more on that purchase than everything else I bought that day, but I left with a renewed sense of optimism. It didn't matter that I've never worn it. Just having it made me feel better. I lifted the set out of the drawer and saw the tags still affixed to them. Fuck it. I was taking them with me. I grabbed all the other pairs I would need and started stuffing them in my duffle.

Just as I grabbed the thong and red lace - practically see-through - bra to stuff into my bag, there was a pounding on the door. Before opening the door, I glanced toward my computer and decided to first check the private chatroom I was instructed by the Colonel to wait in if Jared Trainor was able to respond to my message. I opened the page and saw a message from "Quartermaster" which simply read, *Honey*

R, I can't see you so sent James, the licensed troubleshooter, instead. Trust him. I stared at the message trying to decipher the meaning when another bang on the door pulled my thoughts away. I simply responded with a "we'll see" and closed the chat.

I opened the door and watched as he ran his hands through his already disheveled hair and looked down. "I'm James," he said in a voice so low I almost didn't hear him. He hesitated, then finished with "the licensed troubleshooter."

At that moment, I couldn't help it. The bizarre nature of this whole situation was getting to me and I was unable to hold back my laughter. He looked uncomfortable standing there as I pulled myself together. As my laughter subsided, it occurred to me that Grayson had been telling the truth - at least as far as knowing Jared. I decided to trust him enough to hear him out, but no more than that.

I pushed the door open a little further and gestured for him to enter. In an attempt to extend his discomfort a little longer, I asked, "Do you know why your name is *James*?"

He seemed to regain his composure quickly because his cocky response caught me by surprise. "It got me in the door, so what does it matter?"

Smug bastard. "What do you want?"

He sat down uninvited in the front passenger seat that swiveled to face the inside of the van. He looked up at me and all the cocky attitude was gone. The expression on his face seemed one of genuine concern and that sent me into an immediate panic.

"What?" I asked again, with a squeak in my voice. *Way to stay in control.*

"We have a -" Grayson stopped suddenly and I realized then that his gaze had dropped to my hand that was still holding the racy red lingerie I meant to pack in my duffle. *Shit.* I quickly stuffed it in a drawer that was within reach and turned back to him with an expression that I hoped masked my mortification.

"We have a what?" I asked, annoyed that he was able to unnerve me.

He immediately wiped the smirk off his face and continued. "Problem. We have a problem."

"How do you figure?"

"Can you sit, please?" I had remained standing in my small space. I normally had nerves of steel. The higher the stress in any situation, the calmer I got. I'd actually been in some rather dangerous situations and had surprised myself at how calm I could respond in a crisis. But the combination of Grayson's overwhelming presence and the feeling that all my demons where coming home to roost had me on edge and I couldn't seem to regulate my pulse. It was currently pounding like a John Bonham drum solo on meth. When I looked back at Grayson, his presence that only minutes ago seemed too overwhelming, suddenly brought out a calm in me. I had an inexplicable feeling that I was safe, so I took a calming breath and sat.

He took what looked to be an equally calming breath and began explaining the situation. In the next few minutes, everything I had worked for months on building came crashing down.

CHAPTER 11

Grayson

It felt like one of those defining moments you have in life. The kind where you stand at a crossroads and have to choose a path. You have a fairly good idea where each might lead, but you can never be certain, and you never know the true weight of what hangs in the balance until you start down that road. It shouldn't have felt like this. I should treat Tallulah and this situation as if it were just another op, and once completed, I'd simply move on to the next. But somehow, I sensed that this, and her, were so much more. Despite having to face the Section Chief's ire, I sensed that my career was not in jeopardy. But how I handled Tallulah would affect the rest of my life.

I looked into her eyes and knew I felt things I had never felt before. Somehow, in the span of a few hours - and conversation that was measured in minutes - I had an almost uncontrollable need to hold her, protect her, keep her near. Only my fear of scaring her kept my need, and body, in check. I had to tell her the truth, and in doing so, hope that she would trust me enough to work with me to sort all this out.

I just needed to convince her to take the first step with me. My first instinct that she knew nothing about information the Colonel had was wrong, and I was pretty sure of it. I was also convinced that Jared held things back from me. The fact that the Colonel had prearranged a way for Tallulah and Jared to communicate solidified my belief that Tallulah had information and Jared knew it. I'd deal with him later, but I had to believe that he had a good reason for not looping me in. The people I trusted could be counted on one hand, and Jared represented one of those fingers.

Tallulah, on the other hand, was a wild card. She was smart, beautiful, and I was totally captivated - and screwed. She was dangerous - the first woman that could not only be a hazard to my physical health, but my emotional health as well. I knew I wanted her, but more than that, she tugged on the parts of my psyche that I thought were dormant. But like a volcano, one eruption would forever change the landscape, and simply having her in my presence was causing the heat in my inner core to push closer to the surface. An eruption was imminent, and I found myself looking forward to that moment. But first, we had to deal with the chaos that was about to ensue.

"I work for the CIA." I kept my eyes fixed on hers, hoping she would see the truth in my words. "But coming out here to find you was personal. Jared is an analyst and I've known him for a long time. He trusts me enough to have asked me to find you, and his primary concern was to know you're okay." I kept my focus on her eyes, but her expression gave nothing away. She just stared back at me and waited for me to continue.

"I'm on a medical leave, but my Section Chief found out Jared was looking for you, and when he couldn't get in touch with me, he put two and two together. He knows I've been trying to find you and that I was doing it on my own. Apparently, Jared isn't the only one that thinks you have or know something about whatever information the Colonel may or may not have had. Besides the unknown party that Jared discovered was looking for you as well, the agency seems to think you know something because my Section Chief is on his way to Denver and he wants me to arrange to bring you in."

"I told you, I don't have anything." For a brief moment, a look of fear came across her face, but just as soon as it appeared, it was gone. She was hiding something and obviously didn't trust me. On that level, I understood her concerns, but time was not on our side and I had to find a way to convince her that running wasn't the best option.

"I believe you don't. But what I think doesn't matter." I paused a moment to debate whether playing on her fear was a bad idea, but as a mathematician, she had to at least acknowledge logic. "Whoever is out there looking for you, thinks you have something, or at least know something that will lead somewhere. Right now, it doesn't appear as though anyone else knows where you are, but that can change quickly."

Her expression changed as if a thought suddenly occurred to her. She opened her mouth, closed it, then opened it again with, "how *did* you find me?"

For a moment, I couldn't respond. That slight movement of her mouth had me spellbound. When I regained the motor skills, I simply answered with, "that's not important right now."

"The hell it's not!" Her expression immediately morphed into unmistakable anger. "Of course it's important. If there are others looking for me, there are now several people who know where I am, and you led them to me." Her voice was even, but the expression clearly said she her blood was boiling.

The truth was she was right. And although I trusted Morgan not to reveal the information he provided to anyone else, and to not get Slide-rule involved by disclosing that he coerced the robotic nerd into loaning out is RV, I couldn't guaranty that with sufficient pressure, those secrets would remain safe. Additionally, I couldn't be sure that whoever was looking for Tallulah was monitoring the same databases that Jared was searching and discovered information that either Jared or Morgan had come up with. I also had no illusions that I alone possessed the skill or resources to locate Tallulah. Top that off with the fact that since I had no idea who else was looking for her, I had no clue as to the level of skill or resources that were at the disposal of these unknown parties. I had to be honest without freaking her out to the point she would run.

"You're right, but even though I'm sure we are okay for the moment, we should probably find a safe location to hunker down until we meet my Section Chief tomorrow at nine."

She leaned back slightly, her eyebrows raising up and eyes widening. "Whoa there, Sparky, I'm not meeting anyone. Everything was fine until you came along. You go ahead and report that I don't have anything, I don't know anything, and I'm not particular pleased about meeting with you right now, let alone inclined to meet anyone you work for."

Now it was my turn to have a sudden revelation. "If you didn't want to be found, why come out of hiding and leave a paper trail that anyone with a laptop can find?"

Tallulah looked like she was ready to bolt out of her seat and clock me in the face. The tone and volume of her voice started to rise. "Assuming for a moment that how

I live my life is any of your fucking business, I just wanted a goddamn salt and pepper shaker set, okay?"

The genuine confusion must have registered on my face because she suddenly looked defeated and quietly said, "it doesn't matter. Just leave. I can take care of myself."

"Actually," I admitted, "I have no doubt you can. But there are too many unknowns out there and if you want the salt and pepper shaker set, you need to take the meeting tomorrow and at least learn as much as you can about what's happening and find options for moving forward safely." Even though her statement about the shakers made no sense, I still had a feeling that something about it spoke to me on a level that I subconsciously understood. I knew it related to her weariness at having been hiding for so long, and her desire to stop running. Somewhere buried in the back of my mind was a desire to someday have a regular life, maybe even a wife and kids. I'd miss the adrenaline rush the job gave me on a regular basis, but I also wanted what my parents and older sisters enjoyed – a content and satisfying family life. On that level, I really did get it.

"How can you say that with a straight face?" Tallulah's voice broke my momentary melancholy and brought me back to the problem at hand as she continued. "You know damn well that your boss is only interested in information that flows one way, from me to him. Even if he knew anything that would help me, he wouldn't give it to me until he had all the information he thought he could squeeze out of me first, and even then he may not tell me anything. The only beneficiary of this meeting, if there is one, would be him. Sorry, but no thanks."

I couldn't deny she had a point, but I was far from giving up. "You have to take what you can. You'll learn as much from what he doesn't say as you will from what he does. Just hear him out and if it doesn't feel right, leave. I'll even help you pack up your shit so if the meeting goes south, you can beat a path out of town, but we need to get out of here tonight and find a safe place to wait."

I sat perfectly still, staring into her expressive eyes, seeing a tornado of calculations spinning through her mind. She was sizing up her options and trying to decide whether or not to take a chance. I knew that the odds for her making a choice that would serve us both depended upon my patience to wait it out and let her come to the conclusion I was hoping she would reach.

CHAPTER 12

Tallulah

Logically, I knew my options were limited, but dammit, I at least wanted the illusion that I had a choice that wasn't based on fear. Grayson's gaze was locked on mine as if able to see my thought process and analyze along with me. I held it though whether in defiance or defeat, I wasn't sure. Taking this meeting meant admitting that something was out there that I should fear and that there really was someone who wanted information I had adamantly insisted did not exist. It would require that I tread carefully and disclose only that which would serve to clue me in as to what's been haunting me.

On the other hand, I could just run. I had gotten good at it, after all. Unlike others that had crossed my path who were also running, I had resources that would go a long way to keep me from having to surface anytime in the foreseeable future. But while this was the path I had grown accustomed to for over two years, I had tired of it. I had also, during that time, put myself in a position and environment that proved equally dangerous, albeit for entirely different reasons.

The last six months, however, had shown me a different way of living. Charlie wasn't warm and fuzzy, but in an odd way, he was a friend. And as one tied to the regular world, I had an ally that made me feel I was, at least partially, a part of it as well. I wasn't prepared to give that up just yet, and if meeting with Grayson's superiors eased my way into discouraging any further interest in me, wasn't that worth a shot?

The real problem was whether to find whatever the Colonel had left behind and then, what to do with it once I did. I was pretty sure that I could get my hands on it within a few days, but not knowing exactly what it was meant not being able to plan ahead on how to proceed from there. If it was information or proof that would implicate the government in wrongdoing, wouldn't giving it to the CIA be counter-productive? The Colonel had always intimated that he had something the government would want, but was disinclined to hand over. I never pressed for answers about what exactly that was, and now I regretted it.

Alternatively, since I didn't know exactly what it was, couldn't I just turn it over and walk away with a clear conscious? Good or bad, the decision about what to do with it would be out of my hands. Could I live with that? I could never prove it, but I suspected the Colonel died because of it. Would that make me equally complicit in his death if I chose to ignore his warnings and simply hand it over?

In my heart, I knew the answer, because deep down inside, it was the reason I had stayed underground for so long. I could have easily given every bit of information I had to those suits on the day of the funeral and gone on with my life. Instead, I chose to keep the Colonel's secret buried and go into hiding to protect it and myself. In the end, I realized that it wasn't the faces of the unknown villains after that secret that I was afraid of. It was the secret itself that haunted my dreams at night.

Part of me had always hoped that the Colonel was just paranoid and whatever he had left behind when he died was of no consequence to anyone but him. When I made the decision to reestablish myself in the regular world, I had almost convinced myself that there was nothing to fear and the last two years in hiding were simply a precaution. Sure, I constantly looked over my shoulder, but better safe than sorry, right? Now I fear that my years in exile had been justified, if not necessary.

I gazed back at the table and the salt and pepper shakers. But unlike the last time I held them in my hands, willing them to provide me with answers but coming up short, this time they seemed to speak to me with the solution to my dilemma of which path to take.

I started to formulate a plan in my head, when I realized that Grayson was sitting across from me and waiting patiently for my answer. I don't know how long I had been staring off into space, but Grayson never made a sound. That made me realize why he was probably a very good operative; he knew when to press and when to back off, sometimes that latter being far more effective.

"I'll meet with your boss," I announced boldly. "But we do this my way."

Grayson simply nodded and waited for me to continue.

"First, I need to know how you found me. I don't want to abandon everything I've worked for, so you need to justify the reasons for having to hide out until tomorrow." He hesitated a moment before telling me about Jared's file, some geek named Morgan and his ability to hack his way into government databases, a buddy who, as a U.S. Marshall, was able to convince Joe Sendak to help Grayson set up the meeting at the diner, and his systematic search of RV parks to locate my van and Suzuki.

I took a moment to absorb everything that Grayson revealed. This Morgan guy was the only one outside of Grayson with enough information to narrow down my location. Neither Charlie nor Joe Sendak knew I had a van, let alone where I'd parked it. Grayson's requisition of Slide-rule's Winnebago was only known to him and Morgan, so my decision would be based on Grayson's assessment of Morgan.

"Any chance Morgan would give up the information he dug up on me?" I asked.

"If he were being tortured, maybe, but right now, there's no connection between us." When I shot him a curious glance, Grayson explained. "I lived in an apartment across from Morgan's about eight years ago when I was just starting with the Company. We barely said ten words to each other in the six months I lived there, but we crossed each other's path while coming a going into our respective apartments. Then, about five years ago, I ran into him at CIA Headquarters in Langley. Turns out he's a contractor that probably has a higher security clearance than I do. Anyway, we recognized each other and laughed about not knowing what the other did when we were neighbors. We've done each other favors over the years since then, but only communicate on secure cell or sat phones – Morgan's a little paranoid. We don't run in the same circles, so we've never socialized outside the CIA building. There's really no connection between us that would be obvious enough to warrant a deeper inquiry."

After I thought about that for a moment, I made a decision. "I think this location is safe for now. We can take security precautions in case we have to bolt suddenly, but I'd rather not ditch my van without good reason. As for the meeting, the location needs to be public. I don't trust you enough to meet in some sleazy warehouse in the middle of nowhere."

Grayson frowned, before answering, "I set the meeting for the same diner I was supposed to meet you at yesterday." He smiled and his face relaxed a bit revealing gentle expression that caught me unprepared for the sudden heat I was feeling toward him. That smile was sexy enough to cause serious heart palpitations. I had to give myself a mental head shake before continuing on with my plan. We discussed the layout of the diner, points of entry and exit, the parking lot configuration and agreed to take his Jeep and ride together.

"Well," Grayson said, rising to his feet, "I should probably grab my stuff and get back here before it gets too dark."

The implication didn't register. "Excuse me?" I asked, confused.

"I'm staying here with you tonight."

OH. HELL. NO!

"Think again." There was no way I was letting that man anywhere near my sleeping quarters. He was already messing with my head and I need to keep it clear.

"No way I'm letting you out of my sight until the meeting," Grayson insisted. "And," he cut me off as I was about to voice my objections, "caution dictates I should be close by in case our assessment of the situation is wrong." He looked around the interior of my van. "Besides, your rig is smaller, easier to maneuver, and already untethered to camp. If there's trouble, we can drive out without delay."

I didn't want him in my van, but I had to admit that the thought of having him close was also, in a way, comforting. And even though I was torn, the look of determination on his face said to me that the subject was closed. He wouldn't take no for an answer.

"Fine."

Grayson's expression morphed into one of confusion. "Fine?"

"Yes, fine." I huffed out like a petulant child. "I don't want to argue. Let's just get tomorrow over with. I probably won't be able to sleep anyway."

Grayson stood up indicating the subject closed and looked around as if assessing the next plan of action. He looked back at me and smiled. "We should probably ready

64

ourselves for several contingencies in case things don't go well tomorrow." He spent the next few minutes mapping out multiple plans to cover different scenarios for getting out of town quickly. I didn't want to hear any of it because it meant abandoning the idea of finally putting down roots. While mourning that possible loss, I also had to acknowledge that Grayson was not only smart and careful, but sensitive as well. He seemed to understand how I was feeling, trying to lessen this sting of having to run once again.

It occurred to me that he was making contingency plans as if he would be coming with me. "Hold on," I interrupted. "If things go south, you're not coming with me."

"The hell I'm not. If anything happens, you'll want me around. I have contacts, information and resources so we can figure this out. I get you still don't trust me, but you can. I know that doesn't mean anything right now, but believe when I say I'll have your back. Jared trusts me to make sure you're okay and I want you to have salt and pepper shakers, too."

Suddenly, the fatigue I was feeling grew into full blown exhaustion. It felt at that moment as if everything I had gone through since childhood was catching up to me all at once. The secrets the Colonel left behind and the trouble that accompanied it, coming home to roost. I knew that I was tough, motivated and strong. I had always pushed forward despite any obstacles in my path and forged ahead with steely determination. I always made backup plans so I never felt trapped into submission. But now, all I wanted to do was curl up in bed and sleep.

"Tallulah?"

Grayson's voice broke the decline of my thoughts. It also made me realize I liked that way it sounded when he said my name. He also used my full name instead of calling me Lou. I'm not sure why, but somehow it made me feel better. I looked into his eyes and saw the concern and maybe even encouragement. That looked snapped me back.

Sure, I was tired but I needed to keep it together. My decision to run two and a half years ago stemmed from a belief that the Colonel wasn't entirely crazy. He may have seemed paranoid to anyone who didn't know him, but I had learned to trust in what he told me, even though at the time, I didn't want to acknowledge the value in it. He had information that he thought was dangerous enough to warrant further investigation. And I was sure it got him and Laura killed. I couldn't quit now. That would negate what he had sacrificed so much to protect and I needed to see this through.

"I'm fine," I told Grayson. But I knew that I wasn't really. I had to take responsibility for the fact that the Colonel had relied on me to retrieve all the clues and information he had hidden in various locations around the country. Like a squirrel stashing nuts before winter, the Colonel had stashed all kinds of stuff in all kinds of places, but one thing in particular may have held greater value than the rest. Fear of what I might find prevented me from going after it before, but now I realized that until I did, this would never be over. And I wanted it to be over. I also wanted to know that whatever information the Colonel had made its way into the right hands.

The problem was I wouldn't know which hands were the right ones until I could analyze what he left behind. With Grayson tethered to me, I may not be able to do that without risking it falling into the wrong hands. Well, one problem at a time. First the meeting. I'd hold the Colonel's secrets close to the vest until I had no choice.

CHAPTER 13

Grayson

allulah had just agreed to meet with my Section Chief, allow me to spend the night in her van and make plans to leave town with me in the event of a problem. Basically, everything I was hoping to convince her to agree to. So why did it feel like I just sentenced her to death? I had to hope that other than Dombrowski and Parsons, the information Jared, Morgan and I obtained about Tallulah had been contained. I couldn't assume that, and had to proceed to the meet as though anything were possible, but I didn't want to contemplate every worst case scenario.

We discussed our plans for the night and tomorrow and, surprisingly, had agreed on most every aspect of them. I moved all my stuff to Tallulah's van and unhooked all utilities. We loaded her Suzuki in the trailer and agreed we would each take a "go bag" with us in case the meeting went bad and coming back for the van was out of the question. I knew Tallulah would be armed and that point would not be negotiable.

We worked mostly in silence, each deep in our own thoughts. I headed back to Slide-rule's RV and started gathering the equipment Morgan had provided to transfer to the Jeep. I packed a bag of necessities to take to Tallulah's. When I entered with my bag in hand, I saw she had packed a duffle and left it on the bench seat. Out of curiosity, I looked in the kitchen drawer where I had earlier watched her stash what looked like provocative lingerie. That the drawer was now empty made me smile, as I hoped that the red lacy underthings were safely stowed in that duffle.

I made my way back across the lane to resume my packing. I gathered some of the smaller pieces of equipment and other things I may need in case we had to make a quick escape and stuffed them into a backpack. I loaded a supply of weapons and ammo in a small duffle.

When I returned, I noticed that Tallulah had set a large backpack on the floor and staring at a salt and pepper shaker set she had placed on the counter. I stood beside her and we simply stared at each other in silence. I couldn't tell what thoughts were going through her head, but she seemed to be working through some manner of internal struggle and debating what to say to me.

While normally such silences might become uncomfortable, we both seemed at ease with just letting the moment sit as we gathered our thoughts and contemplated how the next few hours would go.

I was the first to break the silence. "Penny for your thoughts?"

"Seriously?" The look on her face clearly said she thought I was an idiot.

"Actually, yes. I can't imagine what's going through your mind right now, and I'm curious if I should sleep with one eye open tonight." I tried a smile that I hoped would convey my desire to put her at ease, but it seemed to fall short. I don't know why I wanted her to feel safe with me, trust me, when I knew that she had every reason not to.

"If I wanted to kill you....." She smiled, satisfied that leaving that sentence unfinished would either unnerve me or make me laugh. Before I could decide which was her goal, she continued. "You're safe for tonight. What I don't like is not knowing what will happen tomorrow. I don't know what I'm walking into."

"I need you to trust me. Do you trust me?" I asked, not really wanting her to answer.

"Jury's still out," she deadpanned.

She worked quietly to convert the area that was previously utilized as a dining table/work space into a bed. She jumped up on the raised platform mattress and flopped down on her back, her long legs still hanging over the side. "I need some air," was all she said before exiting the van.

I crawled across the bed that now blocked the path between the front and rear of the van. I made my way toward the middle of the van and stood there for a moment staring at the salt and pepper shaker set still sitting on the counter. There appeared to be nothing special about these simple, everyday items. They were small ceramic pieces painted dark blue with little daisies on one side. I lifted them, turning this way and that, hoping to reveal the secret that seemed to hold so much meaning to Tallulah. My observations revealed nothing except that they seemed to be full. Not understanding why, I pulled open a few drawers until I found a small roll of scotch tape. I cut off two pieces, secured them over the little holes at the top of the shakers, then placed them in the duffle bag Tallulah had left on the floor. I couldn't explain my need to do this, but somehow, it felt important to me to make sure she kept these small items no matter what else she had to leave behind.

Later that evening, I went out to do a final perimeter check. When I returned, Tallulah turned off all the lights and climbed into the bed fully dressed while I settled into the passenger seat for the night. It reclined slightly, but I knew that discomfort wasn't the reason I would not get much sleep, though I knew I should try to rest. The attempt was as futile as I suspected. All I could think about was Tallulah. She was so cautious and untrusting, yet she was agreeing to the meeting and having me shadow her for an indefinite amount of time. Was she setting me up for something, planning to escape without me, or just resigned to deal with me because she didn't think she had much choice? The only other option – that she was actually trusting me on some level – never registered as a possibility.

The mystery that was this woman only deepened my need to know everything about her. Her actions baffled me, her conversation surprised me and her beauty left me breathless. She was as much a puzzle, if not more now, than she was when all I had to go on was a file full of cold, impersonal facts.

She was obviously smart and as tough as they come. Her early childhood had to have been a nightmare and subsequent adolescence with Colonel Asshole couldn't have been much of a picnic. Yet she seemed to be educated and refined as if raised a debutante. She dressed casually and had no obvious attachment to material things, yet something in the way she held and carried herself would lead you to believe she came from a life of privilege. At the same time, her observations and movements also suggested someone well trained in military and covert operations. She was an enigma wrapped in an incredibly sexy package. I needed to unwrap the many layers of Tallulah Jean Westfield.

As light began to seep into the tiny windows, I realized daylight was upon us and I had yet to get any sleep. I exited the van to do a perimeter check noting that Tallulah was still asleep. As I re-entered the van, she was up and ready. Her shoulder holster was strapped on and loaded with two handguns and six spare clips that looked to be fully loaded. She was ready for bear.

I started to object, but was cut off before I had the chance.

"Before you tell me I can't meet your Section Chief while armed, I told you before, I'll take the meeting, but only if I do it my way. You don't like it, I have no problem doing whatever it takes to beat a path out of town without you."

"You're fine." Dombrowski will just have to deal with it. Besides, with not knowing enough about the situation, having another set of guns couldn't hurt. I certainly didn't feel Tallulah would direct any violence toward me, but I couldn't figure out why I was sure of it. In any other case, her insistence would have put me on high alert.

I stood and secured my gun and holster at my back and made sure I had two spare clips in my pocket. I threw a flannel shirt over my t-shirt and grabbed my keys. I exited carefully and did another quick perimeter check before crossing the lane to move my jeep closer to Tallulah's rig. We moved quickly and silently to load our getaway bags into the Jeep and lock up her van.

We had decided that I would drive Slide-rule's RV to a highway rest stop about 20 miles away with Tallulah following in my Jeep. We would leave it there for Slide-rule to retrieve once we felt it was safe to let him know where to pick it up. Then we would head to the meeting together in the Jeep. I asked her about the van and its contents, but she simply advised it was handled.

I used that time on the drive to get my head in the game. Last night had my mind spinning in so many directions, I felt I had lost focus, and that can get you killed. I concentrated my thoughts on Dombrowski and Parsons. Jared said they knew about Tallulah, but I couldn't be sure of how far that information extended. I knew Tallulah had something they wanted, and I was almost sure she knew what it was. I was also certain that there was no way she would share it with them. That combination of factors would most assuredly lead to a dangerous stand-off. I had to try and keep everyone on track, knowing that the best outcome for everyone was one in which everybody ended up unhappy. No successful negotiation ever left everyone with what they wanted. And having only one side come out of it happy, meant someone else was getting screwed.

By the time we had Slide-rule's RV parked and locked up tight, my sense of unease seemed ratcheted up to critical levels. My first priority would be safety, with everything else coming at a distant second.

Tallulah got into the passenger side of the Jeep and I drove us down the highway in silence.

CHAPTER 14

Tallulah

My nerves were frayed. I'd slept all of about 2 hours last night and it didn't help that Grayson had that sleepy, sexy look first thing in the morning. I spent the entire night thinking about him and questioning why I felt safe with him around. I had no reason to trust him except that Jared, the one contact the Colonel said I could trust, told me to. Usually, that wouldn't be enough, but Grayson seemed my only way to find out what I could about my situation and find a way to get the Colonel's information into the right hands.

I hated that I was walking into this meeting blind. I hated that I would probably have to abandon my van. I hated knowing that I would probably spend the rest of my life looking over my shoulder.

I hated that I doubted the Colonel and waited to retrieve what he left behind out of fear. I hated that I never got to talk to him about what concerned him. Most of all, I hated that I wanted to trust Grayson and I didn't know why.

He was CIA and lied for a living. He was handsome and charming which meant he was good at manipulation. Whether or not that was his goal where I was concerned was of no consequence at this point. I needed his contacts and information to know what the Colonel hid and to find out who else wanted it. The Colonel trusted Jared and Jared trusted Grayson. But only to the extent necessary to get what was needed. I had to remember that and keep any other thoughts and feelings about Grayson in check.

We arrived at the diner about fifteen minutes early and used that time to canvas the area. Nothing seemed suspicious or out of place. The rooftops appeared clear and there was no surveillance that either of us could detect.

Convinced that the area was secure, we parked Grayson's Jeep in front of the diner in the same spot on the street that I had parked my Suzuki the day before. We took a table in the open seating area of the diner toward the back, near the doors that led to the kitchen, both of us sitting on the same side of the booth, our backs to the wall with the widest view, though not all, of the establishment.

At nine on the dot, two men entered, neither of whom could be mistaken for anything other than bureaucrats. The older of the two appeared to be in his mid-forties. It was clear that his resting face was simply a scowl. The younger man, in his early thirties if I had to guess, looked like what I imagined anyone seeking a career as a government bureaucrat would look like. The only thing that prevented me from underestimating them was the bulges under the suit coats that left no doubt that both men were armed. It was then that I realized that other than a few employees, the diner was empty.

They wasted no time in making their way to our table. They both hesitated before sitting down, clearly uncomfortable with the idea of sitting with their backs to the open areas. The older man spoke first.

"Ed Dombrowski. This is Eli Parsons. You must be Tallulah Westfield." He then shot a pointed look in Grayson's direction. "You, I'll deal with later."

Something about his demeanor and the way Parsons was looking at me as if I were a science experiment that went horribly wrong, just rubbed me the wrong way. Irritated, tired and sensing that introductions were over, I decided to get right to it. Nothing like ripping the band aid off in one swift movement.

"What do you want?" I asked without breaking eye contact with Dombrowski. Clearly, he was in charge and held some influence over, not only Grayson, but this whole situation as well.

Dombrowski slid a glance at Grayson then returned his eyes toward me as he spoke. "You need to come in. We need to be debriefed on everything you know about Colonel Westfield's activities before his death. You also need to be placed into protective custody while we sort out who's been trying to find you – besides Beavis and Butthead over here."

"Yeah, I don't think so. First of all, if you're really CIA, you're not chartered for domestic inquiry. Aren't you playing in somebody else's sandbox? And don't give me a line of bullshit, or I'll walk right now."

Dombrowski looked conflicted. "We can't discuss this here. All I can say right now, is we suspect activity that puts what we're looking into squarely in our lap. That's all I can tell you until you come in. We know the Colonel left information behind that we need to investigate and you are the only one who might know what and where it is."

"I'm not telling you jack. Who else is looking for me?" Tensions were getting high, but I couldn't back down. My entire future was at stake. "I'm going to the ladies room. Think about whether or not my cooperation is worth it, and when I get back, I'll ask the question again."

I got up and started walking toward the restrooms. I know that made everyone nervous because, as it turned out, the restrooms were right next to the entrance. When I veered toward the bathroom door and not the exit, I'm sure I heard a collective sigh of relief from the table.

I stood at the sink and looked in the mirror. Yeah, definitely tired from a lack of sleep if the dark circles under my eyes were any indication. I threw some water on my face. Tensions were high and I knew that one way or another, Dombrowski was taking me with him whether I liked it or not. The meeting and the illusion that I had some control over what would happen was just that – an illusion. He was in charge, though how far he was willing to push things if I refused was the question. Sorting out disagreements while everyone was armed was always a bad idea, so really, this situation was an exercise in compounding one dumb idea onto another. Little did I know how much worse it could get.

As I exited the bathroom, I suddenly realized our one miscalculation. Though Grayson and I chose the rounded booth at the back of the open dining room that gave a clear sight line to the front door, it did not, unfortunately, afford a view into the adjoining parking lot. When I looked beyond the window into the lot, I saw a black windowless commercial van pull into the lot and four men exit the van wearing gray coveralls and pulling ski masks over the heads as they stepped out. And they were armed to the teeth, each carrying modified AK-74Ms, with sidearms and knives strapped to their legs. As the sliding door on the van shut, it pulled away, heading toward the alley. The four men proceeded toward the entrance. *Holy shit.*

Running through the dining room, I made a quick calculation and decided everyone was at risk. "HEADS UP!! Four in ski masks coming in the front. Automatic weapons and coming fast. I got the one approaching from the alley." I ran past Grayson and headed to the kitchen doors. I saw Grayson flip the table on its side and the three of them duck behind it just as I heard the first shot and lost sight behind the kitchen door.

The entire staff of four people happened to be in the kitchen and stepped back as I burst through the doors, their eyes fixed on the weapon I had drawn. Wanting them out of harm's way, I pointed the gun in their direction and simply ordered them into the walk-in fridge. They were practically running into it as I heard the back door open.

The pass-through counter that ran nearly the length of the lunch counter afforded an unencumbered view from the front section of the diner into the entire kitchen. Needing to keep out of sight, I ducked low to the floor and behind a prep station in the center of the kitchen. I heard commotion in the dining area and more shots being fired, but I knew someone was approaching from the alley and needed to keep my focus there until that threat was neutralized.

The short hallway from the alley door into the kitchen gave me just enough of an advantage that I saw the approach before Asshole #1, as I had designated him, saw me. The tip of his gun entered first followed by the rest of his big, burly body. It was clear these guys were not fucking around. They were professionals, and for now, I had to assume I was the target. Even if that assumption was wrong, I was relatively sure that the "good guys" wouldn't enter a diner in ski masks carrying Russian made AK-74Ms, so self-preservation being the overriding factor, I took aim and fired before Assohole #1 could spot me. The bullet pierced his neck and from the amount of blood, probably tore into his carotid artery. He went down in a heap without ever having spotted me.

I made my way to a spot near the far end of the pass though counter that Assholes #2 through 5 would have already passed on their way into the dining area. Sure enough, as I raised myself up onto the work station and peered over the pass though counter, the four remaining Assholes were making their way toward the overturned table. I caught a glimpse of Grayson eyeing the kitchen door as if clocking the distance and calculating whether he could get through it before getting shot.

As I assessed the situation, I heard Asshole #5, who had taken up position at the rear of the line of Assholes shout something in Spanish that made my stomach drop. This was so much worse than I anticipated. The aisle they had to navigate to get from the entrance to the larger dining area where Grayson and company were taking cover had only enough room to pass single file. With all of them in a row, the best way to slow their pursuit was taking out the guy in front. Taking aim, I fired at the back of the head of the lead Asshole and down he went. The one at the back of the line, and the only one who had spoken to that point, turned abruptly and was facing me with his gun drawn. I jumped down to take cover below the counter when more shots rang out. I heard shouting in Spanish and what sounded like retreating steps out the front door.

As I started to rise, Grayson burst in through the kitchen doors gun first. He nearly tripped over the body on the floor trying to get to me. He looked calm as he asked, "are you hit?"

"No." It came out of my mouth with far more steadiness than I felt at the moment.

"Come on." Grayson grabbed my arm and proceeded to lead me back out to the dining area. I stopped at the fridge and opened the door to the sight of four very scared employees looking as though they might pee their pants, if they hadn't already. "Stay in there till the cops come," was all I could manage before shutting the door.

As we exited the kitchen, I saw Dombrowski and Parsons holding guns at their sides, standing in front of an overturned table now riddled with bullet holes. There were a few shots in the wall behind them as well.

We all scanned the room and saw two bodies on the floor several feet away. It took a few seconds to pull it together before Dombrowski broke first and yelled, "WHAT THE FUCK JUST HAPPENED?"

"I'll tell you what happened," Parsons started, drilling holes through me with his eyes. "Somebody wants this bitch dead and we nearly got taken out in the crossfire." There was a shakiness in his voice suggesting he wasn't as composed as he first appeared. "One of you got careless and led these guys here."

As stupid as Parsons seemed, and as ready as I was to lay into him with all that adrenaline still running through me, it was Grayson who bit back. "Hey, shit-for-brains. These guys were pros. This was a planned assault and they knew we'd be here. And this wasn't a hit. They were planning on taking her with them....alive."

"Bullshit. That was an awful lot of hardware. What makes you so sure it wasn't a hit?"

Parsons really was a moron and it was my turn. "Because, you dumbass, the leader clearly told the others to make sure they took me alive, as also evidenced by the head bag hanging from his utility belt. They must have known about this meeting because they were ready to take out anybody who got in their way, and they were loaded for bear."

Dombrowski looked to Grayson. "Columbian mercs?"

Grayson and I answered at the same time. "Panamanian."

"You caught that?" Grayson asked me, referring to the Panamanian Spanish spoken by the leader.

"Yeah." As I said it, another thought hit me like a ton of bricks. "One of *you* dipshits led them to me."

Parsons just didn't know when to shut up. "How do you know they didn't follow you and not us?"

"Seriously? Because where we came from was a better location to hit. They wouldn't have to risk a shoot-out. No witnesses. No security. No chance of cops happening to wander in. They could have slipped in taken out one guy with a single shot, hit me with a taser and been gone before the sun came up. If I knew where to find me, it's how I would've done it. Who knew where we were meeting?"

Dombrowski looked back at Grayson. "The four of us and Trainor."

"Well, since it clearly wasn't me, you three probably have a lot to talk about, so I'm out of here." I started heading for the door, determined to put as much distance from this place as possible.

"Not so fast." Dombrowski's voice was really starting to irritate me. As I turned toward him, knowing this confrontation would not go well, I noticed no one had yet holstered their gun. Not a good sign. Still, I waited for Dombrowski to continue.

"Look, you're the reason for this shit show and I don't give a good goddamn about what you want. You lost that option when the first dead body hit the floor. I'll have cleaners here in five, but I still have two bodies to explain."

"Three." Grayson clarified. "There's one in the kitchen."

"And she's responsible for at least two of them," Parsons chimed in.

I had had enough. I needed to get out of there. "I don't give a shit who you are. I need to leave, so feel free to stay behind and explain the corpses, or try to stop me and I can make *you* one of them." At that moment, four arms raised simultaneously, each wielding a locked and loaded firearm. *Here we go.*

CHAPTER 15

Grayson

As a field agent, you get used to some of the stupid shit you have to deal with from time-to-time. Among the most annoying is the polygraph and the psych eval. One of the strangest parts of the psych exam has been an exercise where the doctor fires off random words to which you are expected to counter with the first word that comes to your mind. I've only done that particular test once, but upon later reflection, I found it very telling about the direction my mind would go in when simply reacting without the time to analyze and evaluate. The words I blurted sometimes surprised even me. That's exactly how this moment felt.

The second everyone's arms began to raise with guns in hand, I realized that the direction in which each was aimed would speak far more clearly than any words could express. Unsurprisingly, Dombrowski and Tallulah had their guns trained on each other. What did surprise me was Parsons' gun aimed at my head. Of equal if not more telling a revelation was that my gun was pointed at Parsons. Not only that, but my body had mysteriously moved slightly and was now partially in front of Tallulah. An instinctual reaction to danger, my first impulse was to protect her against a threat. It just never occurred to me that the threat would come from my agency. I rationalized my decision by viewing the facts at hand: Tallulah was the target; I would not have leaked any information; and I trusted Jared with my life. In the split second I had to make a choice, I was left with the conclusion that either or both Dombrowski and Parsons had set us up or were too stupid to protect against an ambush at a meeting that only five people supposedly knew about. I hadn't said anything to that point, but any one of us from the CIA being armed, especially on domestic soil and for the task of bringing in an asset was against normal protocol. At the moment, though, that wasn't my chief concern.,

Dombrowski looked at me and shook his head. "Quit thinking with your dick and stand down, Daniels. She needs to come in for her own safety, and you know it."

Knowing I had to defuse this situation, I decided a different approach was needed. Keeping my eyes on Parsons, I spoke with as even and calm a tone as I could muster. "Let's look at this logically. Lou, what would it take for you to cooperate with Dombrowski and give the CIA all the information you have? I know you don't think you know anything and you don't have anything of the Colonel's on you now, so are there things floating around that you can secure? What will it take?"

"Let me walk out of here now. If there's anything to be found, I'll find it, but I need time and I don't want these pricks breathing down my neck. I don't trust any of you."

Dombrowski's eyes went wide. "Oh. Hell. No. You're not going anywhere except with us. Whoever is trying to get to you tried to kill me. "

"Well if they'd succeeded, I'd trust you a lot more."

Parsons wisely kept silent through this exchange, but it was getting out of hand. Tallulah, in a voice meant to mimic whispering, but speaking at a volume clearly meant to send a message said, "you might want to back away, Grayson, this is about to get ugly."

I needed to find a solution fast. I couldn't afford to linger on the thought that she was warning me away from danger. No. That analysis could come later; right now, we needed a plan. "How about I stay with her until she's got what she needs to come in?" I'm not sure where that came from, but the more I thought about it, the better the idea was sounding in my head.

"You're already in enough trouble," Dombrowski responded without looking away from Tallulah. "You can't seriously think I'm going to let the two of you go off together? Take Parsons and I'll let you go on your little scavenger hunt, but try to lose him, and I'll never stop hunting you down."

Tallulah shook her head. "No deal. Until I know how Juan Hood and his band of merry men found me, I can't trust you or your sidekick. If Grayson was their inside man, he had plenty of opportunities to turn me over that wouldn't cause this kind of mess, so right now, if you insist on a shadow, he's the only one I'll take. It's that or shoot me."

Dombrowski's eyes kept shifting between me and Tallulah and I know he was assessing his options. When he finally spoke, I knew that whatever he thought Tallulah might have was definitely of some importance because he reluctantly agreed to let us go and find it. As guns began to lower, Dombrowski gestured me aside.

"Don't fuck this up." As pep talks go, this was right on par with Dombrowski's usual style. "Stick to her like glue and if this doesn't result with her or the intel in my hands in 5 days, it'll be more than just me you're answering to."

"You can't put a clock on this. I don't even know where we're headed or how long it could take to get there, or if we have to look in more than one place, for that matter. Plus, we still don't know what the fuck just happened and why. I'll get in touch once I have more information."

"Hah. You're hilarious, you know that?" Dombrowski looked anything but amused. "You think I'm gonna trust you on this? You got 5 days and I get a status report every day. You'll tell me where you are and what you're doing and if you can't get it done in 5 days, then I'm pulling the plug and we do this my way. I'll look into ID'ing the corpses and trying to nail down who hired them and what they were after besides her, but you better have more for me by tomorrow or I'll let Parsons run your next op, which I guarantee you will be somewhere with lots of sand."

I had no response. With all that had happened, I couldn't promise anything. Instead I nodded and walked to Tallulah who was moving pass the bodies toward the entrance. We exited the diner, but when we got to my Jeep, she removed her bags and started walking away. Confused, I asked "what are you doing?"

"Come on!" she yelled and after securing one of the bags on her back, started sprinting north toward a busier part of town. I grabbed my bags and started after her. I tried to grab her as I caught up to her, but she suddenly took a turn down an alley and continued her sprint. Most of the garages down this residential alley had closed doors, but some were simply open carports. She stopped at one and after looking around, started to break into the car parked inside.

Though stealing a car wasn't my first choice in most operations, in this case, I had to appreciate her caution in not trusting that my Jeep hadn't been tagged with a tracker while we were distracted inside. Once she had successfully hot-wired the car, we were on our way taking unfamiliar paths that felt like we were driving around with no particular destination in mind, while she constantly checked in her rearview mirror, watching for a tail.

When she finally spoke, I realized that from the moment we left the diner, she was formulating and following a plan. "I don't think they know about my van yet, but we shouldn't take the chance. I have a friend I can trust to secure other transportation, but you need to let me handle this." Her actions to this point demonstrated her calm under fire, literally and figuratively, and I decided to trust her instincts until I felt it put us in danger. For now, I'd go along with whatever she did.

I also took the time to analyze this crazy situation. Why was it that she'd been out in the open for six months but a move on her was only made once I entered the picture. Or was it Jared's inquires that triggered everything? Could it have been Dombrowski's discovery of Jared's inquiries that led to questions above his head that ended in this chaos? As I sat in the passenger seat contemplating all these scenarios, I was only now becoming aware that we had wandered into serious gang territory. Before I could object to her strategy, she pulled a cell phone out of her go bag and dialed. "Trigger, it's Lou. I need a favor."

There was a brief pause on her end while someone responded. Then from Tallulah, "Yeah. Pretty big. If I have to lose a tail first, I may be coming in hot. I need clean wheels. I'll be at Tony's shop in 10. .... Not cops. .... Something like that. See you then."

She set the phone down and briefly looked my way. "Don't ask. Just don't say anything and when we get there, follow my lead."

A garage door entrance to a warehouse in a sketchy area started to rise and open to what looked like a chop shop. A tall black kid wearing a Lakers jersey and sporting gang tats walked out. Tallulah immediately exited the car and walked up to the kid, then gave him a warm embrace. I noticed he never took his eyes off me, even as he began to speak.

"What's with the Fed?" the kid asked Tallulah, still eyeing me cautiously.

"Later," she replied turning back and smiling at me. "I need to get rid of this car and find new wheels. Can you help?"

"Yeah." He gave the car a once over and sighed. "If you were going to boost a car, couldn't you have at least jacked a BMW? Pull it in." Tallulah jumped back in the car and pulled into the warehouse. Yup, this was definitely a chop shop. Very nice cars in various stages of disassembly were parked along the edges of the warehouse with a flurry of activity by a dozen workers stopping the minute we exited the car. When I approached Tallulah, I also noticed that at least five guys had pulled guns. They were pointed down, but undoubtedly sending me a message.

"Trigger, chill. Grayson's with me." Tallulah obviously new him well and since she looked and sounded calm, I had to assume she had the situation under control. "Grayson, this is Trigger D. Be nice."

Trigger looked irritated. "Really, man? Who is this Barney Fife and what the fuck do you think you're doing bringing a Fed into my house?"

Now it was Tallulah that was getting mad. "Hey, I have a situation here, and not many options. Grayson isn't a Fed, so relax." She pulled her gun from her waistband and handed it to Trigger. "I boosted the car from a house near Rick's Diner. This gun is VERY HOT, as in you need to help me to get rid of it permanently, and I need wheels that will get us out of town. At least two, maybe three states away. Can you swing it?"

Trigger kept his eyes on me during most of the conversation. "How many ain't breathing cause of this?" he asked, holding up the gun.

"Two. I didn't have a choice."

For a moment, Trigger looked like he felt bad for her, then lifted his shirt and pulled out a similar 9mm Barretta and handed it to her. "Take this one. It's clean. T-Bone is on his way with wheels. It'll pass if they run the plates, but if you get pulled over for a closer look, you'll have problems. Wanna tell me what's going on?"

In what seemed like a very maternal gesture, Tallulah touched the side of his face and offered a small smile. "It's better if you don't know." She walked to the car, retrieved her bag and pulled out what appeared to be a small wad of cash. "This is all I can spare for right now, but you know I'll take care of you, Mama and Jasmine."

"Naw man, you hold onto it. Something tells me you gonna need it more than me." Trigger pushed her hand holding the money away from him, then gave me a look that left no doubt he neither liked nor trusted me and that Tallulah's presence was the only thing preventing him from using my head to stop a bullet. "Why do I get the feeling that this mother fucker is the reason you need my help?"

"Look at me, Trigger. You know me and what I was doing when we met. This could be a lot of things, but I'm going to find out what and fix all of it. I won't let this touch you."

"Ain't me I'm worried about. And you didn't answer my question."

Tallulah turned to face me as she answered Trigger. "I don't know Grayson very well, but my instincts tell me to trust him for now. Believe me, if he turns out to be the problem, I'll shoot him myself."

Just as I was about to object, a rather non-descript black sedan pulled into the warehouse. The guy I had to assume was T-Bone exited the car and threw the keys at Tallulah. I grabbed our bags and headed toward the new ride sensing that hanging around any longer would definitely be overstaying our welcome.

Tallulah hugged Trigger and spoke to him in quiet tones. I couldn't make out what was said, but her words caused him to smile.

CHAPTER 16

Tallulah

A s we pulled out of Tony's warehouse, I felt a profound sadness wash over me. Despite his outwardly cruel and careless disregard for societal norms, Trigger D had a good heart. I credited his mom and sister for keeping him from becoming too hardened. He lived in a day-to-day reality that I had only briefly experienced and couldn't imagine surviving in for the long haul. His tough persona kept him alive and high in the ranks of gang culture, which both earned him respect and made him a target for rival gangs. When I met Trigger, we both needed something from the other and a strange sort of friendship emerged. My sadness and regret was not over our friendship but my hypocrisy in wanting him away from this life for the sake of his mother and sister, while at the same time utilizing his position when I needed his unique resources and skill sets. I tried to take care of Trigger's mom and sister with financial help and tried to visit them as often as I could manage, knowing it would probably never be enough.

I suddenly realized I wasn't alone in the car and sensed Grayson had reached his limit for allowing my quiet contemplation and was itching to discuss my plan. Just as I was about to acknowledge his presence, he broke the silence first. "So, where are we headed?"

"Dallas. I have a private vault there. I don't know what exactly is in it, except that it's an envelope the Colonel gave me that I never opened. Just so you're prepared, though, you should know that I don't think whatever it is Dombrowski wants will be there. I suspect that it just has information that will lead me to another location.

Dombrowski wasn't entirely wrong when he called this a scavenger hunt. That was the Colonel's style."

Though I kept my eyes on the road, I could feel Grayson watching me closely. As if testing the waters before diving in, he walked a careful line. "I know you don't trust me yet, but it would help us to be ready for trouble if I know more about that ambush. I don't have any clue who may have hired them, or what level of resources they have access to. Based on their training and hardware, I'd say they are well-funded."

He was right. I didn't trust him yet, despite agreeing to bring him along - it was more a case of a lesser of two evils. Still, he had a point. I didn't know what the threat was any more than he did, but admitting that would also reduce my power position in this partnership and I needed to keep control. I decided on the best compromise. "Why don't we just assume they want me for any intel the Colonel had and are well trained, well funded, and have equal, if not superior resources to yours. If we assume and prepare for the worse, we won't be caught with our pants down. Metaphorically speaking."

That earned a smile, which quickly morphed into a frown. It wasn't the answer he was looking for but it seemed he was willing to let it drop for the moment and focus on the problems at hand. "If that's the case, we need better firepower. What have you got on you?"

I lifted my shirt enough to reveal the gun Trigger had given me tucked into my belt. "This and another 9 in my shoulder holster, plus four spare clips. That's it for now, but I plan on making a stop on the way out of Colorado. I have guns stashed in Pueblo."

Grayson rolled his eyes. "Of course you do. Look, we need to keep moving, so why don't you take the first shift driving and I'll drive at night. If we don't make too many stops, we can be in Dallas first thing tomorrow morning."

I assumed he would close his eyes and drift off, but he sat there staring out the front window. I glanced over then asked, "Aren't you going to try and sleep?"

"Too much adrenaline in my system. Why don't you help me? Tell me something about yourself. You don't have to reveal any state secrets, but help me get to know you a little."

I thought about that and decided he was already at an advantage I didn't like. "Let's start with you first. You haven't exactly been a wealth of information about yourself. I thought Grayson was your last name, but I heard Dombrowski call you 'Daniels."

"He's called me worse." I thought that was all he would offer, but he continued on. "Sorry. Yeah, my last name is Daniels. Grayson Daniels." He paused as if weighing the wisdom of his next question, but sadly for me, he decided to pursue what I had been trying to avoid. "You seem pretty calm after what happened. I'm wondering if you've already experienced something like that before."

I knew exactly where he was going. "You want to know if I've shot anyone before."

"I guess that's what I'm asking. It's just that you don't seem as rattled as I would expect you to be."

"I'm just waiting to be alone before I have a meltdown." I chanced a glance in his direction and though it was brief, he didn't look as though he was passing judgment or being critical of my actions. I think he was genuinely curious. "I've taken a few shots, but until today, I never hit anyone."

I think he noticed a slight shake in my voice at the end of that statement, because his next question was simply, "Are you okay?"

"Yes. Honestly, I think self-preservation was drilled into me by the Colonel with such intensity that processing the consequences of taking those shots won't register until I believe I'm no longer in danger. Until then, the instinct to stay alive will override all else. How about you?" I was desperate to take the focus off me. I knew that if it stayed on me and what happened today, I'd lose it for sure.

"I haven't fired on as many as you might think. It's actually rare that I'm in life-threatening situations. Caution is always warranted, but most of what I do is about working with assets and gathering intelligence." Yeah, I call bullshit. Sensing I was not buying into that statement, he switched gears pretty fast. "Why bounty hunting?"

"Wow. You're good at redirecting conversation that veers too close to you." I paused for a moment, then decided to be equally evasive. "Why *not* bounty hunting?"

'Just seems like an odd choice for someone with a PhD."

"Girl's gotta eat. Math doesn't pay."

"Neither does crime. Doesn't stop people from making a career out of it."

I was getting that tired feeling again. I sighed. "Are we ever going to have a normal conversation?"

"Doesn't seem likely," Grayson deadpanned. "Then again, what's normal? If I had to guess, I'd say nothing in your life has ever qualified as normal. And I'm thinking that's a good thing. I don't think we'd have met if you *were* '*normal*'".

He may not have realized it, but Grayson struck a nerve. He seemed to have an ability to read my mood because he let the conversation drop for now. He leaned his head back and closed his eyes.

I used the quiet time to try and think about the next few days. While I could rationalize having Grayson with me was a way to appease the CIA and escape Dombrowski's scrutiny, I secretly liked the idea of having him along. Even his smart ass conversation style and unnerving perception of people and situations was a welcome change to my solitary existence. I didn't think our partnership would extend beyond this little adventure, and for some reason, that made me sad. I didn't expect us to become BFFs, but part of me hoped there was more to our weird connection than just a mutual need to get to the bottom of this mystery about the Colonel.

I really needed to ignore these thoughts for the moment. I had to prioritize getting to the vault and learning what the Colonel had left for me. We had temporary transportation, but I didn't believe this car would safely carry us into Dallas. Our best chance of avoiding trouble was buying a clean car. I knew a place in Armarillo that would sell us one, cash, without the usual hassle of verifiable identification. We'd need more cash since I was sure I had enough on me to pay for the car, but would leave us with little or nothing for other expenses. I needed Nigel.

I pulled out a different burner phone than the one I used to call Trigger with and dialed the number I knew Nigel would always answer.

CHAPTER 17

Grayson

I must have drifted off to sleep. I awoke to the sound of Tallulah's voice. It took me a few seconds to remember where I was and what was happening, but the sexy rasp in her voice jarred my senses in more ways than one.

As I became more aware, I heard the tail end of her conversation on what appeared to be a different cell phone from the one she used to call Trigger. "Two grand should do it. If I need more, I'll let you know. ..... Probably. I think we'll get there without any problems. .... Make the other transfers like we talked about, but wait until tomorrow for those. ... No, don't call him. I'm fine for now. I don't want him to worry about it. ...... Okay. Thanks, Nigel."

She hung up the phone and saw me staring at her as she put the phone away. I had to ask. "So what was that?"

"We may need more cash. There's a small town about 20 minutes south of Pueblo with a Western Union office. After Pueblo, we can pick up the cash before the office closes and head toward Armarillo."

"Who's sending cash?"

"Fairy Godmother. Pumpkin is out of season."

"Cute. But I'm serious. It's not safe letting anyone know where we're headed." It felt like I was being condescending to remind her of that since she managed to stay off the grid for two years, but I don't think anyone was after her then. Regardless, circumstances had changed, and a higher level of caution was called for.

"Throttle back your anxiety. Nigel manages my ..... financial portfolio, and he's the kind of guy whose success – not to mention his health – relies on confidentiality. Let's just say his clientele would not take kindly to indiscretion."

"So. Money launderer, huh? Handy guy to have around. Find him in the yellow pages, did ya?"

"Craigslist."

I really had to give her credit for her quick wit and dry humor. She delivered every line with a straight face, even tone and mischievous glint in her eyes. Spending any more time with her was seriously going to jeopardize my ability to stay focused on the objective. Before I could comment further on her financial consultant, we pulled into the parking lot of a large commercial warehouse with a retail storefront. The sign on the front identified the business as a plumbing contractor.

"We're here," she announced. She pulled around to the back side of the building where there was a commercial loading dock with a small door right beside it, both at the far right side of the back wall. On the far left was a single door with a lock box hanging from the knob. Below the eaves of the corrugated roof were three massive flood lights wired to a motion sensor that seemed to be directed just a few feet away from the edge of the back wall. Wiring around each door indicated a sophisticated alarm system. She parked just outside the single door on the far left and got out. Figuring she might need helped I followed her out. She had barely removed the key from the lock box, when a guy who looked more like a WWF fighter than a plumber approached quickly. "Hey," he shouted. "Who are you guys?"

"Call Dex," Tallulah responded. "Tell him Marsha is here picking up some of her stuff."

He removed a cell phone from his pocket and within seconds had confirmed the information. "Okay, yeah, you're cool. Dex said it's been quiet and not to worry."

"Thanks. Can you keep traffic away from back here for a while?" Tallulah flashed a pretty impressive smile and the big guy actually blushed.

"Sure thing," he said, and walked back the way he came. I wanted to make a wiseass comment, but thought better of it. Instead I followed her inside.

It turned out to be a small room, unconnected to any other part of the building. It was probably walled off to be a separate storage room, but it was clearly independent of the plumbing business. The room was only about 20' squared, but there were several boxes of various sizes and composition all around the room. Tallulah headed straight for a stack of large aluminum cases and unhooked the latches on two of them. She opened the first and removed two AR-15 rifles, two Colt 45s and two Baretta sidearms. "Grab that duffle bag behind you."

I turned around a saw several large green bags sitting on a pallet against one wall of the room. I grabbed the largest bag and handed it to her. She proceeded to stuff the bag with the guns she just removed and opened the second case she had unlatched. She picked up a briefcase that was sitting next to the boxes and started packing it with ammunition. She zipped the duffle and closed the briefcase and basically, dismissed me from the room. "Here, put these in the trunk."

It was better if I didn't know what else was in this room and how it got here. As I was getting ready to close the trunk I had just loaded with what I would imagine was an arsenal of illegal weaponry, I heard Tallulah exit the building. "Wait. One more thing." I took the box she was carrying from her and loaded it in the trunk as she locked up behind her. We climbed into the car and drove off without uttering another word.

Tallulah stayed behind the wheel and drove in silence. I got the distinct impression she was trying to avoid questions about our little pit stop. I suspect she would have difficulty explaining what else was in the storage room and where it all came from. As curious as I was about that, I had to save the prying questions for subjects that were more important in accomplishing our mission.

It wasn't long before we were pulling down an alley on the south side of building that housed a check cashing store. A Western Union sign hung in the window. Tallulah reached into her bag once again, this time her hand emerged clutching a leather pouch. She unzipped it and removed what looked like some type of ID card. If I had to guess, I'd say it was an out-of-state license with someone else's name on it. In other words, a counterfeit ID. She stuffed it in her back pocket then pulled her hair back in a tight ponytail and secured it with a hairband from her wrist. She reached into that magic bag again and pulled out a baseball cap and a pair of Ray Ban sunglasses and put them on. She and looked at me before getting out. "Stay here. I'll only be a minute."

Sure enough, not more than 10 minutes later, she was back in the car and we were headed southeast. For the first five minutes I debated asking about the cash and why she chose not to ask for my assistance, but I knew it had to do with her lack of trust. She wasn't going to rely on me for anything as long as she knew there were resources at her disposal that she could trust. A gangster named Trigger D and Nigel the money launderer were trustworthy, but me she had problems with. I had to accept that she may never trust me enough to hand over whatever we find, but I had to keep pressing forward. I suppose it was one of those cross-that-bridge-when-we-come-to-it-kind of situations. I just hoped that she wouldn't try to burn this particular bridge before I had a chance to get across.

After a while it seemed like neither of us would be sleeping. It was pretty obvious that between the shoot out this morning and trying to navigate through the day filled with questions, uncertainty and some level of mistrust, closing our eyes was likely off the agenda. Experience told me that, if we didn't take time to calm our minds and rest our bodies, the crash would be pretty brutal. We both wanted to keep moving, and admittedly, time was not on our side, especially with the clock Dombrowski put me on ticking like a time bomb, but I decided to ignore the clock in favor of getting through this unscathed, which meant taking a break to decompress for just an hour or two.

"Hey," I started as quietly as possible so as not to startle Tallulah. "I know we should keep moving, but we're both tired and about to hit a wall. Rather than force a nap in the car, why don't we just pull into the next rest stop. We can stretch our legs, grab a bite to eat, and maybe even catch a couple hours rest before we get back on the road."

Even though she stared out the front window, I could see the frown on her face and hear the sigh that followed. "I was hoping to switch cars before we stopped to rest, but you're right. We could both use a little time to recharge."

A few miles down the road, we pulled into a rest stop. There were a couple of fast food joints open and a cheap chain motel next to them. She pulled up to the motel office but kept the engine running and turned to me. "Why don't you get a room so we can shower and change and I'll grab us some food."

"Sure. Meet me back here." Tallulah pulled away as I entered the office and found a young guy with long blond hair behind the counter. "I need a room. Ground floor, on the end."

The young guy glanced out the window and asked, "one bed or two?" Now there was an interesting question. It was unlikely that either of us would actually sleep, but the idea was to try and get some rest. Being in the same room would be difficult, but separate rooms was unacceptable. For security reasons. As much as I would love to share a bed with her, I had to focus, and I was certain she wouldn't let me within touching distance of her body anyway, so practicality won out.

"Uh, Dude. One bed or two?" The clerk was becoming impatient, and hearing the blaring sound of the television emanating from the back room, it was no doubt because I was keeping him from finding out which Kardashian was doing what to whom.

"Two." He handed me an information card to fill out. When he asked for ID I told him I forgot it in the car, and as expected, he really didn't seem to care. I paid with cash, grabbed the room key and walked out just as Tallulah was returning. I hopped in the car and directed her to the last room on the end of the building. I could smell the burger and fries and realized we hadn't eaten all day. I actually heard Tallulah's stomach growl, but being gentlemanly prevented me from making any comment.

As I opened the door and turned on the light, I saw pretty much what I had expected. The room was typical. There were two double beds, nightstand, dresser, a small closet and a bathroom that would require skills as a contortionist in order to sit on the toilet with the door closed. Tallulah set the food and drinks down on the dresser and headed back to the car to retrieve her bags. Once she returned I did the same, only when I arrived back in the room, the bathroom door was closed and I heard the shower running.

She exited a few minutes later wearing nothing but a towel. With dripping wet hair she pulled clean clothes from one of her bags and walked back into the bathroom. She emerged in jeans and a tank top and bare feet, with the towel now wrapped around her hair.

"We should eat. Food is getting cold," was all she said before she tore into the bag, handed me a burger and fries, and took her food over to her bed and dug in. I decided to eat before taking a shower and polished everything off quickly. Tallulah ate more slowly but still managed to finish everything. I took a quick shower and dressed.

While brushing her teeth, Tallulah came out of the bathroom to discuss the plan. "We shouldn't hang around too long. I suggest we try to get some rest but leave no more than two hours from now. I don't want to arrive in Armarillo too late. I'd like to be in Dallas before the end of business."

"That's fine," I replied. I mentally reassured myself that following her lead was the best plan for now. Nothing she was doing thus far gave me pause to question our security. She was obviously cautious and seemed familiar enough with our path and destination to suggest she had an exit strategy if anything went wrong. She climbed into the bed closest to the door and turned away from me. I notice she had slid a gun under her pillow and while I silently commended her on security precautions, questioned how and why she would think to do that.

I similarly slid a gun under my pillow and tried to drift off, but as I suspected, sleep would not come. I could smell her soap, a lavender scent, and hear her softly breathing in the next bed. Images of her in various stages of dress began to flood my mind. Yeah, forget about getting any sleep.

CHAPTER 18

Tallulah

Two hours had passed and I know I had drifted off a couple of times, though based on the nightstand clock, the longest sleep I had managed was about 15 minutes. Once I realized that trying to sleep with Grayson in the bed next to me was an exercise in futility, I decided to get up and check on a few things. My go bag had the documents I would need to get into the vault, but beyond that was a mystery. I also needed to pick up some equipment. At a minimum, I would need a new computer, wifi booster, and a few other electronics. No matter what we found in the vault, I was never without a way to tap into cyberspace. Information was always the best weapon and I needed every advantage I could get. As I was going through my mental checklist and repacking some clothes, I heard a rustle from the other bed. I looked over and saw Grayson staring at me.

"Get any sleep?" he asked as he got up and started getting himself together and repacking his bag.

"A little," I answered. It was still dark, but I knew we needed to get moving. "We should go."

"I'll load my stuff in the car and jog over to the convenience store and get coffee. How do you take yours?" he asked as he headed out the door.

"Just black. I'll be right behind you."

I watched as Grayson jogged across the parking lot. Admittedly, he was attractive, smart and had an impressive physique. I had to stay focused, but it was hard not to notice there was something strange happening between us. It felt as if we had known each other for years.

I know that I couldn't focus on such things. Any distraction could result in a disaster, but it was hard not to notice that there was something that felt tangible crackling between us. It was an entirely different experience than what I had ever felt before. My first relationship happened while I was in hiding. Ian was dangerous and exciting, and he taught me a lot. I tried not to think about him. But as with many things, sometimes the past is hard to forget.

It occurred to me that all the males around me were dangerous men but for entirely different reasons and in entirely different ways. Ian's dangerous image was an occupational hazard rooted in a cold and calculated persona. Trigger's was born from a survival of the fittest mentality; dog-eat-dog with automatic weapons. Nigel profited from his ability to help you but only with your understanding that crossing him meant he could wipe you out with a few keystrokes on a computer.

Then there's Grayson. I sensed he wasn't dangerous in a cold or reckless way, but rather, dangerously deliberate. I couldn't explain why but something told me he wouldn't hurt me intentionally. I may not be able to trust his end game, but I didn't think he would put me in the line of fire just to get to it, though only time would tell. My biggest concern was over my own self-control. I couldn't let any feelings of lust cloud my judgment, though my inclination to trust him, at least partially, made me think that ship may have sailed.

Once the room was clear, and the car loaded, I found Grayson walking toward the car with two industrial sized coffee cups. He came around to the driver's side. He looked at me questioningly when I remained in my seat.

"Don't you want me to take a turn behind the wheel?" he asked.

"Thanks, but I know the way and I'm already here. If I start to get tired, you can take over."

He shrugged and headed around the front of the car. "Suit yourself."

The ride was almost entirely quite with only a few breaks in the silence for questions about pit stops and Texas geography, both of us seemingly wrapped up in our own thoughts. For me, it was time to better work out the details of a plan for this crazy road trip and playing out different scenarios in my head about what to do if or when we discovered anything of value. I managed to keep my focus on the road, but I also felt better knowing I had a few contingencies in my pocket. The few times I glanced over at Grayson, he seemed relaxed, but I was fairly sure he was on high alert. Something about the brightness in his eyes told me he was acutely aware of everything around him, especially me.

Red's Used Car Dealership appeared to be getting ready to close for the day when we pulled in later that evening. Tommy Orland was locking the door to the trailer that served as the dealership's office. As he turned, he spotted me exiting the vehicle and starting toward him. I caught the moment he recognized me when his frown morphed into a wide smile.

"Marsha!" I cringed knowing there was no avoiding the collision of the life I had under a previous false identify with the one Grayson knew. I counted on his experience as a covert operative keeping him quiet while he assessed the situation without blowing my cover.

"Hey, Tommy," I greeted while allowing him to kiss my cheek without leaning in too closely. Tommy always was a little handsy and the further away I could get the better.

Tommy's expression went through several incarnations starting with confusion as he surveyed the car we arrived in, followed by suspicion when he caught sight of a passenger he didn't know, and finally settling on one of sympathy. "Heard about Ian. I was sorry to hear about what happened. I also heard you dropped off the map. You okay?"

"Yeah, I always knew they'd go out in a blaze of glory."

"They?" Tommy looked thoroughly confused.

"Yeah. Ian and Sean."

"Oh, yeah. I didn't really know Sean, though. Ian was my guy."

"Sure. But look, Tommy, I'm dealing with a situation. Don't worry about him," I added when Tommy kept eyeing Grayson. Wisely, Grayson said nothing even though his expression conveyed a desire to jump in the middle of our exchange. Deciding that ignoring Grayson was best, I carried on. "Tommy, I need reliable transportation and I need you to take your time filing the paperwork."

Tommy waited a beat before moving his attention away from Grayson and back to me. "What about that?" he asked as he motioned toward the car we pulled up in.

"Won't pass muster up close. Can you deal with it?"

Tommy smiled. He held many careers – none legal – and was known mostly as one of the best wheel men around. He was more or less retired from that life, but still helped old friends with automobile issues. "No sweat, Marsha. I've got a midsized Ford. Back fender is a little dinged up but the engine's good. You got twenty-five hundred, it's yours."

"Deal. Get the papers ready and I'll meet you in your office. Can I have the keys?"

I walked with Tommy toward the office, then tossed the keys he gave me to Grayson. I pointed to the last car in the back row. "White Ford," I shouted in his direction. "If you swap out the stuff, I'll finish here and we can be on the road in 10." Grayson just nodded and went to work.

"New man?" Tommy asked while typing on his computer.

"Just a friend."

Tommy stopped typing and looked up. He paused a bit with a curious look on his face. He seemed torn about whether or not to speak. I was about to nudge him along when he finally opened his mouth. "Look. I didn't know Sean well, but Ian was a friend and I know he cared about you a lot."

I met Ian a couple of years ago at a particularly low point in my life. Despite discovering who he was a what he did, I grew to care very deeply for him. I had hoped to have put that part of my life behind me, but it was clear with these recent developments that all those things I was trying to escape were the very things that might help me stay alive.

Suddenly Tommy looked like he had more to say. "What is it?" I asked.

"Nothing. Just be careful. Here you go." Tommy handed me a few sheets of paper that spit out of the printer on his desk. "I know Ian could be a cold bastard, but he would want you to be okay. If you need anything, call me. I owe him that much."

I could only offer Tommy a small smile. Ian valued loyalty and truth from those around him. In the end, his circle of trust was small – just Sean and me. It was ironic that one of us caused him anxiety and the other caused his death. It was also something I wasn't prepared to share with Grayson.

Grayson was pulling the white Ford up to the trailer as I was exiting. We remained silent he pulled onto the highway headed toward Dallas. I was aware of the tension between us and I didn't like it. I wasn't at the point of trusting him completely, but this little adventure was going to be stressful enough without adding this unease to the mix. Apparently, we each hit the wall at the same moment because we both spoke at exactly the same time.

I barely got out my "look, Grayson…" when I heard him say, "I know…." Then simultaneously, "you first." Nervous laughter followed before Grayson took the lead.

"I know trust will always be an issue with us until something happens to change that. I'm guessing that your ability to stay off everyone's radar for a few years relied on using aliases. I figure 'Marsha' is the one known to your storage landlord in Pueblo and Tommy. I don't need to know. My only curiosity is that I caught a glimpse of your ID. It's a pretty impressive fake, clearly done by a pro."

"If you want to know who did it, you're out of luck." Danny, the forger, was among the network of lowlifes I befriended over the years to provide me with things I needed. Danny had sold me a couple of ID packages that had yet to be used, which might come in handy. I had to assume that being out in the open with a CIA sidekick now meant that any alias I used would probably be burned within 48 hours and I would have to cease using it.

"That's fine," Grayson said. "I have a guy whenever good old Uncle Sam can't take care of those things for me, but more than one contact is always preferable. If I need to hire an outside contractor from time to time, I'd like to use a good one. After my little dance with Dombrowski and Parsons yesterday, I imagine any ID I get from them could be tainted, though it doesn't seem like I'll need it for a while. Since you're in charge of this expedition, I'll just provide my charm and good looks. You can take care of the rest."

I couldn't help but smile. He really was attractive and charming, and all evidence so far pointed to a tough and fearless operative. He was also inspiring conflicting emotions. I couldn't trust him, but I still felt safe with him. Something about him made me feel like he would protect me. It was ridiculous, I know. I didn't know anything about him and I couldn't identify what it was but something drew us together, and I sensed he felt the same pull.

Neither of us slept for the entire drive toward Dallas. We decided to take small, less traveled State and county roads instead of using the interstate. Even though this would increase our drive time by several hours and delay our arrival in Dallas, it was better to avoid the toll roads where traffic cams were more likely.

Just on the outskirts of Dallas, we pulled into the parking lot next to a very nondescript, single-story building. A small bronze plaque to the left of the front entrance identified the business as Bingham Securities and Trust. From my go bag, I pulled out the passport and electronic key card that would access the private box I held here, along with a small strapped purse that should hold everything I emptied from the box.

"I'm assuming that passport doesn't say 'Tallulah' on it. Care to share the name?"

I looked up at Grayson and smiled. "No, not really. You've been asking me to trust you. It will help your case if you trust *me* now."

CHAPTER 19

Grayson

We exited the car with Tallulah carrying her go bag. She opened the trunk, put her bag in it and proceeded to disarm, making sure all weapons of any kind were left behind. It was a rather impressive collection of weaponry, including two guns, two clips and a switchblade.

"Your turn," she announced while smiling at me, her eyes scanning up and down my body. For a moment I thought she might be checking out my physique, then realized she was just trying to assess what I was carrying.

I knew places like this existed. They were private companies that offered secured safety deposit boxes that didn't have to comport with standard banking regulations. Clients were more often than not, hiding assets that they didn't want government officials or nosy ex-wives knowing about. Fees for these services would be out of my price range and security would be second to none. There would undoubtedly be sophisticated metal detectors and scanners and strict protocols for access. While I wanted to object, I knew there would be no entry without relinquishing the arsenal on my person, so I reluctantly put my guns, clips and knife in the trunk.

Once inside and through the various layers of security where Tallulah provided her passport – without ever uttering her name - to the manager, she produced the electronic key card. We were led into a vault lined with safe deposit boxes. Instead of keys, the boxes had electronic slots designed for the two keys required to access them. One from the client and the other from the manager. There was also a small touch pad that I later learned was for fingerprint identification. Once the ritual confirmed her identity, the door to the box was opened and a metal box slid out of the opening. We were led to a private alcove and left alone with the box. Tallulah wasted no time opening the box and removing a manila envelope with no markings, a black velvet pouch and two large bundles of cash. She placed all the items in her purse, closed the box and within a few minutes, we were back in the car and driving north, away from Dallas.

She gave me directions to a small motel, similar to the one we had stopped at last night. Once we secured a room, ordered a pizza and settled in, she grabbed her purse and walked over to where I sat on the bed. She sat on the other bed facing me and pulled out the envelope. From the envelope, she removed several sheets of paper, which she slowly looked through. With a big sigh, she handed me the stack of paper, flopped back onto the bed and closed her eyes.

The papers were photocopies of different sections from a newspaper – a weekly shopper from some suburb outside Atlanta, Georgia. There were several obituaries, part of a page that had classified ads, and a few articles, none of which seemed important or in any way significant. In between the papers was a Sudoku puzzle book with a few completed pages. The pizza arrived as I was sorting through everything. Tallulah placed the everything on the small table in the room and said nothing as she started in on the food. I joined her at the table and we ate in silence as I contemplated why something in the air had changed.

"The Colonel did this a lot." At the sound of her voice I looked up to see a sadness in her expression that I recognized as the one I saw when we first met. A sadness born from exhaustion and frustration over dealing with situations not of your own making.

"What did he do?" I asked.

"He was paranoid. When I would come home during school breaks, we would spend that time together going over what I called his 'lessons'. He would come up with ways for us to communicate without others knowing. Design codes and cyphers. I used to think he was nuts, but refusing his command to participate in these lessons was not an option. Anyway, he gave me the envelope a few weeks before he died and told me to stash it until he asked for it or retrieve it if something ever happened to him. It never occurred to me actually go after it until the attack at the diner. I mean, sure, I took off after the funeral and I was worried that maybe something was rotten in Denmark, but everything else he left behind for me to find never led to anything I wouldn't have expected."

"Like what?" I was genuinely curious about this odd relationship they seemed to have.

"Weapons, money, personal papers. Nothing out of the ordinary – for him, I mean."

I held up the papers. "How does that relate to this?"

She signed heavily. "That's how he leaves things for me. I have to figure out where they are based on information that's easily accessible to me, but would mean nothing to anyone else who might find it. Within those papers is the location of whatever it is, and what I will need to gain access to it. Just leave them on the bed and I'll go through it tonight. It shouldn't take me long to decipher. We had several keys to unraveling that mess that only he and I knew about. Once I know where we need to go, we can plan our next move."

My chest suddenly started to hurt. Looking at her, I could see now how truly tired she was. Not just from a lack of sleep, but from the strain of everything the Colonel dumped on her. I wasn't sure if the sadness in her eyes was from the stress of the task ahead of us or because of the pain in recalling her relationship with a man who didn't seem to regard her as a daughter, but rather a conduit for conveying information. The desire to protect her grew larger, but more than that was a need to comfort her and offer security and affection without attaching a price.

She got up and walked to the window. We kept the curtains closed at all times, but Tallulah lifted one edge and peered out. "I really thought I could have a normal life." Though she usually had a raspy quality to her voice, the softened tone betrayed a profound sadness. "I don't really know what normal is, but it was naïve to think that I could live a quiet existence. Just me and my salt and pepper shakers." Suddenly, the significance of keeping those items in her bag made complete sense to me. I could take it no longer.

I got up and stood behind her at the window. Almost against my will, my hands came up and rested on her shoulders. My body seemed to move forward an inch at a time until my chest could feel the heat radiating off her back and the floral scent of her soap surrounded me. On a small sigh, she leaned back until her body was almost completely pressed against mine. As if operating with a mind of their own, my arms wrapped around her body, my hands coming to rest on her stomach. As her head leaned back on my shoulder, I could see her eyes were closed and a single tear had made its way down her face.

My head leaned forward and with my lips nearly touching her ear, I whispered, "I can't promise everything will be okay, but I'll be with you for as long as this takes. We'll work together. You don't have to do this alone."

She turned in my arms, looked up at me with those mesmerizing eyes and I was lost. Unable to stop what was happening, I lowered my head and gently pressed my lips against hers. She responded immediately with her arms coming around my neck. Though I sensed we both felt some level of urgency, the kiss was slow and soft. As it deepened, I felt her move closer, but since our bodies were already pressed together, I interpreted her movements as seeking a feeling of security. That she chose to look for that in the circle of my arms both humbled me and wildly turned me on.

As the kiss went on, articles of clothing seemed to miraculously fall to the floor. It felt like each moment that passed in this embrace exposed more of each other, both physically and emotionally. When be briefly separated, I looked down to find her standing in front of me completely exposed, and never had I seen a more incredible sight. But for the fact that I never took drugs, I would have thought I was experiencing a high like no other. It wasn't simply that she had a magnificent body, but there was an angelic, ethereal quality to the vision before me that injected a level of anxiety I had never experienced with a woman. It was a feeling that I desperately needed to be inside her, to connect with her. Almost to the point of fearing the consequences of failing in that quest.

Even when she turned to pull the covers from the bed, the spell could not be broken. Even when I reached into my duffle bag to retrieve a condom, the spell could not be broken. All I could focus on in those moments was the feel of her skin as my hands moved over her body, the softness of her mouth as I tasted every corner of it, the gentle feel of every curve as I pressed my body into hers, and the feel of her hands that touched me with an intimacy I had never felt.

The exploration of each other with our hands and mouths seemed to go on forever. I knew I couldn't wait much longer to be buried inside her, but this slow discovery felt not only incredible, but also necessary. This was a journey we were taking toward each other to bridge whatever was making us wary.

Every way in which her body responded told me she was building up to the same moment that I could no longer wait for. At the moment we finally came together, I knew my life would never be the same. It was slow and sweet and brought her to the peak more than once. My own orgasm seemed to go on longer than I had ever experienced. As I lay on top of her trying to catch my breath, I felt her hold on me tighten. Her legs wrapped around me and were locked together below my ass. Her arms, which were deceptively strong, had a grip on my body that made catching my breath a challenge. When I lifted my head and looked at her, the expression I saw conveyed surprise. Almost as if the intensity of the experience was as unexpected as it was amazing. I couldn't help but smile.

That seemed to bring her out of her momentary stupor and she released her death grip on me. Separating from her bordered on painful, but I needed the bathroom. Not just to dispose of the condom but to splash water on my face to see if what I had just experienced was real or just a figment of my imagination.

When I exited the bathroom, Tallulah was under the covers and facing away from me. I climbed into the bed with her and spooned up against her. She pushed back into me and took my hand from her hip and wrapped it around her stomach. I inhaled deeply trying to capture not only her scent, but her very essence. I relaxed into her and closed my eyes. At some point, I drifted off into a sound sleep.

CHAPTER 20

Tallulah

*H*oly Fuck! Only a few minutes had passed since Grayson climbed into bed with me and promptly fell asleep. I could feel his warm breath on my neck and the steady rise and fall of his chest against my back. I waited patiently for the panic to set it. This was a major screw up of epic proportions, one from which I would surely never recover. Yet, I couldn't stop smiling. I just had the most phenomenal sexual experience of my life with the one person who had the power to threaten the life I was trying to build, only all I could feel at the moment was safe in his embrace. *I should have my head examined.*

I replayed the entire encounter over and over in my head. The contrast between his hard body and soft touch. The strength in his hold on me and the soft vulnerability in the way he looked at me. The way I mentally fought to treat this as if it were just sex was an epic fail. I never experienced a connection with someone on the same level I just had with Grayson. Once I acknowledged that something was happening between us that went beyond the Colonel's scavenger hunt and need to blow off steam through sex, I had to ask *what next?*

Laying here thinking about the change in the dynamic with Grayson was only going to drive me insane, so I slowly removed his arm from around my body and got up. He stirred only slightly before falling back asleep. After cleaning up and dressing, I grabbed the papers off the other bed and started going through them. I sat at the table where I could watch Grayson's face at rest. That made it hard to concentrate, but eventually, I was able to focus on the task at hand.

By the time Grayson started to wake an few hours later, I had figured out what we needed. His eyes slowly opened and fixed on mine. A wide smile spread across his face. He sat up against the headboard, rubbed the sleep from his eyes and ran his hands through his hair. I intended to tell him what I discovered in the papers but was momentarily distracted by the sight of his exposed chest and arms and the outline of certain body parts under the sheet covering his lower half.

"Did you get any sleep?" he asked.

I mentally threw cold water in my face and shook my head. "Not really. I spent the time going over these papers. I think I know what we need to do next. We have to pick up a few things on the way, but Atlanta is our next destination."

"Okay." He gestured to me with a crook of his finger and slow smile. When I walked over to the bed, he reached up, pulled me into his lap and pressed his lips to my forehead. "Can we take a minute?" he asked.

Rather than answer, I simply wrapped my arms around him and pressed my face into his neck. I couldn't explain why, but sitting on his lap with his arms around me calmed my nerves and lessened my anxiety. I knew, however, that as much as I wanted to stay like that indefinitely, we had to finish what we started if I had any hope of putting this nightmare behind me.

"We should pack up and get on the road."

Grayson gave me a gentle squeeze. "Just let me get in the shower. We'll grab some coffee from that convenience store down the street and you can fill me in on the plan."

I was suddenly overcome with the need to feel him again. "I haven't had a shower, either. Do you think we can work up more of a reason to need one?" Before I could consider why I said that, I found myself on my back, Grayson above me and my clothes strewn around the room.

CHAPTER 21

Grayson

The minute we started the drive toward Atlanta, I knew that the change in our relationship was sealed and I was happy about that. Every distinguishable difference was an improvement, starting with the physical. It wasn't just the unbelievable connection while making love, but it was also our mutual need for constant contact. In the car, walking through the electronics store to buy a laptop, it didn't matter. Whether I was holding her hand, touching her face or running the back of my hand down her arm with a gentle caress, the need to be constantly touching her was overwhelming. And I sensed the same from Tallulah, if her reaction to my touch or the actions she initiated were any indication.

There was also a noticeable change in her willingness to include me in her thinking when formulating strategy. I wouldn't go so far as to say she trusted me completely or showed any willingness to impart more information about her past on me, but there was definitely more of an openness that didn't previously exist.

The downside was that she would expect me to demonstrate the same willingness to share information if there was any hope of building up to some level of trust. I decided to take the initiative and talk to her before the issue came up in a context I couldn't control.

Tallulah had asked that we drive around a suburban area as she unpacked the laptop she purchased. As she was unpacking some of the accessories that she also purchased, I decided now was the time. "I need to talk to you about something."

She immediately stopped what she was doing and looked up at me. I found an open spot on the street, pulled over and parked.

Best to rip the bandage off in one quick pull. "Dombrowski put a clock on this mission. He only gave us five days, and he expects me to check in every day. I haven't been in contact since we left Denver, but I suspect if I don't call with an update soon, he'll send out a posse to find us, including law enforcement, military, even the boy scouts. I told him the five day rule was a no-go, but I'm concerned that dismissing that possibility out of hand will make him twitchy." I waited patiently for her reaction, which up to that point was a blank expression. Then she broke into laughter.

When her laughing subsided, her response surprised me. "So give him an update. I imagine the Redskins not making the playoffs would make his ass twitch. He could probably use more fiber in his diet."

"What would you like me to tell him?" I asked, surprised she was more amused than concerned.

"Tell him we're making progress, you'll start checking in daily and we'll turn over whatever we have in five days."

"Really?"

She suddenly looked at me with an expression that conveyed the sentiment: *you're kidding, right?* "I saw the sat phone in your duffle. I suspect any kind of tracker or GPS is disabled or its encrypted, so there's no chance he can trace our location, right? So calling him isn't a problem. We are making progress and there's no reason to think we won't continue to do so as long as we keep moving. As for the five days, if we have nothing in that time, that's exactly what he'll get."

She was so matter-of-fact that I was actually impressed, but I also had other concerns. "He may want more details."

"I know you have divided loyalties here, but let's be clear. I'm the one with a bullseye on my back. If I don't come back with something he wants or we don't find it soon, I've got bigger problems than Dombrowski's pucker. At least agree that we can't give any hint about location or otherwise give him any details unless or until I know there's value I can bargain with. I won't try to tell you how to do your job, but for safety sake, let's acknowledge the possibility that if anyone starts shooting again, they could miss me and hit you. I don't think I could handle knowing you were hurt because of me. We still don't know what happened in Denver."

It took me a moment to process what she just said. I understood the practicality of her statement, but the idea that she worried for my safety touched me. Only my family gave a shit about me in that way. They may not know what I did for a living, but they cared about my safety nonetheless. But my everyday experiences were different. Anyone in my job assumed the risks, so the knowledge that your life was sometimes on the line was a reality you simply learned to live with and accepted for others similarly situated in this profession.

It also sobered me to the situation more quickly than a bucket of cold water over my head. While I sat here waxing poetic about the feelings she invoked in me and the changes between us, I completely ignored the fact I had broken my cardinal rule of operations. I slept with an asset. The agency never discouraged that behavior as long as it had purpose and resulted in a successful mission or cultivation of a valuable intelligence source. The bigger problem was I also started developing feelings for her that destroyed my objectivity and could negatively affect my judgment in life or death situations. Admittedly, the overwhelming need to protect Tallulah started from almost the second I saw her picture, but now, all bets were off. I was certain I'd risk everything for her and she needed to know that. Consequences be damned.

"If we're going to be clear about anything, it's that my priority is you. Any deals we strike with Dombrowski are simply a means to an end. Rendering you useless to anyone who wants the intel is the only way to extract you from this insanity and give you a chance at a real life." I thought I may have said the wrong thing because it looked as though she was about to cry. Instead she leaned over, kissed my cheek and said, "you better call Dombrowski."

The conversation with him didn't go well. He was not happy about being kept in the dark about our location or details of our quest, and despite spewing all kinds of threats, some of which included removal of a key appendage from my body and sticking it in an orifice where it clearly didn't belong, I stood my ground and promised to check in, not the next day, but upon arrival at our next destination.

During most of my conversation with Dombrowski, Tallulah's shoulders appeared to shaking indicating her silent laughter at my dilemma. Once I ended the call, she turned to me and smiled. "Sounded like his head was about to explode. Or at the very least, he was having some kind of aneurism."

"On this list of things I need to worry about, Dombrowski's neurological condition ranks pretty low on the food chain. I'll deal with him when I deal with him. So, what are we doing?"

She finished setting up the computer. "I need to find a strong wi-fi signal I can hack and use to get a few more pieces of information before I know exactly which cemetery to go to."

"Come again?"

"You ever watch those spy movies that involve these complicated codes and clues to find state secrets? They're always designed so anyone with the knowledge and ability to decode the message could find the prize. The difference here is the Colonel designed his codes so I was the only person who could translate the message. If I couldn't do it, or something happened to me, the information was forever lost, and I think he was okay with that possibility. I don't think it was ever essential that someone find it. Just that I could."

I said nothing, so she continued. "He had different kinds of locations that he favored for stashing stuff. Federal land was good for burying stuff, but landmarks and terrain changed over time, so those were for short-term storage. He kept a few safe houses. But something everyone might want? It's buried in a cemetery."

"We need to go grave digging?" I'm pretty sure I looked sufficiently shocked.

"In a manner of speaking. It will be an old cemetery protected by historic preservation laws and the grave will belong to someone who died around the time of the Civil War, so unlikely to have recent visitors. It'll be buried a few feet down, but not to the coffin. Just deep enough to be unaffected by natural erosion, but not so deep to make it real hard to get to."

By this point, she had the laptop up and running. "Actually," she smiled, "we don't need to drive around. I found a signal close by that I can use. We can stay here." Her fingers flew across the keys and within minutes, she had what she needed. She closed up the laptop. "Let's go."

"Want to let me in on where?"

"A historic cemetery south of Atlanta with a Confederate monument at the entrance."

As I pulled away, she elaborated further. "The numbers in the Sudoku magazine are a book cypher. The puzzles with incorrect answers tell me which numbers are relevant and that gave me the location and name on the grave we're looking for."

"Cool." As we traveled east, I felt an abundance of conflicting emotions running through my blood and a host of thoughts jumbling through by head. Yet I couldn't bring myself to feel guilt or regret. Sure, I made a few questionable decisions in the last couple of days, but despite the danger, I wasn't sure there wasn't anything else I wanted to be doing in this moment. The irony was not lost on me. Tallulah was someone the agency would classify as an asset, yet she was the one manipulating me. That I recognized it was happening didn't really matter, since it changed nothing. The only thing I had difficulty figuring out was how it happened that my current mindset or behavior didn't match up with the person I was up until the meeting with Jared. The transformation of who I was and how I defined myself altered in the blink of an eye and I was fine with that. Something for a shrink to dissect. For now, I'd accept that everything for me had changed. Whether or not it was for the better would reveal itself in time.

I could only surmise that the restlessness I'd been feeling lately was only in part due to being on medical leave. There was also an unacknowledged desire for something more in my life, and perhaps, Tallulah was that something. Sure, there was so much more about her I didn't know, but I couldn't imagine any revelation about her being a deal breaker for our relationship. Even referring to whatever this was as a "relationship" was evidence of a change I was more than willing to pursue.

At the moment, though, I needed to bring my focus back to the here and now. Curiosity about an unknown past or hoping for a different future, would do nothing to survive the present.

CHAPTER 22

Tallulah

The first hour of our drive was is silence. It was a comfortable silence, which itself, felt like proof that we had a connection that went beyond sexual. Still, I wanted more. I thought about all the questions I wanted to ask; things I wanted to know about him. I've never had friendships where you just talk to someone, ask questions about their past and learn about their personality and quirks. All my relationships were pretty far from traditional, so navigating that getting-to-know-you phase felt foreign. But everything I had been doing up till a few days ago, was done with the goal of trying to have a regular life. Recognizing that this was just part of the process, I decided to wade in, knee deep. As I was about to venture into uncharted territory, it was Grayson that took that first step for me.

"So," he started, "I've been meaning to ask about something."

"You can ask," I replied in a tone suggesting that asking didn't guaranty getting an answer. Okay, so I needed some serious work. But bantering with him was fun.

He gave a cocky smile that implied it wouldn't stop him from trying. "Jared dug up information about you when you disappeared, hoping to find some clue about how to find you."

He waited while that tidbit sunk in. He seemed to be waiting for my reaction to see if it was safe to keep going. I schooled my expression and decided to see if he was brave enough to continue. Seems he was.

"There was an admission record from a base hospital in Germany. The injuries you were treated for looked familiar because I had the same injuries a few times – after getting into fights. Funny thing was, there was another record from the same hospital on the same night at around the same time. Seems three enlisted guys returning from leave got smacked around good. I didn't know why Jared included that in your file, but I think he thought the two were related."

"Was there a question in there?"

He laughed. "Not really, no."

I couldn't help but let out a loud sigh. I knew questions like this would always come up. Maybe not about this incident in particular, but about my life as the daughter of Colonel Marshall Westfield.

We had started sharing little pieces of our lives with each other and so far, the sky didn't fall. Seems opening up about things in the past wouldn't hurt me. I just had to be careful about how far back those disclosures went. Ultimately, some of it had the potential to do harm.

"The Colonel was strict and I was bound by a set of unbreakable rules. While he was stationed in Germany, I went through a rebellious phase that didn't last very long, but I'd been out that night when I wasn't supposed to be. I was trying to sneak back to our house when these three drunk assholes tried to have a little fun with me. They didn't know I was 15 or that I was the Colonel's daughter."

"You kicked their asses, didn't you?" He actually sounded impressed, much like the Colonel had after he slapped me around a bit for breaking a rule, or two, or three.

"They were drunk. I mean barely-able-to-stand drunk. The Colonel always felt it was important for me to react instinctually to danger, so he pounded it into me – literally – until I automatically reacted to any perceived threat. That particular smack-down didn't take much effort since they were halfway there already."

Grayson didn't say anything for a minute, but it was just enough time for me to realize that I wanted someone else to know what my life with Colonel Westfield was like. I'd already given Grayson a glimpse into some of our bizarre life, just by virtue of what we were doing now. It was then I made the decision to tell him anything he wanted to know about that time of my life.

The next two hours passed with questions from Grayson about my childhood. He was careful not to ask about my life prior to my adoption. I assumed he must have seen information about the overdose and death of Diana Roberts and surmised, since I volunteered nothing, that this painful part of the past was best left alone. It was refreshingly easy to talk to him about my time with the Colonel. What I did find a little hard to talk about was Laura Westfield and my regrets about our relationship. She did so much for me, not just my education and tutoring in social norms, but just by being the only mother figure I had during those formative years of my life. Yet in all that time, I never acknowledged her as such, and I would always feel bad about that. I don't even know why I treated her that way. I knew I had to own my part in causing some of the sadness I saw in her eyes and that was a hard pill to swallow. Though I had done my fair share of damage, it was never inflicted upon anyone who didn't deserve it. It was tough to acknowledge that with Laura, I had caused pain to someone who loved me.

We were inching closer to a conversation that would move toward the death of my family and my subsequent Houdini act, but that was where I slammed on the brakes. Any inquiry that originated from that point in time was a non-starter. Time to quickly change the subject.

I think he sensed my change in mood. Before I could start on my inquisition of his life, he switched gears into safer territory. "What about your van? I still don't think anyone knows about it."

"I asked Trigger to get it and make sure it's clean. He was the one who helped me build it so I'm hoping that, if all goes well, I can still keep it."

"You did the build-out?" Grayson asked, seemingly impressed.

"Yeah. I was torn about whether to stay in one place and the van gave me options. I needed to be able to live off the grid, but still have a home base. Trigger let me use the shop to do the build and even supplied some of the materials. You know, stuff that 'fell off a truck'."

I thought about all the hours we had put in to get it done, but in the end, I thought it had been worth it. Not just for the great result and pride I felt whenever I was in it, but also because the time we spent together on it brought my friendship with Trigger and his family closer. It also endeared me to other gang members who quickly learned that, by Trigger's decree, me, my van and my motorcycle were off limits.

Grayson, it turned out, was more fascinated by the technical. He questioned me about the solar panels and charge inverter, electrical wiring and insulation, water storage and pump, and a surprisingly odd curiosity about the custom built composting toilet.

"I had to leave some of Morgan's equipment behind in your van. I'm not sure how to explain why I can't return it when I get back."

I could have let Grayson sweat, but that just seemed too mean. "Assuming it was still in there when Trigger picked up the van, your stuff is safe. Trigger won't let anyone touch it without his say so. The guys will know anything in the van is mine, and therefore, off limits. It'll be okay."

Grayson looked surprised and a little angry. "Why? What's the deal with you and Trigger?" Was that jealousy I heard in his voice?

"Trigger is a good friend. He does a lot for me, so I try to help him out with his mother and sister."

A look of understanding crossed his face before he said, "that's where your mail goes, right? Cora Mae Brooks is Trigger's mom?"

I smiled thinking of the woman who welcomed me into her fold. "I try to visit as often as I can. I pay her a generous rent to use her address. Besides, the kids in that neighborhood are better than private security contractors. No one gets in or out of the area without being spotted and reported to Trigger. If anyone starts poking around looking for me, I'll know about it."

I let Grayson chew on that information while I thought about the remainder of our travel time to Atlanta. We were approaching evening and needed to take a break. "We're coming up on Jackson. Up for making a pit stop in good 'ole Mississippi?"

CHAPTER 23

Grayson

I was still thinking about her friendship with Trigger and his family, when she asked about stopping in Jackson. "Sure. We can grab a bite and decide if we want to keep going or stop for the night."

"I'm up for the food, but I think we should try and make Atlanta tonight. If we have to dig up a historic cemetery, I'd just as soon do it in the middle of the night and not broad daylight. If we wait to drive out tomorrow, it will be late tomorrow night before we can dig."

I agreed and we pulled into a rest stop just outside Jackson. We gassed up the car and headed to the Denny's across the lot. As we sipped coffee and waited for our meals, something occurred to me. "Are you concerned about Dombrowski's deadline? If you are, then don't be. I won't let him dictate our actions like this is some kind of agency op."

Tallulah had been quiet since pulling off, and it was starting to concern me. Even now, as she looked in my eyes, there was something there that hadn't been before, though I couldn't figure out what it was exactly. My spidey senses were definitely off. I wanted to be reassuring, but I didn't know what her concern was.

Finally, she responded. "I just feel like the sooner we find something, the sooner I'll be done with this nightmare."

"Tired of me already?" *Wow. Did that sound as needy as it felt.* I suddenly wanted to take the question back, but rather than laugh at me or question my masculinity, Tallulah looked worried, and I started to panic.

She looked down, her voice so quiet, I barely heard it. "That would imply that once this is over, so are we. I guess I didn't consider what would happen when you didn't need to shadow me anymore. I'm sorry."

No, no, no. She couldn't possibly think we would ever be over. "Whoa. Stop right there. First of all, I was joking about being tired of me. Second, I haven't considered anything beyond this hunt, but I assure you, ending whatever this is between us is not even up for consideration. I may not know what this is, but I know I want to see where it goes. I want to table this conversation for now, but not unless I know you understand this discussion is far from over." I looked in her eyes and saw what I thought could be a glimmer of hope. Then it faded.

"We can table this for now."

I reached across the table and clasped her hands in mine. I had meant it to be a reassuring gesture, but heat from our touch sent signals that my body was processing incorrectly. *Down boy.*

It also briefly crossed my mind that we could chuck this whole shit show and leave the country. I had a lot of contacts in Europe and she obviously knew a forger that did first rate ID packages. Then it hit me. The salt and pepper shakers. If we left now, we'd be on the run forever. That's exactly everything Tallulah wanted to stop doing. She wanted to put down roots. I understood that better than she might think I did, and because I understood, running was out of the question.

So back to Plan A. It was better to stay focused in the present with our eye on the ball. I decided more detail was in order. "Do you know what we're looking for in that grave?"

"No," she replied, not appearing to be eating, but just pushing her food around her plate. "The Colonel would normally draw this out with more clues, but that takes time, and given the dates on the newspaper clippings, I'd be surprised if it pointed to other locations. He couldn't leave the base on extended trips without drawing attention, so my guess is, he kept it simple. I think he was worried and wanted to set things up for me to find, but knew he only had a short window of time to get it done. If I look at the overall picture, I would guess he knew something bad would happen. He was prepared for this."

That part this excursion didn't occur to me. My original question was actually about size, not circumstance. "What I meant was, will it be bigger than a breadbox?"

She laughed. Finally, a genuine smile, followed by, "not a clue. My bigger curiosity is whether or not its booby-trapped."

"Is that a possibility?" I asked, a little worried that was something we have to consider.

"Yeah. I found some C-4 in one of his hiding spots and it looked like part of it was missing. "

She said it so casually, it was as if we were talking about some missing socks from the laundry. I guess growing up the way she did, explosive materials would naturally come up in casual conversation. Even with three older sisters, I began to really appreciate the normalcy of my youth.

"If you were the only one able to decipher the clues, why would he booby-trap the intel?"

"Habit."

While that simple word raised more questions than it answered, I still had major concerns. "I'm going to assume that you would be the only one able to diffuse a booby-trap, should there be one."

She smiled again. "Yeah, no sweat."

Once we were back in the car and on the road again, I thought about everything I learned about her since we met. I certainly gained some insight into her life, but what I learned were details of information that I already knew. Her file gave me knowledge of her adoption and what I suspected was a strained relationship with the Colonel. While Tallulah expanded on that knowledge with stories and anecdotes, it only served to confirm what I already thought or knew. I suspected she had resources that helped keep her underground for over two years, but all I discovered was the identity of a few of them. What she was actually doing during that period, where and with whom remained a mystery.

She seemed open to talking about her life from her adoption up to the point of the Colonel's death. Everything before and after appeared to be off limits, if her rapid change of subject at any hint of those topics was an indication. I had to respect her reluctance to talk about her childhood before the Colonel, since by all accounts, it couldn't have been good. Roaming the streets with a drug addicted mother could have led to some traumatic experiences that she blocked from her mind. Though whether that was done intentionally or subconsciously, I didn't know.

It was the secrecy of her activities from the point she went dark until she began slowly emerging back into the mainstream that was starting to bother me. If the scumbags we were meeting gave any clue, I knew whatever she did during that time could not have been good, safe, or legal. Association with the parade of lowlifes I've met so far led to a narrative I may not want to explore, but would definitely need to. I was willing to let it go for now, but I knew there would be a point when I'd have to press the issue if there was any hope of moving forward with her.

Conversation for the duration of the drive was light. She offered a few more stories about the Colonel, but for the most part, she was fairly quiet. She did educate me on her knowledge of explosives, in particular, the homemade kind. It seemed more the Colonel's style to utilize military weaponry and ordinance that was "borrowed" or bought and sold on the black market. Homemade seemed out of character for a guy like him, but it wouldn't surprise me that he learned to improvise. It was just that some of the components and techniques Tallulah referred to were the kind utilized by groups like the IRA from back in the day. It made me wonder if the Colonel had his own bevy of scumbags on his contact list.

We arrived just outside Atlanta a little after midnight. We gassed up the car and Tallulah took over the driver's seat and drove us to the cemetery. She drove past the front, where a statute of a Confederate solder adorned the entrance. The opposite side of the property backed into a wooded area. She followed that property line until she was able to pull the car up behind some brush at the edge of the woods. The detour we made leaving Dallas to the small hardware store now made more sense. We removed the shovel, gardening tools and small bag of soil from the trunk and hopped the fence.

Tallulah moved in silence, checking markers on the various paths and names on headstones. She shone her flashlight on a marker at the intersection of two walking paths, and whispered, "we're close." She moved methodically from this point, appearing to count her steps. We stopped at a small section of graves that were isolated from the rest of the cemetery. She moved to one of the headstones near the center and set down her tools. "This is it."

It was a rather non-descript headstone that simply displayed a name and a date of death as August 1873. Tallulah walked off a short distance from the edge of the headstone and motioned for me to kneel on the opposite side. Using the garden tools she carefully removed the top layer of sod. Using the shovel, we carefully began digging down in an area about three feet squared. We reached a point about three feet deep, when the shovel hit something metallic. "Careful," she whispered as she guided my shovel from the hole.

Using the hand tools, we began carefully removing more dirt around a metal box wound in several layers of shrink wrap. Once we were able to remove the box, Tallulah emptied the bag of soil into the hole and used the hoe to compress the dirt as she added more back into it.

I was a little confused by her need to restore the gravesite. I had no idea what, if any, kind of security was in the area or if she felt the need to hide the fact that we had been here.

"We should get out of here. Why are we taking the time to put things back instead of just leaving it?" I asked, as she continued to put the grave back to right.

"Respect."

Requiring no further explanation, we worked together until the top layer was returned and came pretty close to looking undisturbed. I grabbed all the tools, Tallulah grabbed the box and we made our way back to the car. With the box on the back seat, the tools in the trunk, and me at the wheel, we made our way out of the brush and back onto the main road.

"Head north toward Marietta," Tallulah instructed. "There's a safehouse there that I don't think has been compromised."

"How can you be sure?"

"Because the Colonel didn't set it up. Just trust me."

I gestured to the box in the back seat. "What about the box? Should we stop to look inside?"

"No. I have a storage unit nearby. In case there is a booby-trap, I don't want anything happening where there are people. Hang a left here and it's on the next block."

We pulled into a storage facility and Tallulah gave me the code to the gate without hesitation. We headed toward the back of the yard where the largest units were located. When we reached her unit, I saw that it was secured with a combination lock. Once inside the unit, she turned on an overhead light and I noticed boxes had been strategically placed to obscure the view into the back of the unit. There, I saw a small utility table was set up and boxes and containers lined up on the back wall. She opened one of the boxes and removed a small tool chest. Placing our treasure on the table, she carefully removed the shrink wrap from around it.

The box resembled a standard fire resistant lock box that you could purchase at any office supply store, only the electronic locking mechanism on this box looked significantly more complicated. After a brief inspection, Tallulah announced, "yeah, we have a problem."

"How so? Can't you disarm it?"

"Sort of." She gave me a sheepish look. "This lock is a decoy. If I try to open it with the code, it'll blow. The good news is, whatever he ultimately hid, it's in here. If it were just a clue to another location, he wouldn't have rigged the box this way."

"What's the bad news?"

"I'm going to need more tools. Better tools. What I have here won't do the trick."

I looked at the box with my frustration level ratcheting up a few notches. I wanted to get this over with but I needed to be patient. "Are we taking the box with us?"

She looked at it a moment before deciding it would be safe in the unit for a few hours. While she assured me that the Colonel was skilled in his use of explosives and that the trap was stable enough to move without the risk of triggering the device, she didn't want to take the chance around innocents who could get caught in the blast.

We locked up just as the sun was coming up. We started toward the safehouse with my hope that Tallulah would get some much needed rest. We'd been up all night and I questioned the wisdom of asking her to disarm an explosive trap while sleep deprived.

CHAPTER 24

Tallulah

We arrived at the safehouse which was just an apartment on the ground floor of a four story building. I entered the security code on the door to the main entrance and walked to the last door at the end of the hall. Pulling out my trusty lock kit from my bag, I picked the lock, knowing there would be a key inside.

There were only a few pieces of furniture that were covered with sheets. It had been some time since anyone was here, but as I expected, the lights and plumbing were all functioning normally. We pulled the sheets off the furniture and sat on the couch.

Just before I felt myself fall asleep, I stood abruptly. "I can disable the emergency alarm on the back door. If you pull the car around to the back, we can unload the stuff and bring it in."

I opened a drawer in the kitchen and pulled out the door key, a small tool kit, then followed Grayson out the door. He headed toward the front of the building and I ducked into a small alcove at the back. The sign on the door clearly warned against setting off an alarm if opened, but a few well placed turns of some screws and clips of some wires and I had the door opened just as Grayson approached, loaded down with bags and one of the boxes we had retrieved in Pueblo. It took one more trip before the car was empty and everything piled in the center of the living room. Before returning I reconnected the emergency alarm. It could work in our favor if someone tried to enter from the rear.

Grayson and I passed each other at the entrance to the apartment. "I saw a convenience store on the corner," he said. He gently caressed my face. "How about I pick up a few snacks, then we try and get a few hours of sleep before we head back to the storage place."

"Okay." I pulled the key out and handed it to him. "I'll clean up. Grab a bunch of protein bars and bottled water. Oh, and a bag of pork rinds." I heard Grayson laugh as he headed down the hall.

I found cleaning products under the kitchen sink and laundry soap in the hall closet next to the stacked washer/dryer. I wiped down the kitchen and bathroom. There were clean sheets in plastic bags in the closet and I made up the bed. Grayson walked in just as I was carrying my bag to the bathroom. He was carrying several plastic bags and sporting a grin on his face. I couldn't help but smile and call him on his attempt to be sneaky.

"Did that Snicker's bar do the trick?"

His expression immediately turned perplexed. "How did you know?"

I dropped my bag, walked up to him and smiled. "The wrapper sticking out of your pocket was a dead giveaway, but my first hint was the chocolate stain at the corner of your mouth." I reached up behind his neck and eased his head down to me. With a quick swipe of my tongue, I removed all trace of the candy. "I thought you were a spy? You know you're not supposed to leave evidence behind. Lucky for you I took care of it."

Before I had a chance to gloat, I found myself pressed up against the wall by 190 lbs. of very turned on male devouring my mouth. His hands seemed to be everywhere and all I could do was hope he packed the condoms. So much so that I was a little disappointed when he backed away slightly, his breathing a little heavy. He looked down at me with a gentle expression and said, "why don't we wash the cemetery off us first?"

It turns out that all those movies that show sex scenes in the shower are full of shit. There was no way for any action to happen in that bathroom. The Four Seasons or the Plaza, perhaps, but there was no hope in a standard apartment bathtub. We settled for helping each other wash the dirt off with a few strategically placed hand movements, and turns under the spray of water. It did, however, serve to ramp up our mutual need for each other and moments after exiting the tub, found ourselves tangled up on the bed.

I realized that those small touches and his gentle caresses over the last day did nothing to sate the desire that only our bodies joining could satisfy. I also felt the same sense of urgency I saw in Grayson's eyes that conveyed his need to be inside me. Even as we lay in bed, mutually satisfied grins on our faces, I knew our connection was growing stronger and becoming more necessary.

Unfortunately, as anxious as I was to test the connection theory with further carnal experimentation, the metal box in the storage unit was causing distraction to my lustful thoughts. Grayson, however, had other concerns. "Please try to get a little sleep. I can hear the wheels in your head turning, but you need to shut down, if only for a little while."

I knew he was right. Without responding, I took a few deep breaths, closed my eyes, relaxed my mind and drifted off. I woke a couple hours later as Grayson was climbing out of bed. I took a minute to admire his incredible physique before getting up.

"What do we need before we head over there?" Grayson asked as he pulled on his shirt.

"We need to stop at a hardware store. I'll need a heavy duty drill, some chemicals and a few other tidbits. There's one about a mile from here. It's a little out of the way, but it's our best bet for carrying all the stuff I need."

We grabbed what we needed and headed out. After picking up supplies at the hardware store, we arrived at the storage unit early that afternoon. I took my time setting up, for obvious reasons, while Grayson stood silently, acting and assisting only when asked.

I used a tape measure to find and mark a spot on the top of the metal box, then using heavy clamps, secured the box to the table. The extension cord I had in the unit was long enough to reach the outlet at the end of the row of storage units. Working carefully and methodically, I drilled a half-inch hole at the mark. Pointing to one of the boxes on the back wall, I asked Grayson to remove the scoping equipment.

While pulling out the equipment, he perused through the other contents of the box when recognition dawned on him. "Want to tell me what all this stuff is for?" he asked.

"Nope. But if you insist on knowing, it's very complicated security by-pass tools."

"Used for safe-cracking."

"It has many uses. You shouldn't fixate on one thing."

"Like safe-cracking." Jeez, he was like a dog with a bone on this.

"Or in this situation, defusing an explosive trap. Want to hand it to me already?" Grayson handed me the scope and stood very close to me at the table. He bent down and with his breath on my ear, whispered, "I wonder where, when and why this stuff was last used."

We were again drifting into territory I wasn't yet ready to discuss, but more than that, was keeping my focus where it needed to be. "Why don't you ponder that question on the other side of the table. I need to concentrate."

"Sorry," he mumbled as he moved across from me.

It took some time and slow movements, but using the scope and a copper wire fashioned into a hook, I was able to expose part of a length of clear tubing. Filling a syringe with the chemicals I had premixed, I injected the tube with the chemical mixture. The air in the tube turned a bluish color indicating part of the trigger had been neutralized.

"Hand me those clippers." Grayson handed me the clippers which I used to cut a green wire that caused a loud beep. "Should be good now." I said, hopefully. I could now safely input a code into the keypad and open the box without setting off the explosives.

As I carefully lifted the cover of the box, I heard the pop of the tube pulling away from a vial. When nothing further happened, I knew it was safe. I gently removed the remaining wires on the trigger and the detonator from the small amount of C-4 packed inside. There wasn't enough C-4 to do more than destroy my storage unit and the contents in it, but it certainly would have done damage to anyone standing near it if it went off.

Grayson inspected the box and looked up confused. "I've never seen a set up like this before. Do you know how he came up with this design?"

"He taught me about all kinds of stuff, including explosives, but I always knew never to ask questions about any of it." Returning my attention to the box, another smaller metal box rested inside. I carefully removed it and did an inspection. There was a simple clasp and nothing appeared to be rigged to another trap, so I slowly lifted the lid. Inside was a plastic sleeve with a flash drive and sheet of paper with a series of numbers. I shoved it all in my pocket then separated the C-4 from the rest of the components. I placed the explosive material in another box and left everything else on the table to deal with at another time. "Let's go."

Grayson said nothing. He simply returned the extension cord to the unit, closed it up and replaced the lock. We drove back to the apartment in silence.

CHAPTER 25

Grayson

I f the tension for what just happened wasn't enough t spike my anxiety, certainly the increasing list of questions rattling around my head was. The Colonel's methods called into question the past that was commonly known against what was demonstrated by his actions. His absolute trust in Tallulah's ability to decode his clues and defuse his traps spoke to something in their relationship that became more evident with each story she told and now, in the way he left this information for her to find.

Speaking of which, the intel was now in our possession, or rather burning a hole in Tallulah's pocket. I could tell she was uncomfortable with it and was considering how to broach the subject of what was next to come.

Tallulah parked the car a block away from the apartment, I assume for security reasons, and we continued to walk in silence. By the time we entered the apartment, I couldn't take it anymore.

Needing to reaffirm our connection, I held her face and gently kissed her before looking in her eyes. I wanted her to see the truth in my words. "I'll leave the decision to you about what we do next. Do you want to look at the drive before we decide?"

"I need to see what we're dealing with." She pulled out the plastic sleeve from her pocket and removed the sheet of paper. Grabbing the laptop, I watched her fingers fly across the keys once again. At one point, she opened the sheet of paper and began simultaneously scanning it and typing information into the laptop. Finally, I had to ask. "Are the numbers on that sheet a cypher of some kind?"

"Yeah. It's a book cypher but we use published legal opinions from the Supreme Court. Book and page are always consistent because they are cited to in legal briefs and arguments, so they never change. You can even look them up online and be assured that page references will be the same. The patterns were pre-designed so I would always know where to start."

"Smart. So what is this code telling you?"

"That I need an air gapped computer in order to see what's on this drive."

I was confused until I realized what she was saying. "You mean a computer that's never been connected to the internet?"

"Any signal from the outside and the data gets wiped," she explained. "There will be several levels of encryption and three separate password access points to get into the files. One mistyped password and the data gets wiped. The Colonel wanted to make sure that only me or someone I chose to receive this information could open it."

She looked too tired to take on anything else at the moment, so I offered to run out and get another computer. As I headed toward the door, she stopped me.

"Wait," she said. She looked down at the flash drive in her hands then closed a fist around it. She seemed to be waging an internal battle that I was helpless to fight for her. Finally, she looked up. "I don't want to know what's on the drive. It's better if I just hand it off, but I don't trust Dombrowski or his sidekick. Can you get in touch with Jared?"

"They'll be monitoring him closely. Don't you have a way to contact him? I thought you could email him."

Her expression looked fallen. "It was a one-time thing. If we weren't able to connect after one attempt, Jared would shut down the email account. I have no way of reaching him now, at least not covertly, anyway."

I hated the expression of defeat on her face, but I still had options. I knew Jared was the only government person she would trust, so I had to find another way. "We should get on the road and head to D.C. Once we get closer, I have a couple of contacts that I can use as cut-outs to get a message to Jared."

"Is there any chance Jared told anyone about the meeting at the diner. Anyone who might have arranged that clusterfuck?"

I knew she was worried, but I've known Jared for a long time. "There's no way. I trust Jared with my life."

It seemed she would accept that for now. "Okay then. Why don't we eat, clean up and get ready to head out first thing tomorrow." She got up, moved toward me and walked right into my arms. We stood there and held each other, just trying to draw strength. It was killing me to feel her pain and not be able to alleviate it.

She tightened her embrace and asked, "why do you think the Colonel did all of this? What would be worth his life, Laura's life and throwing me into so much chaos, I may never have a regular life? I always thought his 'training' was all about being able to take care of myself. It didn't occur to me that he was preparing to throw me to the lions."

It occurred to me only then that she was viewing this situation as a punishment. That somehow the Colonel heaped all this upon her shoulders as a means to hurt her and I couldn't let her think that way. I considered the big picture and realized the truth.

"I knew the Colonel only by reputation. He may have been thought of sometimes as an asshole and known to be a real hard ass, but he was also respected as a man of integrity and a true patriot. That you are the only person in the world who could have deciphered his clues and found this flash drive only shows his utmost confidence in you and belief in your character. He may have been hard on you, but I think he did it to prove to himself and to you that you are worthy of his faith and trust. It says a lot about how he felt about you."

Her grip around me tightened, making breathing a little tricky, but I didn't mind. If I could provide her just a little bit of comfort, it was worth it. When she loosened her embrace, she reached up to kiss my cheek, then walked to the bedroom.

As I walked in behind her, my excitement diminished when I saw her gathering clothes and tossing them in the washer. We spent the rest of the day cleaning, packing and getting all our bags ready. I grabbed burgers from a fast food joint a couple of blocks away, but when I returned, Tallulah was on high alert. She stood at the window, peering through the blinds that had remained closed. All the bags were sitting in the center of the room and the gun in her hand rested as her side. I closed and bolted the door behind me, dropping the food to the floor, and removing my gun from holster at my back. "What's wrong?"

"Did you catch that van parked out front on your way in?" She was right to be cautious. Having possession of that drive raised the degree to which we needed to be careful. It was one thing to be chasing clues that no one could decode, but having the actual intel ramped up the risk. I knew that, so had already become extra diligent in observing everything around me, watching for any sign that our location had been discovered. I'm not sure that would ease her worry, but we would be out of there soon enough. I just had to make sure she acted cautiously without overreacting.

I looked out the blinds and calmly set a hand on her shoulder. "Drug deal," I advised her. "The south end of the park is out of your line of sight, but those two guys in the van are waiting for the foot traffic to clear before making the approach to the dealers standing on the corner of the park. I watched them as I came down the street and they've been casing the park. Trust me. As soon as the time is right, they'll make their way over there. That is, if they can. They both looked pretty high." I felt her body relax under my hand.

Somehow, I had managed not to spill the contents of the paper bags when they hit the floor, so I picked them up and brought them to the counter. "Come on. Try and eat something." As she walked toward me, she looked worried, not about what was outside, but about her own behavior. I noticed she would look at her hands whenever she was feeling some self doubt. Wanting to remove it, I decided on a plan.

"Look, we need to be careful now that the drive is in the open. Only one of us should sleep now while the other keeps watch. If you want, I'll take first watch. I can sleep tomorrow in the car."

"Actually, I think we should leave as soon as it gets dark. Get on the road now and take driving shifts. With a short break along the way, we can be there in about 12 hours." Tallulah was clearly anxious to unload this drive quickly.

"Okay," I conceded, "but eat first."

With the laundry done, the garbage emptied and the furniture covers back in place, we packed up and headed out. Tallulah took the first shift driving and though I was concerned about her state of mind, I thought the quiet was a better option. I knew if we started talking, I'd end up employing those tools of investigation and manipulation that I use when cultivating an asset. I didn't want to learn her secrets that way. I wanted her to tell them to me and trust that I'd keep them. She needed to come to that decision on her own. I closed my eyes and drifted off to a dreamless sleep.

CHAPTER 26

Tallulah

I didn't participate in social media, but I wondered if this is what people had in mind when they listed their relationship status as "its complicated." For the last hour, all I've had to keep me company were these thoughts rattling around in my head that I couldn't get a handle on.

I told Grayson a lot about the period of my life with the Colonel and Laura. I had even revealed thoughts and emotions that opened me up and made me feel vulnerable. I realized that it didn't make me weak, but actually helped give me strength. For as long as I can remember, I've always had to keep secrets from the people in my life for both my protection and theirs. Since I preferred not to lie, I often held things in, managing my issues independently and silently.

Telling Grayson about my fears and self doubt was a show of trust I never thought I'd have with anyone, let alone an operative of the CIA. Yet any concern I would have had about telling him those secrets in my past simply didn't' exist. Okay, sure. I had many, many more secrets lurking in the shadows that Grayson would have no idea about. Secrets that might lead him to walk away.

I also knew that we were nearing a point where I had to decide if or when he should know more about me. Other secrets. Bigger secrets. Some of them would have no effect on my life now, so why open that can of worms? Some of them could expose Grayson to danger, so why would I put him in that position. And some required the kind of trust that was too big a leap of faith for me to take.

What pissed me off more than anything was that some of these secrets were the result of decisions I had no control over or the product of actions I was forced to take because of the decisions of others. I was perfectly fine with taking responsibility for my own mistakes, but suffering the consequences of things I had no part in creating was making me angrier with every passing hour. What's worse is knowing that none of the actions of others were necessarily bad decisions. Sometimes being backed in a corner made you react in a way that can cause unending pain, but even in hindsight you can honestly say there was no other way. I would have more of a legitimate complaint if the secrets I held were the result of someone else being irresponsible or stupid. Since that wasn't the case, dwelling on how I got here would serve no purpose, especially since, at this point, none of it could be undone.

It was time to move on and make a decision for myself. How much can I trust Grayson with before he decides I'm not worth the trouble, or even worse, feels the need to betray me because of his job or his own beliefs and morals? I knew he had some moral flexibility since he had, at least for now, overlooked Trigger's occupation, and hadn't pressed for more information about Dex the gun keeper, Nigel my money guy, Tommy the wheelman or Danny the forger. It seems he understood that some of these resources were unavoidable contacts needed to stay hidden these past years, but how about those relationships that weren't entirely borne out of self preservation?

I wanted things in my life to be different, but how much of that would rely on my ability to trust others? I couldn't say I was completely without trust. I trusted everyone I kept in my life, but only to the extent that was needed to maintain that relationship. Charlie, for example, was entrusted with limited contact information and had gone a long way to bring me back into the mainstream by helping me procure legitimate licenses and permits, but only because it was in his own best interest to do so. My success in fugitive recovery saved him a lot of grief, but more importantly, it saved him money. As long as he had just enough information to get what he wanted, he was fine with ignorance of the rest.

Trigger was another story. I trusted him with my life, just not my secrets. My reason for keeping secrets from him was not my lack of faith in our friendship, but the belief that everyone had a line in the sand. You understand that having information others may want would be testing those limits and everyone had a breaking point. Threats to his mother and sister would be his. Letting him see what he already believed to be true protected him. As long as everything he thought lined up with his reality, Trigger and his family would be okay.

I was good at keeping things compartmentalized. As far as I knew, only two people knew my entire history and both were dead. Though neither death had any direct connection to my life or my past, I couldn't risk that opening up to anyone could put them in danger. Despite that fear, I wanted connection to someone who knew everything about me. I wondered what life would be like without these secrets.

Maybe I just had to learn to trust someone, to trust Grayson. I wanted to believe that our connection and feelings toward each other were enough to begin a journey toward that goal. If I wanted a regular life, I had to acknowledge that if you're constantly looking over your shoulder, you can't see what's in front of you. At some point you have to trust someone to watch your back and I want that person to be Grayson.

Once again, I was getting ahead of myself. I needed to get rid of this drive, and hope passing it off to Jared was the right call. After that, I needed to know why I was ambushed at the diner. Who was behind it and why? The likelihood was that it had to do with the Colonel's information on that drive, but I couldn't discount the idea that there was another possibility. One I wasn't prepared to explore just yet.

I had to admit that I also wanted to find a way to gage how invested Grayson was in pursuing our relationship beyond this assignment. Unfortunately, it seemed as though that would forever be shoved on the back burner until other issues were dealt with first. It seemed like taking control of my life was only possible at the expense of actually having one.

Grayson started to wake up just as we were approaching a rest stop outside Durham. With a very attractive, sleepy-eyed smile, he sat up, rubbed the sleep from his eyes and finger combed his hair. Once he got a handle on the time and our location, he offered to take over behind the wheel.

"I could use a little break from the car," I told him, as I climbed out and stretched my tired muscles. "Can you gas up the car? I'm going inside to pick up some snacks and splash some water on my face."

"Sure. Do you have any clean burner phones? I need to get in touch with someone who can help get a message to Jared."

I pulled out the last clean burner I had and handed it to Grayson, then headed toward the convenience store.

As I was coming back out, I heard the tail end of his conversation. "...I told you, he's a creature of habit. Just make sure it's charged and you program the speed dial with the number I gave you.... Yeah, I'll owe you a big one.....Thanks, Maddie."

We got back in the car and headed toward Virginia. But before I paid a visit to sleepy-time junction, I was definitely going to hear about Maddie.

CHAPTER 27

Grayson

I knew Tallulah heard the end of my conversation with Maddie and from the looks of it, she wasn't particularly pleased. And not unlike a sensitive rash, this wasn't going to go away on it's own, but required delicate handling in order to prevent making the problem worse. Simply trying to will it away wasn't going to work. Maddie could have easily been one of those contacts that necessitated an awkward conversation to explain, but fortunately, she wasn't. That didn't mean I got a pass on having to explain.

"I found someone to act as a cut-out and get to Jared. She'll buy a burner phone and pass it to Jared. It will be pre-programed with the phone number for this burner and he'll be instructed to call me as soon as he can." I waited to see her reaction. Though her eyes were focused on the road ahead, I knew she was digesting the information. Before I could offer more, she spoke with a concerned tone.

"How do you know you can trust her?"

"It's a long story, but the short answer is, she 's a hooker and Morgan's former neighbor. He was doing some unauthorized surveillance on her and I needed to get him out of a jam. So I created a problem for her then solved it, so now she turns to me to fix things for her and in return, she'll help me out or pass me information."

"What do you mean you 'created a problem'?" I could hear the slight irritation in her voice.

"My cover ID is a security consultant, so I know a lot of law enforcement types in D.C. and Baltimore. I got her busted for solicitation then used some of my other contacts to get the charges dropped. She doesn't know Morgan and I are friends because I told her I was hired by someone else to 'deal' with Morgan. He moved out of her building the next day, and I got her busted a couple days later to use as leverage in case she wanted to pursue charges against Morgan. I made sure she knew that I was the one who took care of her 'problem', but since it turns out she wasn't planning on filing a complaint against Morgan, I never had to leverage the bust and she thinks I'm just a good guy. So now we do each other favors."

Oh shit. I just heard how that sounded. I quickly added, "not *those* kind of favors. I've never slept with her."

She briefly pulled her focus away from the road to shoot me that *are-you-kidding-me?* look. Followed up with, "I didn't ask, and it isn't any of my business."

"Hey," I said, a little confused by her reaction, "I want to be honest, so I'm telling you the truth about Maddie. Why are you upset if I didn't sleep with her?"

She was quiet for so long. As a man, I would have felt compelled to keep talking. Even though I don't think I did anything wrong, growing up with three sisters and a very strong mother taught me that it's sometimes better to apologize, even if you know not for what, simply to keep the peace.

As an operative, however, that instinct is almost always wrong. You don't offer up anything until you know the other position first. You may be giving up something you didn't need to if you had just waited it out. It turns out I was smart to wait, because when she finally spoke, I realized I was looking at her reaction as if it were coming from a woman, and not an asset.

"I don't care if you slept with her." She paused briefly which is when I noticed her expression seemed to convey a sense of sadness and disappointment. When she started speaking again, I realized why.

"I assumed you were good at your job. The way you found me at the trailer park, the way you handled yourself at the diner, your instincts when it came to sketchy situations with Trigger. I just never considered your skill when it came to manipulating people, which I assume is a big part of your job. Makes me wonder." And there it was.

I needed to nip those thoughts in the bud. "Nothing between us has been a manipulation." I should be angry that even after everything I thought we were feeling and the connection we shared, she would question it. But that's what secrets do. They make you cautious of little things, suspicious of lots of things and question everything. There were so many things in my past I could never tell Tallulah about. Not because I didn't want to, but because I couldn't. That was the job, and hence, her doubt.

If my actions on this scavenger hunt didn't put my career in jeopardy yet, handing over the intel to Jared would probably end it. At best, I'd be put in a debrief that could last days, followed by some kind of suspension or censure on my record. It could even pull me from the field. Given the way I'd been feeling of late, it didn't surprise me that I didn't really care. If my days at the agency were numbered, so be it. Tallulah was going to come first.

There was one way to prove it. "Okay," I said, needing to see this from her perspective. "Assuming I've been manipulating you, it would be to bring you in or secure the information we just retrieved. So I'll make this easy for you. Pull over and destroy the drive. I have a safe house in upstate New York. We can make our way there now. I have money and passports stashed and we can head to Canada. From there, we can go anywhere you want. I know you don't want to keep running, but I know a few places we'd be able to stay put for a while. It's your call."

I knew that running was an unappealing option for both of us, but part of me wanted her to choose it. To say that being with me, whatever the cost, was more important. Every thought I had and decision I've made since I met her was so contrary to the person I had been, it only served to reinforce the belief that my priorities had radically changed. Tallulah now topped the list and my career had plummeted so many rungs down the ladder, it was no longer visible. I had done my service to my country, first in the military and then with the CIA. I gave everything I had, and it was long past time to take something for myself. Whatever her decision, my path would forever be entwined with Tallulah.

After a few minutes of silence, we came upon an offramp for a small rest stop. She pulled off and parked. I assumed she decided to run. Despite my anxiety over the consequences, I was going to stay true to my word.

We exited the car and met at the front. She reached into her pocket and pulled out the drive. I waited for her to toss it to the ground and crush it. Instead she reached out with her free hand and grabbed my wrist. She lifted my arm, put the drive in my hand and wrapped her hands around my closed fist with the drive inside. Silently, she brought her arms around my body and rested her head on my shoulder. I returned her embrace and waited.

Her voice was so quiet, I barely heard it. "I'm sorry. I don't want to run, but I don't need you to make me any promises. Let's just get the drive to Jared, then whatever happens next, happens next."

I knew she still questioned my sincerity, a problem that only time would fix. Still, I needed her to feel that the connection between us was real. I gently lifted her face and kissed her. I started off wanting her to feel secure, but the kiss went on and with each passing moment became so much more.

The loud roar of a passing tractor trailer served as the bucket of cold water we needed to bring us back to the here and now. "Let's go," she said as she moved away. I gently grabbed her arm and pulled her back into my arms. She gently rested her hands on my chest. She looked up and smiled as she pulled away and got back in the car.

I knew sleep wasn't possible right now, but we needed time for Jared to get the message, and at the same time get some rest. It was also unwise to wait it out too close to Washington. We agreed to try and close our eyes at this rest stop. Once we got back on the road, we would take back roads heading north to avoid prying eyes and kill time.

About an hour outside of Washington, the burner phone rang. On the other end of the phone, Jared sounded very unhappy. "There's a lot we need to deal with starting with who's the bimbo who passed me the phone in the bar and how did she know I take lunch there?"

"Best if you don't know," was the only response I could give in that moment.

"You should know that Dombrowski is apoplectic over not hearing from you. He's had guys watching me. Luckily your girl was able to slip me the phone without drawing attention. She made it look like she was trying to score a john. Covered her tracks by walking out with some other guy. So, you want to tell me what's going on?"

"Go to the same place we last met. Be there in two hours. Can you lose the tail?"

"Yeah, I have one option for emergencies. I think this qualifies. I'll see you then."
He disconnected. I was worried about Jared being followed, but I had already scoped out the area of the last diner we had met at. The location was such that surveillance was not possible. Anyone watching would have to do it from a fairly open position which would make them easy to spot.

I turned to Tallulah. "We're meeting Jared at a diner. We have just enough time to get there first and scope the area and watch his approach. At the first sign of trouble, we're out of there."

As she followed the directions, she stayed silent until we were just about there. It was that moment that she chose to ask, "do you think I'm doing the right thing by giving this to Jared?"

I told her the truth. "Honestly? I prefer it to the alternative. I don't want to hand it over to Dombrowski. I'm still bothered by the fact that both he and Parsons came to the diner armed. They're bureaucrats. They don't go out in the field, and especially not to just bring in an asset and they certainly wouldn't do it carrying a gun."

Tallulah looked confused. "You sound as if you're not entirely comfortable with handing the drive over to Jared."

"Part of that is for safety reasons. Absent another explanation coming to light, that drive and your knowledge of it is the only reason for the ambush at the diner. Without any more to go on, I have to proceed with the facts that I have. That means putting it in Jared's hands puts him at risk."

"You said part is for safety reasons. Why else would you be reluctant?"

"Jared isn't as jaded as guys like me who spent a lot of time around really bad guys. He wouldn't intentionally put either of us in harms way, but he might be trusting something or someone he shouldn't, and that's how we got tagged."

"So why would we put Jared in that position?"

"Not only is he someone I trust, but within that circle of people, he might also be the only one who will understand any data that might be on it. Jared isn't just an analyst. He has degrees in math and chemistry. Even if he doesn't understand the information, he's smart enough to know who we'd need in order to get to the bottom of it." I waited to see if that would satisfy her, knowing we only had a couple more minutes before we would be close to the diner.

"Let's get this over with."

CHAPTER 28

Tallulah

We carefully approached a diner that appeared to sit in the middle of nowhere. The approach allowed a view of the surrounding area without obstruction and left no place from which to covertly surveille the diner. The few abandon buildings in the vicinity were boarded up and could not be entered without exposure. Set up for surveillance would require a minimum of three people and a couple hours prep time.

We decided to take position near one of the abandoned buildings knowing full well that any trained operative following Jared would spot us watching the approach and back off immediately. It didn't seem like we had much of a choice, so we just waited.

Within a few minutes we spotted a single car approaching in the distance.

"I don't recognize the car," Grayson said, "but that looks like Jared. It doesn't look like he's being followed."

As Jared drove past us, he glanced over and acknowledged Grayson with a subtle nod, then proceeded to the diner. As he walked into the diner, we remained in the car and continued to watch the road to determine if he had, in fact, arrived alone. A few minutes later, satisfied the meeting would be secure for now, we entered the diner.

Grayson took my hand as we walked in the door. At first, I assumed it was a gesture of support, then I realized he was placing the drive in my hands. I looked at him questioningly, but he just smiled and moved to the back of the room where Jared sat at a booth. Grayson gestured for me to sit across from Jared, but remained standing.

"Hey, Jared," Grayson started. "I think we're okay for now, but we shouldn't linger. You two need to talk, and I should keep watch. I'll be outside." With that, he turned and left.

"Okay, well I guess I should get to it," I said. Jared just smiled. "I know the Colonel reached out to you, but never gave you anything tangible. To be honest, I never wanted to know what he had. I've managed to go more than two years without ever looking."

"I'm sorry if I was the one that forced your hand. I've been worried about you since you took off. I only wanted to be sure you were okay."

I knew he felt bad that he may have been the catalyst to all the drama, and despite my irritation for the disruption in my life, I couldn't live with him feeling guilty. He was only looking out for me because of his friendship with and respect for the man that raised me. "It's okay, but I think I'm done with all of this." I placed the drive on the table, which he took immediately, then continued to explain. "I didn't look at what's on it. All I can tell you is it has to be viewed on an air gapped computer. There will be three password protected access points into the files. In order, the passwords are *disclosure*, *evidence* and *burden*. If you don't follow this instruction exactly or input any password incorrectly, the data will be wiped and you'll never recover any of it."

Jared reached across and put his hand over mine. "Don't worry," he said. "I'll find out what this is all about. I have a head start on all the assholes chasing after this. In the meantime, watch your back. I'd also appreciate it if you watch Gray's back, too. He's risking a lot and I'm kind of fond of the guy. And by the way I saw you look at him, I'm guessing you're fond of him, too."

"I am. And I will." Just then Grayson walked back in.

He looked at Jared as he took my hand. "We should go," he said. "It's clear right now, but we're too exposed. Jared, where are you headed from here?"

Jared responded as he started to stand. "I'll head toward Fairfax and pick up a computer. I'll find someplace to hold up and work. Dombrowski's goons think I'm still at Debra's place. I've been known to hang out there for long stretches of time."

Grayson looked shocked. "You're still sleeping with your ex-wife?"

Jared smiled again. "I'm still boinking her on occasion, but mostly we hang out, play cards or go out from time to time. We actually get along better since the divorce."

Grayson laughed. "So how did you get past Dombrowski's guys?"

"Debra keeps her car at a neighbor's place down the back alley. I can get to the car and pull out without being seen from the front. I guess my lack of field experience only warrants the need for two babysitters and no coverage out the back. I don't think they'll get suspicious unless I don't leave tomorrow morning. I'll call you once I've had a chance to look at the drive."

We waited until Jared was out of sight before heading out. Since I had no idea where we were going, I made no objection when Grayson opened the passenger door for me to get in. I was, however, curious about our next move. "So, what now?" I asked.

He looked at me like he wanted to say something, but wasn't sure if he should.

"Just spit it out," I said with a touch of irritation. This whole experience was getting to me.

"If Jared gets back without tipping anyone off that we've made contact, we're safe until he tells us what's on the drive. After that is anyone's guess. Until then, we should stay away so no one suspects we've been in touch. We should head up to my place in New York. We can try to relax for a while and decide what to do when I hear back from Jared. How about it?"

That sounded as appealing an idea as I've heard in quite a while. "Sure. Let's go. Where is it?"

"It's a small cottage on three and a half acres east of Buffalo."

"Head to Philly. We can get a new car there. We've been in this one long enough."

Grayson gave me a look. "You got a handle on the Criminal Car Max in every state?" Despite his attempt at humor, I knew he was frustrated about the lack of information concerning my past associations.

I knew this would be an issue, but I just wanted to get where I could calmly have this conversation in a place that wasn't moving.

"I'll tell you about it once we get to your safehouse. Let's just get out of here."

The drive to Philly was mostly in silence. Both lost to our own thoughts, until we reached a warehouse on the outskirts of town. The sign on the door identified the business as Nicholas Brothers Collision Repair. I parked on the side of the building and walked to the entrance.

"Can you stay with the car a minute?" I asked. I knew there was a chance Grayson would object, but he just nodded and stayed in the car.

I entered the front door and looked around. Activity seemed light, but everyone was on alert. That's when I spotted Henry coming toward me. His scruffy beard had grown even fuller, but his oddly bright white teeth shown through the bush of facial hair.

"Marsha. Goddamn. I heard you fell off the map. What the hell?" He embraced me in a big bear hug and lifted me off my feet. When he set me down and I could breathe again, I decided to get right to the point.

"It's good to see you, Henry. I'm in a little bit of jam. I picked up a car from Tommy in Armarillo, but I've had it a few days and I've got a few miles left to cover. Any chance we can deal on a swap?"

"Car's clean?"

"It's Tommy-style clean. I got it parked outside."

Henry smiled. "Sure, sweet-cheeks. Anything for you. I'm sorry about Ian. You ever hear from Sean?"

"Sean's dead." I was surprised Henry didn't know that.

Henry appeared shocked. "Huh. Well, that's not what I heard. Word is he got away and took off. Last I heard, he was somewhere in Turkey. Istanbul, I think."

Panic started to set in. Sean was supposed to be dead. He was the only person who may know more about me than I cared for anyone to know. I wasn't sure since he confronted me on the night Ian died. We never got to finish that conversation, but what he managed to communicate led me to believe he knew more than just the fact that my real identify wasn't Marsha, as I had claimed. I had to know for sure.

"Do you know anyone who's actually seen him?" I asked.

"Not really. I mean, you know how it is. Somebody heard from somebody who talked to a guy who knew something. Is this a problem?"

"No." I tried to appear calm and nonchalant. "Just curious. What about that car?"

"Come one." Henry gestured toward the door at the other end of the warehouse. "It's out back." There were several cars parked behind the warehouse. Henry handed me a set of keys and pointed to a dark blue pick up with an extended cab. "What are you trading?"

I led Henry around the corner to look down the side of the warehouse. His first reaction was much as I expected. "Who's the dipshit?"

Yup, Grayson was out of the car, leaning against the hood and staring at Henry with looks that could kill. "Don't worry about him," I advised. "He's a friend helping me out." Henry started down the alley toward Grayson, who thankfully, didn't move. Grayson continued to lean against the hood, his arms crossed, eyes following Henry's movements as he circled the car.

It was clear Henry was suspicious, but not enough to sink the deal. "I'll make the trade," he said. "But I'll need three grand for the upgrade and to offset my expense to unload Tommy's piece of shit."

"Deal." Then, looking and directing my instruction to Grayson, "Can you pull around to the back? We're taking the dark blue pickup." Without a word, Grayson drove behind the warehouse.

As we walked toward the back, Henry could contain his comments no longer. "Where'd you find the stiff. Guy looks like he's battling a hemorrhoid."

I said nothing else, and once everything from the car had been moved to the truck and money and paperwork had been exchanged, we took off headed northeast

CHAPTER 29

Grayson

I waited as long as I could, then prepared to start my inquiry. I'd been patient and understanding of Tallulah's trust issues and knowing her background, shouldn't have been surprised by the characters we've encountered thus far, but enough was enough. I wanted to understand the life she led while in hiding. The endless parade of scum was starting to leave me cold. I just needed her to open up and trust me.

Just as I was about to launch into my first question, Tallulah stopped me in my tracks. "I know you're dying to ask, so anything I say now is a preemptive strike against interrogation. I got involved with people who helped me while I was laying low. And yes, people with those types of resources are rarely upstanding members of society. I promise I'll give you more, but I really want to have this conversation when we're not in a moving car. Besides, it's not like you've been a wealth of information about your life."

Wow. That's when it hit me. All the questions, doubts, suspicions and concerns about her past, were part and parcel of things that came up in the course of doing my job. Sure it was one-sided, but that was how I became successful. Learn how to extract information and get others to reveal their secrets then use that information to manipulate them into doing what I wanted them to. There was no need for them to know about me. It served no purpose. If I had to reveal something to get something, it was always a fabrication and never the truth. Perhaps that's why I never had any level of intimacy in my own life because giving of myself was something I could never be comfortable with. It went counter to the very training that made me effective in the job.

I suddenly realized that while she may not have divulged secrets about her time on the run, she had shared many parts of her life with the Colonel and had trusted me with confidences I was sure she had shared with no one else. Insignificant as they may have been, they were still parts of her that only I had the privilege to hold. And yet, for all she had shared, I gave nothing. That was about to change.

I mentally readied myself then let the floodgates open. "What do you want to know?"

"I don't know," she replied, almost as if resigned to get nothing of value from me. Then something flashed in her eyes. "Tell me about your family."

Okay, this I can do. "I'm from an Indiana suburb just across the border from Chicago where my parents still live. I have three older sisters and nobody in my family knows what I do for a living."

That cute little furrow in her brow I saw whenever she was confused reappeared. "What do they think you do?"

"I work for a security consulting firm called Hamilton Security Consultants. It's an actual consulting firm that advises on security for high risk properties like banks and such. It also holds a few government contracts to consult on security at embassies, smaller airports and military facilities. They advise on things like manpower needs and procedures, camera placement for maximum coverage, protection for points of ingress and egress with equipment like motion sensors and metal detectors. Stuff like that. Because of government contracts, they allow placement of operatives like me to use their firm as a cover for work I'm doing for the CIA. Most of the employees at Hamilton believe I actually work there, but don't know exactly what I do because of the high level security clearance required for the projects I'm assigned to. Only a few of the top tier executives know who I am and they're all former spooks."

"Do you ever want to tell your family?" she asked.

"No. They would just worry. I may be the only male, but I'm still the baby of the family and for the most part, that's how they treat me. My oldest sister in particular is very protective."

"What is she like?"

"Lizzy? About what you'd expect in the oldest sister. She's maternal, responsible, always looking out for everyone. She's a nurse, married a doctor, has two kids, two dogs and makes sure they have dinner with my parents every Sunday."

"Must be nice to have a sister like that," she said with a dreamy look in her eyes. It hit me then that Tallulah was an only child and had no concept of what it's like to have siblings.

"Yeah, well, she can also be a pain in the ass sometimes. She didn't like that I joined the military and that I don't come home that often. Even though it's work that prevents it, she thinks it's a lame excuse and never fails to give me grief over it." I loved Lizzy and if there was someone I would want to tell about my real job it was her, if for no other reason, to let her know that my absences from the family table were due to a desire to serve the greater good. Honestly, she'd still think it was a lame excuse, but maybe she might be a little less pissed at me.

"Who's next in line by age?" Tallulah seemed really interested in my family, so I would indulge her curiosity.

"Lainey. She's the peacemaker. Always trying to broker a truce during family arguments. She's a high school English teacher."

"Is she married?"

"She married her high school sweetheart. He's the manager of a pub that specializes in these homemade craft beers. They have a three-year-old daughter. She a real beauty." In my circle of friends and acquaintances from Langley, no one ever discussed their personal lives. It helped keep focus on the job, and held those feelings of longing for family and personal connections at bay. As Tallulah asked questions about my family, I started to feel those pangs of sadness you feel when you really start missing the people in your life. Even now, as I thought about Lainey's daughter, Fiona, I longed to see her happy, chubby face when she laughed at the silly faces I made.

Before she could ask, I volunteered information about the youngest of my sisters. "Maggie is the wild child. Lizzy and Lainey went to college in Indiana, but Maggie left and went to NYU. She ended up taking a job on Wall Street, so she lives in the West Village. She gets less grief than me because she always makes it home for the holidays."

"What about your parents?"

"Pretty typical. They both grew up in Chicago, but decided they didn't want to raise a family in the city. They liked Indiana because of the lower cost of living and taxes, but it was still close enough to Chicago to take advantage of the culture and activities only a big city can offer. We still went to museums and the theatre, but my parents felt like they could provide a better environment outside the city."

"What do they do?"

"My father is a retired lawyer. Mom was a secretary but she retired, too." I thought about my parents and how, after the drama of raising three daughters, they didn't pay much attention to my shortcomings. Lizzy liked to say that I was raised more in the "free range, organic style" of parenting, being more or less left to my own devices. I thought it made me independent, but Lizzy liked to psycho-analyze me and once told me that I probably joined the military because I craved the kind of discipline and structure I never got at home. Frankly, I think she underestimated her dictatorial style of taking over where she thought my parents overlooked.

But for all of my family's quirks, I knew I was lucky to have them. We had our share of dysfunction like any middle class American family did, but it felt like we were a pretty strong unit nonetheless. That kind of love and support could get your through a lot.

I thought about Tallulah's youth and how she spent most of it as a soldier in the Colonel's army. She was learning to load guns when she should have been playing with Barbies, yet I wasn't prepared to judge him for that. Until we knew what was on the drive, it was unreasonable to assume his motives for the necessity of Tallulah's training had no purpose. Still, there were so many things I didn't understand. Like why, when by all accounts the Westfields had no desire for children, did the Colonel adopt Tallulah in the first place? She spoke fondly of Laura Westfield, but admitted to never having a close relationship with her. Despite her obvious affection for Laura, why was she not closer to the only mother she really had? Sure Diana Roberts was her mother, but it was Laura who provided the nurturing care a girl needed.

I don't think she actively set out to distance herself from people. It was just the unfortunate by-product of a history filled with uncertainty and pain. Now I realized that asking her to change her natural inclination to hold everything close to the vest might push her away from me. Every attempt she made at giving me information was a step she was taking to try and change that part of her. And because of habits I developed on the job, I was on my way to screwing it up.

Realizing that my mind had wandered away from our conversation, it also occurred to me that she stopped asking questions. I looked over and saw a contemplative expression on her face. I wondered what she was thinking, but my gut told me she might be a little envious that I had those kinds of stories to tell. I told her about my crazy sisters and she told me about defusing a bomb. *Shit.* I seriously needed to lighten up.

Wanting her to feel like she wasn't alone, I reached across the console and grasped her hand. I was comforted that she reacted by closing her fingers around my hand. Even though she didn't look at me, I'd like to think she understood the feelings I tried to convey in that small gesture.

I estimated a straight drive would take around six hours, but I knew we would need to make a few rest stops and stay off stretches of larger highways likely to be monitored by traffic cams and toll booths. That would delay our arrival until sometime tomorrow morning.

A little more than halfway there, we decided to take a few hours rest. The small truck stop provided gas, food and a small motel. With the truck parked right outside our room, we brought our drive thru burgers in, along with a couple of bags and settled in. I knew Tallulah wanted to wait until we reached the safehouse before diving into any serious conversation, so I allowed her to silently move about. We took turns in the shower and ate in silence.

When I emerged from the bathroom after washing my hands, I saw her standing at the end of the bed, just staring at it. As I came up behind her, she immediately turned and leaned into me. For the next hour, nothing was said. It was as if we knew that all we needed was to feel each other without fear or apprehension. To forget any secrets and bury the past. It was a slow exploration of body and soul where words would have been a hinderance on that journey. Instead we spoke with our hands and caressed with our lips. We touched and felt, and when we were finally joined in the most intimate way possible, we held that connection for as long as we could. As we reached the peak together, I knew that nothing else would ever matter as much to me as Tallulah.

CHAPTER 30

Tallulah

N othing ever quite prepares you for those moments in life when you know everything changed. Even without the words, more was said between us in the last hour than had been said all week. The question now was what to do about it. Never more had I wanted anything the way I wanted Grayson. But in the back of my mind, I knew it wasn't likely. My past decisions effectively killed any chance I had with a man like him. Especially after hearing about his family, I knew I'd never fit in to a world like that.

I'd use the next few days to decompress and wait to hear from Jared. Once I knew what the drive held, decisions could be made about what to do next. In the meantime, Grayson deserved to know a few things about me, starting with my past associations with men like Ian. There would be difficult stories to tell and truths that I would hesitate to admit, but Grayson deserved no less.

With just over an hour of actual sleep, we packed up and headed north. I don't think we spoke a single word since arriving at the rest stop, but the comfort in that silence soothed me as we traveled further into uncharted territory.

When we finally arrived at the safehouse, I was surprised to discover how isolated it was. A long drive off a county road led to a small cottage and barn on three acres, bordered on two sides by woods. After messing around in the barn and cellar to get the power turned on, we started carrying in the bags and boxes from the truck. The cottage was small and cozy. There was a nice sized kitchen that opened to an eating area with a table and chairs. The living room seemed tiny because it was dominated by a fireplace that was too big for the room and an oversized sofa. When Grayson removed the sheet that covered it, I almost broke out into laughter at the bright floral print that was so out of character for a tough guy like him. The bathroom was small, but I saw it was a wet room.

The bedroom was at least large enough to navigate around the sides of the queen size bed. The three-drawer dresser wouldn't fit many clothes and there were already several shirts hanging in the tiny closet. Only the bed was protected by a dust cover, so there was a thin layer of dust over the remaining, albeit sparse, furnishings.

I pulled out some cleaning products and Grayson headed to a market about two miles away to get us a few supplies. I poked around as I cleaned the cottage. There were several cases of bottled water in the pantry, along with quite a few canned goods. There was a washer, but no dryer and all the stuff in the closet were men's clothes in Grayson's size. By the time he returned, the house was sufficiently cleaned and the bed made.

We worked silently to put the groceries away, then Grayson started fixing some bacon and eggs. I wanted to maintain some distance until we sat down to talk, so I offered to start a fire.

"There's wood stacked up behind the barn," he said, "and a box of kindling on the back porch."

As I walked out to the barn, I laughed at the picture we were painting. We were acting like an average couple, coming up to our upstate getaway for a relaxing weekend. The normalcy I craved was right at my fingertips, yet it was anything but. This wasn't a casual weekend, and relaxation was just a pipe dream while we waited for the other shoe to drop. In some ways it felt as though I'd rather have not gotten a glimpse of something I couldn't have. I felt like a child being brought to the amusement park to walk around and watch everyone having a good time but being told I couldn't get on any of the rides.

Ever since we had arrived, Grayson seemed especially quiet, yet chose every opportunity to communicate with his touch. As we moved around the small house, he never missed a chance to gently stroke his fingers down my face or arms. He laid small kisses on my head as he moved from one room to the next. Finally, as we sat down to eat, he reached over, placed his fingers under my chin and gently lifted my head until our eyes met. "There's no time frame on this," he said. "I don't expect you to tell me everything now. Or ever. It's not important that I know everything about your past before we met. But if you want to tell me, I want to know. I just don't want you to feel any pressure about being here with me now. This time is for us, and if all we use it for is to play Parcheesi, I'm okay with that."

"You have a Parcheesi board?"

Grayson smiled. "Battleship, actually. And a deck of cards." I returned his smile and we ate in silence.

When we settled on the sofa and took in the warmth of the fire, I decided I had put off the conversation long enough. "Grayson?"

"Hmmmm?"

"I think we should talk."

"Okay."

I moved out of his arms so I could turn and face him. It would be so much easier to talk to him if I didn't have to look in his eyes. I think I feared he would look at me with disappointment or disapproval and I didn't want to see that on his face. *Well, too bad. Pull up your big girl panties and get this over with.*

"After the Colonel died and I took off, I used part of that time in the first couple of weeks checking all the slicks I knew about, safehouses and storage units and anything else I could discover. After I found a few stashes of weapons and cash, I decided to wander around for a while. I was hiking up in the Angeles mountains when I met Ian Maguire."

Grayson's expression transformed to shock. "Ian Maguire the arms dealer?"

"One in the same. I didn't know who he was at first. He was laying low at a cabin he kept in the mountains. It was a chance meeting while hiking. He seemed taken with me, and it wasn't long before his business started picking up and he needed to travel, so when he returned to his home base in L.A., I went with him.

"I had a couple of aliases, courtesy of the Colonel, before I met Ian. Marsha Bradley was the only ID had on me when I first took off, so it was what I used. Ian knew it wasn't my real name, but he never seemed to care. He never asked me to tell him my real name and he never questioned my past. He said things that made me believe he thought I was some kind of grifter, but he never pressed the issue.

"At first, he kept me away from his business, but over time, he wanted me with him all the time, so I traveled with him more often than not."

"By then, did you know what he did?" Grayson asked.

"Yes." I lowered my head. It was hard to look at him while talking about Ian.

"Hey," he said as he lifted my face and looked into my eyes. "I'm not judging. You should see the list of people I've done business with to serve a mission. I'm not proud of it, but sometimes you have to do what needs to be done."

"I know. Ian introduced me to people who ended up being useful, including Tommy. But you should know that I genuinely cared for Ian. He was cold and ruthless, and god knows how many people were hurt because of him, but he made it easy to put it out of my mind. He took care of me in the same way the Colonel did, but gently and with more affection and caring. He taught me a lot about surviving and moving in different circles from the ones the Colonel prepared me for."

"Were you in love with him?"

Grayson's question caught me by surprise. I didn't know how to answer since it wasn't something I spent any time considering. Ian and I just . . . . were. Still, Grayson deserved an honest answer. "I cared for Ian very much, but no, I wasn't in love with him."

An expression something akin to relief crossed his face before he asked, "How long were you together?"

Suddenly horrible images of the last time I saw Ian filled my mind. I tried to erase those pictures and any memory of those events, but despite the passage of time, I still saw that day with absolute clarity.

Grayson must have misunderstood my silence. "You don't need to say anymore. We can take a break if you want."

"No," I continued, "I'm fine. It's just that Ian died last year. One of the guys Ian trusted most, his second in command, turned on him. I'm pretty sure he was an undercover cop. A huge buy was set up and the exchange was set to go down at the Port of Charleston. Something went wrong and Ian was shot and killed."

"What happened to the other guy? The second."

"Sean Barrett. I saw him go down in the gun fire. I thought he died."

"He didn't?"

"Henry, the guy who did the deal on our truck out there? He told me he heard Sean was in Istanbul. I honestly don't know what the truth is."

Grayson was quiet for a second, then asked, "What makes you think Sean was a cop?"

"Ian rarely left Sean and me alone together, but on the day of the buy, Ian had to leave to meet with somebody. While he was out, Sean came to my room and told me he knew my name wasn't Marsha. I wasn't concerned 'cause I just assumed Ian had told him as much, but then he called me Tallulah. That sort of freaked me out. Even Ian never suggested he knew my real name, and there was nothing that I knew of that connected the two identities. Some of the information Sean had about me would have had to come from someone with government access."

"Do you think Ian knew about Sean?"

"Normally, on any deals that made Ian nervous, Sean would provide back up at the exchange from an elevated position. That way, if anything went wrong, Sean could cover the area with a high powered rifle so that Ian could get out. I knew Ian didn't really know the buyer, except by reputation, and he was worried about the deal, only instead of putting Sean in a nest, he asked Sean to stand with him at the buy. I had a perch on a warehouse roof just watching. Next thing I know, gunfire erupts and everyone scattered. I saw Ian and Sean hiding behind some shipping containers when Ian pulled a knife and tried to stab Sean. I heard gunshots and both of them went down.

"The news said four suspects were killed. Brian was his regular driver tasked with driving in the shipment on a truck once payment was confirmed. I don't know what kind of arms were part of the deal, just that they were on that truck. Emmett took Sean's position on top of some shipping containers. It was a smaller contingent than Ian normally took with him on a buy, but as far as I know, the four of them were all that were there that day. It wasn't until later that I put it together with what happened earlier that day. With the change in Ian's MO on this deal, it started to make sense that Sean was a cop and if Ian hadn't figured it out before the exchange, he certainly knew in that moment everything went to hell."

Grayson thought about that for a moment, then asked, "why would Ian go through with the deal if he thought Sean was a cop?"

"Honestly, I really think Ian's suspicions had more to do with me. He told me once that he suspected that Sean had feelings for me. I think he knew Sean had been in my room that day. Even though nothing happened between us, I was still a little jumpy after our conversation, and Ian picked up on that."

"What else did Sean know about you?"

And this was where things would get complicated. How would I explain this to him without opening up an even bigger can of worms? Just then, Grayson's phone rang. Saved by the bell. Literally.

CHAPTER 31

Grayson

Mother *fucking shit*! Talk about lousy timing. Tallulah was really starting to open up to me. To trust me. The phone ringing stopped her momentum, and by the look on her face, pulled her back within herself. I knew restarting this conversation would require patience and finesse, but I had to deal with this call first.

"Yeah," I said with some irritation.

"You wanna tell me what the fuck?" Jared responded, equally irritated.

"First, what crawled up your ass and died? And second, what the hell you mean by that?"

"You're on speaker with me and Dombrowski ....." Just as I was about to lose it, Jared quickly continued. "...and before you get your panties in a wad, the intel you gave me is worthless."

Dombrowski piped up, "I don't give a shit what or who you're doing right now. Get your ass in here right now. You violated protocol, defied my direct orders, in short, you've strayed so far off the reservation, I don't know if I can bring you back. On top of which, you did it for nothing. Now listen to me and listen good. You've got 24 hours to get your ass to Langley with the Westfield woman. End of."

"If the intel is worth –" the phone disconnected. "less. Well, okay then."

Tallulah, who had been watching me the whole time looked confused. "The information on the drive is worthless?"

"I don't know. Jared was in the room with Dombrowski and both told me the intel is shit. If that's true, it doesn't make sense. Why were you targeted at the diner if you didn't have something of value? Is there any possibility we missed something? Could there be more out there that we just haven't found yet?"

"I don't know, but I doubt it. I got to every slick the Colonel used in the house he lived in. I looked at most of what he left behind except for the envelope we retrieved from the vault in Dallas. There may be a couple of slicks I didn't get to in his safehouses, but he wouldn't hide anything of value there or rely on me to find it. The Colonel had money, but his resources were limited. He was able to arrange for automatic payments from a private account in the Caymans to pay for the safehouses and storage units, but those funds wouldn't have lasted more than another six months. He wouldn't take a chance that I couldn't get to it before the money ran out."

"Well, we need to get to the bottom of this. Do you have clean ID we haven't used yet?" As I asked the question, I reached into the pantry and pulled a crowbar out from behind the cases of bottled water.

"Yeah. I grabbed a clean ID package I had stashed at the safehouse in Atlanta. Why?"

Tallulah followed me into the bedroom. As I tossed out the shoes and boots sitting on the floor of the tiny closet, I explained. "We need to get to D.C. tonight. We'll have to take a commercial flight." Using the crowbar, I pulled up the floor boards at the bottom of the closet and removed with a wooden box. Inside were guns, money and passports. I shuffled through the passports, took one out, grabbed some cash and closed the box. Returning the box to the space under the floor, I spoke to Tallulah over my shoulder. "Grab one bag and pack the bear minimum. Lose anything that could get us in trouble if we get searched. We'll stash the rest of the stuff in the cellar."

I hated going anywhere unarmed, particularly in light of recent events, but getting to D.C. and talking to Jared was imperative. I felt like time was not on our side. With the motive for the shit show in Denver now in question, we needed to figure out why Tallulah was targeted. We started moving the boxes and extra bags to the cellar. A false wall hid the location of a concrete room. There wasn't much in there. I hadn't had this place long, and it had taken me some time to do the necessary renovations that would serve my purposes, and I had just started feeling comfortable coming here.

I caught a glimpse of Tallulah as I locked up the cellar. She looked a little despondent and I had to attribute that to the revelation that we went through all this trouble for information that was useless. I didn't know what to say to her to make her feel better, so I chose instead to hold her. As we reentered the living room, I wrapped my arms around her and just held on.

When I couldn't stall any longer, I reluctantly released her and said, "there's a shuttle to Washington out of Buffalo tonight. If we hurry, we can make that last flight."

Without saying a word, she picked up her bag and headed for the door. I had a small Toyota pick up in the barn, but I didn't have time to mess with it to make sure it would run okay. I didn't like the idea of taking the truck we bought in Philly to the airport, but not enough to delay our plans. I locked up the house and we headed for Buffalo.

With the truck tucked away in long term parking, we purchased our tickets and were on our way to D.C. without any problems. Tallulah remained understandably quiet for most of that time.

We had purchased a couple of new burner phones on the way to the airport, and I used one of them to call Maddie once we landed. Despite the hour, I knew she would answer.

"Hey, Maddie. Sorry to ask for another favor so soon, but I need you to get a room at the Hilton in McLean for two nights. Check in and meet me in the hotel bar in one hour. Can you do that?"

"Babe, you're really racking up the IOU's," she said with humor in her voice. "Or should I take this as an indication that you're changing your mind about sampling my goods?"

"Tempting as that is, I know you're too much woman for me. One night with you could kill me."

I heard her laughter. "You got that right, honey. I'll see you in an hour."

It took a while to get a cab, but once we were on our way, Tallulah leaned up against me and laid her head on my shoulder. I felt I needed to offer an explanation. "I just want to keep our identities under wraps for now. If anyone gets wind of the names we're using, the agency will burn them, and we'll have to get new IDs. We're less likely to get made staying in a room booked and paid for by Maddie. If there's a leak on the inside, they'll know we're coming and will have their contacts watching the cash motels."

"I get it. You don't have to explain about Maddie. But what about the plane tickets?"

"Too many flights arriving at Dulles and Regan to monitor them when they don't know where we're coming in from or if we're even flying."

When we arrived at the hotel, Maddie was in the hotel lounge, as promised. She sat alone at the bar with two empty stools to her right. I took the seat directly beside her with Tallulah on my other side, and ordered two Scotches on ice. Maddie slid the key card toward me which I pocketed immediately. In return, I slipped her two hundred. She smiled at my reflection in the mirror across the bar, stood up and left. I thought we'd finish our drinks and head upstairs, when I noticed Tallulah had already downed hers. Guess she needed it.

We took turns in the bathroom, moving silently. It was killing me not to talk to her, but she clearly had a lot to process. As I came out of the bathroom, she was sitting on the edge of the bed staring at the TV which had yet to be turned on. She remained quiet for so long, I assumed she didn't want to talk, but just as I was about to give up on getting an indication as to how she was feeling, she spoke.

"I just can't stop thinking about the Colonel. In the last few years before he died, he kept acting oddly. I was used to his training and lessons, and at first, I understood them because in his mind, they had purpose. Later, his behavior seemed erratic, especially right before the accident. I was studying at CalTech and when I'd call to check in – the Colonel's requirement – more often I was reaching Laura and told the Colonel was nowhere to be found. Laura never seemed to know where he was or what he was doing. He gave me that envelope and told me to stash it somewhere safe and out of reach. He said I'd know when I needed to find it. I presume he meant I'd retrieve it after his death. I can't imagine he would assign so much importance to information that was useless."

I didn't want to freak her out any more than was necessary, but I needed her to be prepared. "Look. The debrief tomorrow is going to be rough. They'll be watching Jared too closely now to get him away from Dombrowski. Because we didn't look at the drive ourselves, the only hope of getting any information is to go in.

"You should understand that procedurally, I didn't always know the nature and scope of the information I obtained unless it was crucial to achieving my objective. Sensitive information is only disclosed on the basis of need-to-know. My job is to manipulate situations and assets to obtain information. Sometimes the content and what to do with it was above my pay grade. If this had been an actual CIA operation, my knowing the contents of the drive would not have been necessary to getting it into Dombrowski's hands. Once I turned it over, I wouldn't be told what it was or the significance of the information.

"But this isn't a CIA operation as far as I'm concerned, and I don't give a shit if Dombrowski thinks otherwise. Knowing what was on that drive and how the Colonel got it is essential to keeping you safe, so it's going to be a fight."

"I understand." She turned and looked in my eyes. "Grayson? Can we just forget all this shit tonight? Tomorrow will take care of itself."

I watched silently as she stood up and walked to me. In the four steps it took to reach me, she managed to remove half of her clothes. There was more that needed to be said, but my tongue seemed more anxious to explore her body than to form words. As she requested, we spent the night trying to lose ourselves in each other. With the outcome of tomorrow unsure, she was determined to make tonight count. Every movement was slow and deliberate. Everything in her eyes asked me to love her, and I was powerless to stop myself from doing exactly that.

As much as I wanted to use my strength and confidence to take her hard and overwhelm her senses, it was Tallulah that grabbed the reins. From the first moment we touched, she took charge of everything that happened. I lay on my back while she looked down at me. I felt myself buried deep inside her as I looked in her eyes, and I knew at that moment she needed to take control, if only for a short time. Since the day she was born, everything in her life happened to her. Even the choices she made were decisions she arrived at as a result of situations she was thrust into. If it meant letting her feel a return of some power, even if it was only in bed, I would submit to her demands. I would follow her lead, guided by everything that I know connected us.

We managed a little sleep that night, most of it instead spent silently conveying emotions that neither of us were yet prepared to express out loud. As the sun began to rise, I assumed our conversation from last night would continue, but as I broached the subject, Tallulah shook her head. The brightness in her eyes seemed dulled, but she held my gaze with a look of determination.

Her voice was steady. "Any leverage I may have had to get information about who is after me, disappeared the moment CIA learned the information had no value. There's no incentive for them to help me. Since I don't know what was on the drive, I certainly would have no earthly clue how he got it. I don't trust the CIA to do anything for me, but as long as they don't do anything against me, I'll be okay. The only way to ensure that is to tell them whatever they want to know about the Colonel. It's not like there's much more I can offer in that regard. I may have held the secret of this drive, but I'm sure there were other things in the Colonel's life that I knew nothing about."

I was hit with the fear that she was right. The Agency had no incentive to help her. I realized that the need to keep her safe outweighed any hope I had for her to have a normal life, one with me in it. I had to protect her. "Maybe you should go back to Colorado."

She looked up at me with surprise. "What are you saying?" she said with a touch of anger in her voice.

"What I'm saying is you're right. Letting me bring you in nets you nothing. I may have more luck getting information if they don't have you to try and squeeze it out of. You can take a return flight to Buffalo. Get to the safehouse, take your stuff from the cellar and drive the truck back to Denver. Lay low until I find out who came after you. Once I have more to go on, I'll get in touch with you through Trigger."

"No."

"No?"

"No. If I run, I'm gone. Denver is where shit went down and I'm not putting Trigger, his family or any of his guys in the line of fire. I'm probably burned there anyway and I can't go back. If I'm going to face this, it'll be head on. Bring me in to Langley or we leave the country. Together. I don't want to go without you. So choose."

I knew she was asking me to make a decision, but I couldn't get past the part where she was talking about our options as if we were acting as a team. She never told me she didn't want to be without me. It was implied in her actions but never definitively declared. There was no turning back now.

"We're going to Langley. Get dressed. Oh, and I love you."

CHAPTER 32

Tallulah

I watched Grayson get up from the bed and walk into the bathroom. He probably realized what he just said and needed to hurl. Then he walked out of the room before I could formulate a coherent response. But what would I have said?

What *would* I have said and why didn't he give me a chance to say it? *What the hell? Were you so sure you knew my response that you didn't need to stick around and hear it? Is my side of this conversation such a foregone conclusion that it wasn't required to be verbalized? Do you even care what I had to say?* In my shock and confusion, the internal monologue in my head had officially gone completely off the rails, but I couldn't hold back the anger. *How dare he?*

I proceeded to march to the bathroom door. He was about to get a piece of my mind. "Unless you've got a good goddamn reason...." I swung open the bathroom door. And caught sight of the most gorgeous naked ass I've ever seen. Facing the toilet. With the seat up. *Ah shit.*

"I get our relationship is evolving," Grayson said while barely containing his laughter, "and admittedly, I don't know the rules, but don't we have to be married at least 10 years before it's okay for you to just walk in while I'm taking a piss?"

No hit squad required. I was about to die from mortification.

I slipped on a towel on the floor, and it took three attempts to grasp the door handle to shut the door, but that was about as dignified an exit as I could have hoped to achieve.

I heard the toilet flush and water running in the sink. When Grayson came out, I was still standing in the same spot facing the bathroom door. His eyes gave my body the once over, and I suddenly realized what the picture looked like. Not only was I naked, but the contrasting color between the redness of my face and paleness of the rest of my body must have been comical. But the look in his eyes didn't reflect humor. It was more like .... *Oh boy.*

"If you have something to say," he said in a husky voice that couldn't disguise the lust, "please put some clothes on, otherwise I won't be held responsible for my actions. You'll be too occupied to get it off your chest. Your really magnificent chest."

"Okay, down boy," I said, still unable to shake the humiliation. "We should probably get going."

He walked up to me and brought his body oh so tantalizingly close to mine. His hands running gently up and down my arms, he lowered his head and with his lips on the base of my neck, whispered, "we have time."

By the time we emerged from beneath the bed covers, I couldn't remember what started everything. I could barely remember my name, though given the long list of names I had gone through in my life, that really couldn't be considered surprising. And that thought brought me back. Reality check. We needed to get to Langley. There was so much left to resolve.

Grayson dressed and grabbed the plastic laundry bag from the closet. He placed his ID in the bag and asked for my ID. I gave him all the paperwork I had, along with a burner phone and all but a few bucks in cash for us to carry. The plastic bag was folded up and stuffed into a dark colored sock. It surprised me when he reached into his bag and pulled out the Colonel's knife that I had tossed at him the first day we met. He walked over to a return air vent near the floor beside the bed and proceeded to use it to unscrew the vent cover. When he stood up after stashing the sock in the vent and replacing the cover, he noticed my shocked expression and asked, "what? What's wrong?"

He followed the line to where my eyes were fixed and held up the knife in the palm of his hand. "Oh," he said, looking somewhat embarrassed, "I meant to return this to you at some point." He held it out for me to take.

"Just hang on to it for now," I said. I wanted to give it to him, but the moment didn't seem right. I knew we had the room for another night so we left our bags and headed to the lobby.

We got in a cab and Grayson directed him to an address across the river.

"Where are we going?" I asked.

"Get some coffee." He smiled and pulled a phone from his pocket. The next thing I heard Grayson say into the phone was, "yeah, yeah, yeah. I want Jared. You can send him with Carson or Baker, but no Parsons. .... Hernandez is fine. ... We're getting coffee. Twenty minutes," then he hung up.

We arrived at a coffee shop a few minutes later. We grabbed a couple of coffees and a table near the entrance and waited. On schedule, a black Suburban pulled up in front of the shop and Jared emerged with young Hispanic man. Both men entered the shop and Jared walked directly to Grayson.

After a quick embrace, Jared turned to me. "Lou, it's been a while. How are you?"

"Ducky."

His smile was uncomfortable. I wasn't trying to be a bitch, but despite Grayson's trust in this man, I had a problem trusting him completely.

Jared returned his attention to Grayson. "Sorry, buddy, but we have to leave now. Dombrowski is about to lose his mind. We can't talk until we get to Langley. I'm under orders to keep my mouth shut until we get back."

"Whose driving?" Grayson asked, having noticed that both men had emerged from the back seat.

The young man who I assumed was Hernandez, answered. "New guy from Logistics. Dombrowski wants someone in the car who will make sure we follow orders."

Grayson looked at Jared, who just shrugged.

Needless to say, the ride to CIA was silent and uncomfortable. I started to question the wisdom of this decision. Maybe running wouldn't have been so bad. Too late. Time to suck it up.

When we arrived, the vehicle was allowed to pass through security with relative ease. We all walked toward the main entrance, flanked by two agents as Jared let the way. Just as we were about to enter, I asked for a minute. Alone. With Grayson. Everyone hesitated, then walked through the entrance and waited just on the other side.

I turned to Grayson. "Please keep the Colonel's knife. I want you to have it. Oh, and I love you, too."

Before Grayson had time to react, I opened the door and waltzed through, leaving Grayson standing there with his mouth open. *Hah. Back at you, Mr. Smugness.*

We were ushered to a security desk and issued guest ID badges. Without a license or passport, I was required to jump through a few extra hoops, but in the end, we were led to what I assumed was an interrogation room disguised as a conference room. Grayson, Jared and I took a seat, while Hernandez stood behind us. The other agent left the room, and within a few minutes, Dombrowski and Parsons entered, looking ever like the assholes I knew them to be. They sat and Hernandez walked out.

Dombrowski wasted no time. "If it were up to me, you three would be in separate rooms under hot lights, but I'm getting a lot of heat on this one, so when I ask questions, I better get answers." He directed his gaze to me. "Where did you get the thumb drive?"

"Now hold on," Grayson started, looking as if he were about to leap out of his seat and dive across the table. To avoid losing control of the situation, I held up my hand before Grayson could do or say anything that he'd regret.

"It's okay. Look," I turned my attention back to Dombrowski, "if you want the Reader's Digest version, I was adopted by Col. Marshall Westfield and the guy was an asshole. He was also paranoid and a little nuts. He invented all these ways to hide shit and for me to find shit. I grew up thinking it was some kind of game, but as it turns out, joke's on me. After he died, I looked for everything he left, except this one thing. The level of crazy attached to it was just a little more than I was comfortable with, so I chose not to go get it until you fabulous people forced my hand. I played his little scavenger hunt game, found the drive and gave it directly to Mr. Trainor. I didn't look at it, I have no idea what's on it, and I have even less of a clue where he got it. That's it."

Everyone just sat there and stared. "You don't seem satisfied. Too bad. Want to tell me what you found out about the ambush at the diner?" Silence. "No? Okay, then I think we're done." I started to stand.

"Not by a longshot," Parsons chimed in. Man was this guy an idiot. Grayson looked as though he was ready to strangle Parsons. Luckily for him, Jared, who had also noticed Grayson's agitation and was sitting on his other side, put his hand on Grayson's arm. I sat back in my seat to bring the tension down a notch.

"Anybody here heard the name Pavel Vasiliev before?" Dombrowski asked? I noticed he was staring at me, and by the looks of it, watching closely to see my reaction. I wouldn't give him the satisfaction.

From Grayson, a simple, "nope." From Jared, a more respectful, "no, sir."

"Why? Who is that?" I asked with as neutral an expression as I could muster.

Dombrowski waited a beat before answering, never taking his eyes off me. "Ukrainian born scientist. That thumb drive? Hundreds of pages of research and notes. As best we figured from the content, they belonged to Vasiliev."

"If you want to know how the Colonel got them, why don't you ask Vasiliev?" Grayson asked.

"Because he's dead. He died in the spring of 2000. Car bomb. Took out him, his wife and two kids. I tried to get more information, but everybody's being tight lipped. FBI, ATF, State, military. What little I'm getting just leaves more questions and now I'm getting heat from over my head about where this intel came from."

"I told you," I said with as much calm as I could muster. "I don't know how or from whom the Colonel got this information. He didn't tend to loop me in on specifics. I was just a foot soldier in his little army. I did what I was told and I didn't ask questions. For all I know, he could have been preparing for the zombie apocalypse. Besides, what does it matter? You said the information was useless."

"That's what I was told. Deputy Director Bedford ordered the information returned to Vasiliev's employer, Frazier Biotech Labs, which as it turns out is government funded. And he's wants to know how Col. Westfield got it."

Now Jared joined in. "I did as much digging as I could, but I couldn't find any connection between Marshall and this scientist in the public records. But there was a connection." Jared was now glaring at Dombrowski.

I was starting to get anxious when Dombrowski decided to share. "A while ago, I found out the Colonel's name had come up in reference to chatter we heard that a couple of known members of a Ukrainian mob had entered the country. Because they were tied to an organization that had arms deals in parts of the Middle East, the intel came across my desk. There was talk that they were looking for Col. Westfield. We had nothing actionable, so we notified FBI they were in the country and closed our file. Then the Colonel died in an 'accident'. I don't believe in coincidence, but the Feds and State Patrol both said 'accident.' The whole thing stunk, so I kept my file open."

"So you laid the trip wire that Jared triggered when he searched for Tallulah," Grayson surmised.

"Actually, no," Dombrowski said. "I found out about Trainor's search purely by chance.

"I was scheduling polygraphs for some of the guys in your section," Parsons said with that snooty tone. "I walk by Trainor's cubicle and saw a copy of a bail enforcement application for Ms. Westfield sitting on his desk. It was partially obscured, but I saw enough. We ran a log of all inquires made from his terminal and found out he was doing searches for her."

"And," Dombrowski added with a pointed look at Grayson, "when I couldn't reach you, I knew what was going on. When Trainor told me about the electronic trip wire, I got concerned. There was no way to know if it was set by someone inside the agency or not, and I couldn't take a chance that it was just an overreaction, so I decided to go out to Denver in person."

"At this moment," he continued, "I only know slightly more than I did that day. We ID'd one of the bodies in the diner. Arturo Guzman. Scumbag for hire. Last known to be working with a team run by Diego Escarra. He used to be known for using only top notch guys. Military training, English speaking, highly skilled. I checked with the Central American desk and they tell me Escarra lost a few guys in an op that went bad in Venezuela last year. He doesn't cost as much using less experienced guys, so word is, he's been taking jobs for less money from groups coming out of Eastern Europe."

"Didn't you find anything else?" Grayson asked.

"Actually," Dombrowski said, "we had to use 'national security' to keep the locals out of that mess in Denver, but the FBI got cranky so we didn't linger. They're still pissed about that, which is why they won't cough over their file on the bombing that killed Vasiliev."

"Wait," I chimed in. "I still don't understand the connection. Other than Vasiliev being Ukrainian, and rumors about their mob looking for the Colonel, nothing ties one to the other except coincidence. And being told the information is useless doesn't make it so. How do you know it really is?"

Dombrowski looked around and appeared to hold his breath for a moment. After a loud exhale he explained. "I should ask you to leave the room," he said to me, "but since you brought us the intel, I have to trust that even if you didn't look at it, as you claim, you still would have had the opportunity to, so I'm not compromising security by telling you this. We took a copy of everything on the drive before we returned it. Then Frazier Biotech asked if we altered the file or documents. They were particularly interested in one subfile that contained a lot of DNA test results. We ran those results through the national database and got no hits on any of them. What I was able to learn from their contact is that those tests results were never a part of the original Vasiliev files maintained at Frazier.

"Also, they did tell us that there were flaws in Vasiliev's research that made the original objective unattainable, but some of his experiments could produce viable data in the future. Because of his deal with State regarding immigration, which included safe haven for his family, any work he produced as part of the deal belongs to us and is proprietary.

"Even though I don't know enough yet about the research, Vasiliev did have a CIA file. The information on him is limited because a big part of his work was done for the Soviet Union before the collapse. Guys who work Eastern Europe tell me that some of the scientists who were part of the old Soviet research programs were abducted by the Ukrainian mob in the chaos that followed the collapse and forced to continue their work in the hopes that they would develop weapons that could be sold on the black market. At this point, it's all speculation. We don't have anything that definitively ties Vasiliev to the mob or to the Colonel, but it's a logical assumption that it's all related somehow.

"Unfortunately, we're not chartered for domestic inquiry nor are we law enforcement. There's no actionable intel that makes this a CIA matter. Once we returned the information back to Frazier Biotech, it effectively ended our participation in any of this. The only question left is whether or not you're still in danger."

Grayson turned and looked at me with concern. "Until we know who hired Escarra and why, we have to assume the threat still exists. We also haven't addressed the issue of how our Denver meeting location got compromised. The people in this room were the only ones who knew where or when."

"Look," Parsons interjected, "much as you don't want to acknowledge it, you can't say with a hundred percent certainty that you and Annie Oakley got made somewhere along the way. You can't reject the possibility that your location was discovered too late to move on it before our meeting, so they had no choice but to make their move at the diner."

Much as I hate to admit it, Parsons had a point. I couldn't discount any possibility without knowing more, so I had to accept every scenario lest I shoot myself in the foot by ignoring something just because I didn't happen to like it. When I glanced over at Grayson, he seemed to be considering the same argument.

"Be that as it may," I reluctantly acknowledged, "without more information, there's no way to know for sure. I can go underground with the possibility of never being able to live out in the open, or I can stick my head up and see who takes a shot."

Grayson immediately shot to his feet. "OH. HELL. NO." he shouted rather loudly.

"It's not your call," Dombrowski responded in a heated voice of his own. "Parsons may be right about the clusterfuck in Denver, but if not, there's a pretty significant leak with the ability to get information that supposedly only the people in this room had. And I really don't trust you," he directed at me, "but until I know what connected Colonel Westfield and Vasiliev, you're the best shot I have at finding out how all this went to shit."

Tired of this insanity, I reverted to wise ass. "Dombrowski, please, ease up on the charm or I just may orgasm on the spot."

Grayson sat back down, Jared laughed and from Dombrowski, I got what I expected. "Fuck you, lady."

"You kiss the Director's ass with that mouth?" Now I was being a bitch.

But Dombrowski wouldn't let up. "You're nothing but trouble and if I find out you held back, ..."

"Don't finish that threat, Dombrowski," Grayson stepped in. "I can't stop her if she wants to trot around like a carnival game target while some asshole with a gun takes a shot, but I'm not trusting anyone but me to watch her back."

"You're already in enough trouble, Daniels," Dombrowski warned. "You participated in, if not are responsible for that disaster in Denver, you failed to follow orders or check in, and now it turns out that the intel your turned over was procured through questionable sources from a government funded lab, was possibly stolen, and only because the shit is worthless are you unlikely to be charged with espionage. You'll be lucky if your debrief only takes a week. I'll put an agent on her, but seems to me she can handle herself just fine without you."

"She can, but she won't. She has to be able to trust whoever you assign." Grayson's decibel level went up a notch.

"If you think that's gonna be you, then I'd say she's dragging you around by your dick."

Okay. Time to end this. "You guys know I'm still in the room, right?" I asked as I caught everyone's attention. "Now let's be smart. We all want to know the same things, even if the motivations behind it aren't aligned. We need to know how the Colonel got his information and where the leak came from. Denver is ground zero, so I can start there. If you send Grayson with me, we can move around gathering information and send you reports. If our efforts draw attention, we can narrow down how. You just need to make sure the information chain stays the same."

"I don't like it," Grayson muttered.

"I don't care," I replied. "But I will need a copy of the research. We have to figure out what it is and why you're being told it's worthless, because I don't buy it."

"You get caught with it, it's my ass," Dombrowski said.

"Then I better not get caught with it."

"I'm with Gray. I don't like it." Jared had remained relatively quiet until that point, but I could see the concern in his eyes. "This can't be a sanctioned op and if anything goes wrong, you and Gray will be out in the cold."

I looked at Grayson. "Aren't you still on some kind of medical leave?"

"Yeah."

"So it won't look like an op if you and I are just traipsing around while you finish out your leave. Only a person worried that I'm still breathing will send someone after us. If we find out who and why, we will at least have gotten some answers. Being on leave gives everybody else in the room deniability, but sending reports on the down low leaves bait if the leak is on the inside."

"Look, Westfield, I'm sorry," Dombrowski said to me, looking anything but contrite. "I don't think you've been forthcoming about everything, but I get it. You're smart not to trust me either, and your assessment of the situation is more intuitive that I gave you credit for."

He turned his attention to Grayson. "I don't like her, but she makes sense. If there's no immediate security threat, I can't technically hall you in and reprimand you until you're cleared to return to duty. Since you're officially still on medical leave, and we're not facing any imminent danger, I can wait to bring you back for a debrief until after the doctor releases you. If you want to use that time to hang out with your crazy girlfriend, I can't stop you. I can, though, require regular status updates on your medical condition."

"You're a real charmer, Dombrowski," Grayson said. "It's almost hard to believe you've been divorced three times."

I couldn't resist. "I think the bigger surprise is how he got any of them to marry him in the first place."

Dombrowski slid a thumb drive across the table to Grayson. "The research. Be careful with that. I want regular reports." He then slid a cell phone to him. "This is a secured encrypted phone. Now get the fuck out of here."

"You son of a bitch," Grayson responded in anger, looking at a copy of the drive and an encrypted phone that were obviously prepared in advance of this meeting. "You planned this all along. You knew Tallulah wouldn't or couldn't supply answers, so you were ready to serve her up as bait."

Dombrowski said nothing which only confirmed Grayson was right.

There were parts of this plan that scared the shit out of me. Some information was meant to remain unknown, but it was entirely possible that keeping my secrets might only be possible if I sabotaged the plan.

CHAPTER 33

Grayson

Hernandez met up with us as we exited the conference room and advised he would take us wherever we needed to go. I asked he drop us at the same place he picked us up. Jared caught up to us as we reached the elevator.

"I don't like it, Gray. I also don't think Parsons is telling the truth. When I got up from my desk, that bail enforcement application that Parsons claims he saw was inside a file folder under a bunch of east Asia reports I was working on. No way he saw it unless he was looking."

"Don't worry about it," I tried to reassure Jared. "I've never trusted Parsons and I'm not about to now. Just keep your eyes and ears open."

"Will do," Jared said with a slap on my back. "Watch your back." To Tallulah, he said, "I'm sorry we won't have more time to get to know each other. Maybe when this is all over, we can grab lunch or something."

Tallulah flashed that smile that took your breath away. "I'd love that," she said to a now blushing Jared. That was the second time I saw a grown man have that reaction to her. It didn't surprise me so much as it tickled me.

As we were exiting the car at the coffee shop, Hernandez stopped me with a hand on my arm and said, "I don't know what's going on, but for what it's worth, I don't trust Parsons. If you need anything, I've got your back."

"Thanks."

As Hernandez pulled away from the curb, Tallulah dropped her forehead on my shoulder and signed. "Can I assume you have a plan?"

"I found life is more interesting if you don't make any assumptions, especially about the usefulness of having a plan." Tallulah's head shot up in surprise.

"Hey," I said with a smile, "just kidding. Of course I have a plan."

"Does it entail my dressing in costume disguised as a space alien?"

"If you're up for some role playing, I prefer the French maid outfit, but as long as they come with crotchless panties, I'm okay with either."

"Don't be ridiculous. You don't wear panties with a French maid outfit." Tallulah gave me a small smile. Her eyes still reflected the sadness she was carrying, but I had to feel encouraged that she was at least trying to maintain her sense of humor.

I wanted to act as if everything were okay and we were just deciding on a vacation destination, but I knew that's not what Tallulah needed. She needed to be secure in the knowledge that I would tell her the truth about every situation, and allow her to participate in decisions so she could feel as if she had some semblance of control in a reality where she had none. I decided to lay everything out for her and not only seek, but seriously consider her input. I figured we should keep moving while discussing options, so I took her hand and we started walking to the end of the block.

"I don't think there's a big threat here in Washington. Being on my turf is a huge disadvantage, even if the leak did come from the inside. I have a place a few blocks from here that I think is safe. We'll case the area before we go in, but if it looks okay, I want to grab a few things we might need. We'll take a cab back to the hotel in McClean and retrieve the rest of our stuff. From there, I want to take the bus to New York City. My sister, Maggie, has a place in the West Village and I'd like to see her."

"I'm okay with that, but is there any particular reason why?" Tallulah asked.

"Yeah. I don't think we'll be back to the east coast for a while. I don't know when I'll be able to visit my parents, so this is my best shot at seeing her. We're the

179

closest in age, so I've always had a tight bond with her compared to my other sisters."

"Why don't you think we'll be back?"

"I think you were right about Denver being ground zero, since that's were you first came up for air. I figured we start there and send up our first flare. We'll move around from that point sending messages that might help us narrow down where the leak is coming from."

We spent the remainder of the walk hashing out some of the details. I led her to the back side of a parking garage directly across the street from my apartment. We ascended the structure using the back stairwell, being sure to check every floor for any surveillance. My Porche was parked on the second floor of the garage, and since we weren't taking it, I chose not to approach or check on it. I can always send someone else to do that at another time. It reminded me that my Jeep was still in Colorado. I'd have to figure out what happened with it after we got back there.

Once on the roof, I was able to observe my apartment and the surrounding buildings. As I had hoped, everything seemed quiet. As we stood and watched, I observed one of my neighbors come home, a young man named Seth who worked as an aid to Congressman George Meyer. He exited a cab and walked to the front door. My apartment was one of four units in a converted brownstone. I had an apartment on the ground floor across from Seth. As he entered, nothing seemed out of the ordinary.

After sufficient time had passed to convince me that it was safe, Tallulah and I made our way across the street and entered my apartment. After gathering the few things I thought we might need, we took a cab back to the hotel in McLean. Before long we were on a train to New York.

I was able to reach Maggie on the phone when we arrived, and after the requisite ass-chewing for having been out of touch for too long, we agreed to meet for dinner at a little bistro near her place. We had just enough time to check into a small, cheap hotel to shower and change.

As we made our way to the bistro, I figured I should warn Tallulah about what to expect where Maggie was concerned.

"Maggie isn't as pushy or bossy as Lizzy, but she's a force in her own right. She'll definitely give you the third degree and she'll want to know what we are to each other."

"What are we to each other?" she asked with slight smirk on her face.

"What label would you prefer? Girlfriend? Lover? Partner? Sex slave?"

"No label required," she replied. Just then, Maggie walked up silently behind Tallulah. "As long as you acknowledge I'm the one in charge, it doesn't matter what you call us."

Maggie, whose presence was not yet detected by Tallulah, raised an amused eyebrow and smiled.

"Yes, Master." I bowed. "Or should I call you 'baby cakes' or 'my little lamb chop'? I know how you love a good pet name."

"Whatever you want, Pumpkin Patch," Tallulah countered.

Maggie could hold back no longer and burst into laughter. Tallulah swung around to Maggie. When she turned back to me, she poked me in the chest and glared at me, although it might have had a scarier effect if she hadn't turned as red as a beet.

"Maggie, this is Tallulah," I introduced. "Tallulah, this is my sister, Maggie."

With a final sneer in my direction, Tallulah turned to face Maggie, who had already extended her hand and a smile. "I like her." Maggie said to me. To Tallulah, "It's really nice to meet you."

"It's really nice to meet you, too," Tallulah replied.

Dinner turned out to be a really great time. Tallulah and Maggie got along as if they'd been friends forever. Since Maggie was a financial analyst and Tallulah a mathematician, they seemed to share the same love for numbers. It surprised Maggie that Tallulah worked as a bounty hunter, but when she explained it was just to help supplement her income while designing computer programs and phone apps, Maggie just accepted it as perfectly normal.

It wasn't until Tallulah excused herself to the ladies' room that Maggie turned on me. "Okay, Gray, what's the fucking deal?"

"First of all," I answered, "watch your mouth. And second, what the hell are you talking about?"

"You know I have a Masters Degree from Columbia, right?"

"Yeah, that's a good school."

"Yes, it really is. So why do you treat me like you think I'm stupid?"

"Huh?" Just when I thought I was starting to understand the women in my life, Maggie throws a curve ball.

"I don't hear from you in I don't know how long. You pop in for a surprise visit with a woman I didn't know anything about, but really like. You gallivant all over the world, but I've never heard you mention going to Denver, yet here you are with a new girlfriend who lives there. When I ask you what brings you to New York, I get an answer that's a cross between Forrest Gump and Abbot and Costello. You may be able to keep your secrets from Lizzy, Lainey and the folks, but you need to come clean. It's me, Gray. The one that always covered for you. You know you can trust me. So, what the hell is going on with you?"

"It's complicated, Maggie."

"No, no, no. Playing that card is reserved for relationship talks and explaining to mom why we're still single. You can't use that with me. Whatever this is about, does Tallulah know?"

"Yes, but we can't get into it now."

"This conversation is not over," she said as she looked up to see Tallulah approaching and smiled.

"Well," I said as I decided this was as good as time as any to make a quick exit, "while this has been a real slice of heaven, Tallulah and I are taking an early train, so we should probably get going."

"Oh, you mean to get to that business meeting in Boston, or uh, no, um, that vacation at Niagara," Maggie mocked our poor attempt at an earlier explanation.

"Yeah, exactly." I wouldn't give her the satisfaction of getting flustered over our little flub.

"Okay, sure." She turned to Tallulah and gave her a hug. "My parents want everyone home at the holidays. If you're still with my loser brother, and I hope you decide to keep him, it'll be great to see you there."

Tallulah seemed at a loss for words, so I stepped in. "I may need to rethink showing up if you're going to be there," I told Maggie.

"Everybody loves me better anyway," Maggie replied.

We said our goodbyes and Tallulah and I walked back to our hotel. I was starting to get better at reading Tallulah's expressions, but while getting ready to turn in for the night, I caught a glimpse of one I had not really seen before. Her mood seemed a bit melancholy as she walked to the window and looked out. I walked up behind her and wrapped my arms around her. She laid her arms over mine and leaned her head back against my shoulder.

She spoke in a quiet voice. "Sometimes I wish I had a sister. A confidant that you can tell all your secrets to. I kept to myself in college. I always felt like such an outsider. I didn't seem to fit in with the other girls. I didn't go to a regular high school, so I couldn't relate to the stories other people told. I felt like a freak. I could disassemble and clean a firearm, but trying to have a conversation terrified me."

Now I understood her expression and mood. In an attempt to relate, I said, "For the record, no one in my family knows what I do for a living. Even Maggie. I have to keep secrets, too. And keeping them from Maggie has been especially hard, because she suspects I'm not completely honest with her, and I know she feels hurt that I won't confide in her."

"Don't you want to tell her?" Tallulah asked.

"Reading in your family carries another set of issues I'm not prepared to deal with yet. Even though I'm rarely in life threatening or even dangerous situations, I know they would still be worried. Even if they knew what I did, since assignments are classified, I wouldn't be able to talk about it and that would bother them. It's easier to project a fiction and let them think what they think."

"I guess we both have had to keep our secrets."

I realized then how much stronger our connection truly was. She was the only person outside my colleagues that, not only knew what I did, but could relate to the kind of life that keeping secrets required. We understood each other in a way that only two people like us were uniquely suited to empathize with. Despite being for entirely different reasons in entirely different circumstances, the difficulties we faced in navigating personal relationships were eerily similar.

As we made love late into the night, I held her with a renewed sense of purpose. I would protect her and her secrets. If she needed a confidant, I would always be there to listen, but it was also important for me to understand that she may not be ready to reveal all her secrets for a very long time. Keeping things locked up inside her had become a tool of her survival and asking her to change that would do nothing more than scare her. Because learning about them wouldn't change the way I felt about her, no matter what it was. Of this I was certain.

CHAPTER 34

Tallulah

Something had shifted last night. I couldn't put my finger on it, but it felt as if Grayson was determined to take care of me while simultaneously treating me as a partner on equal footing with him in every way. He acted like my personal protector, while making sure I was as heavily armed as he was. He hovered around me like a shield, as I carried my own bags. He moved quickly with planned purpose, yet asked me to make decisions. He was adapting to the changes that were defining the evolution of our relationship. I just wasn't sure if that was because of the kind of man he was or if his training and experience as an agent developed that ability. I guess in the end, it really didn't matter which. Either way, we were becoming closer and I was feeling more confident in our mutual trust.

The silences between us were becoming more comfortable, the dialogue being replaced by constant, yet gentle caresses, suggestive glances, and quiet contemplation. During the train ride to Buffalo, we barely spoke, but it felt as though so much was being said.

The truck was exactly where and as we left it in the airport long-term parking lot, with a quick inspection revealing it had remained untouched. We decided to spend an extra day at Grayson's cottage which turned into two days. We spent lazy days eating peanut butter sandwiches and playing cards, and yes, even Battleship. We made love on the overstuffed sofa in front of a fire and discussed ideas about how to figure out what was on the drive.

We finally decided it was time to leave and packed up the truck. We closed up the cottage and made sure we had everything we needed to take before heading out on the long road trip to Denver. Despite having an available route to Denver that would take us within a few miles of his parents' home, we chose a more southerly path. Grayson explained not wanting to go near his parents or his other sisters until we resolved the question of whether I was still being targeted.

We decided to drive at a leisurely pace, use highways less traveled and make frequent stops. We also made several stops to purchase computers and burner phones. We were somewhere in southern Kansas when we decided to take an extended stop. We found a small, out-of-the-way motel and a convenience store nearby where we picked up a few supplies.

Once we settled in, I opened up the laptop and, disabling all connectivity functions, loaded the contents of the flashdrive. My training as a mathematician gave me some insight into the research and data, but for the most part, it was all Greek to me. Jared had added a notation as to which subfile had not been included in Vasiliev's original file and decided to start there instead.

When I opened it, I immediately recognized the data as results of DNA testing. The focus seemed to be on specific elements of the results, but the subjects of those tests were only identified by assigned numbers. Nowhere was there any index to the names of any individuals who may have been the actual subjects. I was able to translate some notes written in Russian, enough to know several of the subjects were related and particular common markers of these subjects was of interest. I went back to the research notes starting in the beginning by chronology. Unfortunately, I wasn't conversive in these scientific disciplines to make sense of any of the notes.

When frustration set in, I set the laptop aside and crawled across the bed to where Grayson was leaned up against the headboard, reading a newspaper. He put down the paper, wrapped me in his arms and kissed my forehead.

"Getting frustrated?" he asked.

"I can't make heads of tails of some of this stuff. Is it possible to call Jared?" I asked. I knew that, while he may not understand the research either, he may have had someone else look at it and at least have some idea of what it was.

"Yeah," Grayson said as he reached down into his duffle and retrieved the encrypted phone Dombrowski had given him. "I'll get him for you." He dialed and handed me the phone.

Jared began speaking before I was able to say hello. "By the way, I forgot to tell you before you left, keep your hands to yourself. You both have enough going on without getting tangled up in the sheets, you know what I'm saying?"

"Sorry, Jared, but that horse left the barn." Silence from the other end.

"Ah shit, Lou. I didn't mean anything by it. I just don't want either of you hurt. Gray's a good guy, but there's a reason he's one of the best operatives out there. I just think that while all of this is going on – "

"Jared," I interrupted. "I know you mean well, but don't worry, okay? Right now, I need to know who else reviewed the intel, and was anyone able to analyze the data."

Jared paused a moment before continuing. "Because of the leak, we didn't approach any outside experts. I showed it to one guy inside the Agency that has knowledge in this area without telling him anything about the data. He was only able to view it on a computer screen in a locked room for a couple of hours for security reasons, but I had to pull it before he got very far because Dombrowski shut down any further inquiry. The most I was able to get was that the research was focused on a new method for delivery of an infectious pathogen that targets victims with specific DNA markers. The idea being a biological weapon that could target only certain groups people. He couldn't tell me the kind of pathogen or who would be targets, but he said Vasiliev was collecting a lot of DNA samples. The subfile that Frazier didn't have contains the only samples that weren't part of Vasiliev's original file."

"Do we have any clue as to who those samples belong to?"

"Not a clue. Like Dombrowski said, they didn't match any samples in the national database. Dombrowski is still trying to get more information on Vasiliev from State and FBI, but so far, no one is sharing."

"Okay, thanks. And don't worry about us. Grayson and I are fine."

I handed the phone back to Grayson and he just smiled. "Jared's heart is in the right place," he said. "I think he's more worried about you than me. I don't have the best history where women are concerned."

"I'm sure he means well. I just don't like him thinking this thing between us is superficial, or worse, taudry."

"That's not what would make Jared say something. I'm sure his concern is that starting something while we're amidst all this uncertainty about everything else is a recipe for disaster."

"Do you think it is?" I asked, suddenly unsure.

The next thing I knew, he pushed me back on the bed, pinned me down, with his eyes focused on me with intensity. "I need you to hear me. I love you. I can't promise anything about this crazy situation except one thing. No matter what happens, we deal with it together." He kissed me hard and smiled. "Besides, if you dump me, Maggie will probably disown me."

"Well we can't have that now, can we?" I paused and returned that laser focus with our eyes meeting. "I love you, too and I'm sorry. I usually don't care what other people think, but Jared is your friend and he obviously cares about you."

It was then I started to question any kind of future with Grayson, not because of the mess we where attempting to untangle, but because our histories would make combining our lives impossible. For me, while Grayson's family could eventually accept me despite a dysfunctional upbringing, my history could jeopardize Grayson's career. It was possible that he could lose the ability to maintain a high security clearance and even prevent him from seeking positions higher up in the organization that required more sensitive access.

For Grayson, he may be able to deal with my association with a bail bondsman with questionable character, like Charlie Brodsky, but he would have to overlook my friendships with guys like Trigger. And no matter what I said about Grayson, Trigger would never trust him. Trigger would never have to know that Grayson was CIA, but he would make other assumptions that made Grayson a liability to Trigger's way of life.

There was also one huge factor I kept trying to ignore. The one secret I had yet to tell anyone. Every step we took in this journey kept bringing me closer to the point where I feared keeping the secret was no longer possible. It also confirmed my suspicions about how this all came about.

After having heard everything Dombrowski had learned, it seemed that the connection between the Colonel and Vasiliev was clear. The Colonel had somehow secured possession of that research and the Ukrainian mob had discovered that. How that information came into the Colonel's possession and how that fact was leaked may never be known. What we needed to confirm was whether the mob or their contractors still believed the information was valuable and in my possession.

I didn't realize how far off my thoughts had drifted until I heard Grayson's raised voice. "Tallulah!" When I finally glanced over, I saw mix of curiosity and frustration in the expression he wore, followed by, "Did you hear anything I just said?"

"Sorry, no, I had a thought."

"What is it?" he asked, looking concerned.

"Let's make a few assumptions. One, the Colonel obtained Vasiliev's research. Since it contained information not available in the files kept at Frazier, we can also assume it was not stolen from the lab but from Vasiliev's personal stuff. "

"Don't we need to know how they were connected and how the Colonel got it?"

"No," I replied, trying to deflect the conversation away from that aspect of our inquiry. "For our purposes, we have set aside those questions. We may never know how or even if they knew each other. It's possible that the Colonel happened upon the intel by chance. I mean, think about it. Dombrowski said Vasiliev died in 2000. That means either the Colonel knew Vasiliev and held onto this information for all this time, or he didn't know him and just came into possession of it. Even if the Colonel's possession of it came to light and leaked to the mob three years ago when he and Laura died, that's still 15 years that he just hung onto it? Does that seem reasonable to you?"

Grayson said nothing, but I could see the wheels turning in his head. He patiently considered my analysis, waiting for me to continue.

"Second assumption. Sketchy as it is, the story is true about Vasiliev working for the mob after the Soviet Union collapsed. He was working on this research for them at the time he fled Ukraine and made his way to the United States. In 2000, the mob discovers his whereabouts and take him and his family out with a car bomb."

"So you think the mob sent assassins to the US to take out one lowly scientist?" Grayson wasn't convinced.

"We're talking about the Ukrainian mob. I learned a lot about different groups and arms traders while I was with Ian, and I can tell you one thing for sure. The Ukrainian mob guys that Ian had dealings with were evil bastards. They'd shoot you just to make sure their gun worked. It wouldn't be outside the range of possibility that they'd take out Vasiliev as payback for fleeing with what I'm sue they would have considered their property."

"Say you're right," Grayson conceded, "why kill the Colonel and go after you in the diner?"

"Third assumption. Few people knew the research was actually worthless. If the standard was whether or not the information could be converted into a viable delivery method for biological weapons, the mob may not have known that there was no value in the intel. Who cleared out my house on the day of the Colonel's funeral?"

Grayson thought for a moment. "Jared's file on you said he was never able to confirm who. He assumed it was FBI or military police, but I don't think he dug too far."

"If it was the mob and they didn't find anything, that would explain why they took notice when I came back into the picture, and why they were careful not to kill me. The last time they did that with the Colonel, they weren't able to retrieve the research."

"Okay. So why did it take over six months to make a move on you, and at the worst possible time – while you were meeting with CIA?"

I thought about it. "Jared told you no one was actively looking for me, right? They just set up a way to be alerted if anyone else was looking. Until Jared resumed his search, they didn't know I had returned to the mainstream. I don't want to brag, but I was good at staying off everybody's radar. Even Ian didn't know who I was. I had resources and contacts. Even if they tried locating me when I first went underground, I don't think they'd have a clue where to start." I didn't mention Sean, knowing I had to figure a few things out before coming clean with Grayson.

I had to know if Sean was still alive. I was 99.5% sure Sean was some type of undercover law enforcement, but I wanted confirmation. I needed to know exactly what Sean knew about me and how many others he may have told. It was possible he was the leak, but his motive was unknown and that scared me. Once we arrived in Denver, I needed to find a way to get in touch with Sean. If he was alive, he might have some of the answers I needed.

Since Ian's death, I had cut off all contact with any of the people associated with that life. Until now. Having to use those resources, guys like Tommy, to move across the country, would spread gossip about my reappearance pretty quickly. I didn't like the exposure, but the necessity of it helped me move past the panic.

I stared at Grayson's expression which told me he wasn't convinced. "Look," I said, "I don't think any of those assumptions are that far off the mark and it gives us something to start with. The one thing that bothers me is the diner. I can't accept that you or I didn't spot a tail on the way to the meeting. I really think it was Parsons. He's ambitious and inexperienced. When he saw what Jared was looking into, he probably pulled information from unreliable sources to keep it off Dombrowski's desk and may have unknowingly been the leak. Once it was known that Parsons knew where to find me, he wouldn't have been hard to track. Sitting behind a desk makes you forget to take simple precautions."

"That makes about as much sense as anything else right now. Starting with your premise being correct, where to you think we should start?"

I picked up a burner phone and called Trigger. "Hey, Trigger. Is everything okay?"

He sounded upset. "You wanna tell me what the fuck? I got rid of the piece, but Iceman told me the Feds were all over Rick's Diner. The news said something about Homeland Security. That your mess?"

Time for a subject change. "Did you get my van?"

"Oh. So that's how it's gonna be. Okay then, yeah, I got the van. It's clean. I had to pull stuff out to be sure, but I put it back together and left it at Ma's house. Neighborhood has eyes on it and no one's messed with it since. The trailer and your bike are at Tony's. Where have you been, man?"

"It's a long story. I need to pick up my van. I'm about a day out."

"You with that asshole? The Fed?"

I knew this would be an issue. "He's not a Fed, so lighten up. We're together, so yeah, he'll be with me. And don't give me any shit about it. I'll be stopping in to see Ma and Jasmine, and Grayson will be with me, so ease up, will you?"

"You know if Ma don't like him, it's gonna be a thing."

"I'm not worried."

"You should be. What else you need?" he asked.

That's why I loved Trigger. He was like my brother. Even amidst disagreements, he would always worry about me and want to know I was okay. "There's stuff I have to work out when I get to town. I may need your help."

"You know you can ask me for whatever, right? You know I give you shit, but I owe you big."

"First of all, you don't owe me shit. Same goes both ways."

"I know," he said. I heard the smile in his voice.

"Just one other thing. Do you know what happened to a Jeep that was parked in front of Rick's?"

"Fed-mobile? Yeah. Local cops impounded it. T-Bone found it on the lot on 26th Street. I had T-Bone and Scar make a few passes while it sat in front of Rick's. Doesn't look like anyone messed with it, but we left it alone, like you asked."

"Okay. Let Mama and Jasmine know I'll be by around 6. I'll bring dinner, so tell her not to cook."

"Sure thing. See you then."

I looked over at Grayson and he was sitting quietly, watching me intently. "You want to let me in on the plan?" he asked.

"Trigger made sure my van is clean. I think the best strategy is to move around in it. We'll road trip leaving markers where we need to. Trigger has it sitting at his mother's house. I haven't visited in a while, so this will be good chance to see her and his sister, Jasmine."

"Sounds like a plan," he said. "So I've been curious about what the story is behind your friendship with Trigger." The question was posed so casually, but I knew he was chomping at the bit to get more information. It was, after all, an odd pairing for us to be friends.

"I met Trigger shortly after Ian died. We were in a position to help each other out, so we did. I wanted a permanent address, but one that would keep inquiring minds at bay. I pay rent to Cora Mae and all my mail gets sent there as my legal address. I don't want to talk to you about Trigger's business, so I'll just say that I've helped him out from time to time."

"Okay," Grayson replied. I knew he wasn't particularly happy with that answer, but it seemed he wouldn't push for now.

CHAPTER 35

Grayson

A short time after our conversation about Trigger, Tallulah and I were on the road. I didn't like that Tallulah seemed protective of her relationship with Trigger or that she wouldn't tell me more about their dealings. Given the promises I made to myself about backing off and giving her some space, I knew I needed to let it go for now.

In spite of that promise, I decided it couldn't hurt to try the back door to get information. "So tell me about Cora Mae. You call her 'Mama', right?"

Tallulah smiled. She obviously felt affection for Trigger's mom. "Yes," she said, "Cora Mae is a headstrong woman. Unfortunately, she's cursed by poverty, geography and circumstances outside her control. She works hard to take care of her family, and despite hardship, raised two great kids. I know Trigger seems like a punk, but beneath the gang persona, he does have a good heart. Cora knows what Trigger does to bring in money is wrong, but her daughter, Jasmine, has a chance to get out. She's smart, beautiful and has a real shot at going to college. Cora will do whatever it takes to see that through, even if it means looking the other way when it comes to Trigger."

We arrived in Denver with enough time to find a motel and get cleaned up. Tallulah called an order into a popular restaurant that prepared a variety of foods. I questioned whether we were feeding the entire neighborhood since she got two large pizzas, a large tray of fried appetizers, two buckets of fried chicken, french fries, biscuits, green beans, and an apple pie.

After picking up the food, we entered a neighborhood and saw first hand what Jared had only been able to provide a visual of by satellite photo. It reminded me of some of the worst areas of D.C., Harlem, south central L.A. and Gary, Indiana. A network of young kids, mostly boys between 10 and 14, seemed to be patrolling the area. Several of them scattered when we entered the street where Cora's house sat. Within a minute, several gang members appeared on the street staring us down. As I suspected, this area was perfect for anyone hiding from the outside world, provided you could either blend in with this environment, or in Tallulah's case, had an inside connection.

One of the gang members seemed to recognize Tallulah and gestured a greeting. Tallulah pulled up to Cora's house and exited quickly. Trigger exited his house and was making his way down the front stoop when he was almost bowled over by a very exuberant young girl. Her long, dark hair fell in dozens of intricate braids, adorned with decorative beads. She practically slammed into Tallulah and wrapped her in a bear hug.

"Lou!!" she screamed. "Where have you been? I missed you sooooo much. Trigger told me you were coming to pick up your van. What happened? Oh my god? Who's that hunk in the truck? Mama's waiting for you. I think she wants to scold you for something, so be ready." I don't think the girl took a breath.

Tallulah gestured for me to join her. As I walked up to stand beside her, Trigger held out his hand. I couldn't quite understand what was happening since I know he didn't approve of my being with Tallulah, but if he was making an effort, so would I. As I shook his hand, he laughed and said, "Ma wants to meet you. Good luck, man. You're gonna need it. This is my sister, Jasmine."

"Hi, Jasmine." I tried to flash my most disarming smile. I'd like to win over at least one member of this family and I figured the young girl was my best shot.

"Are you Lou's boyfriend?" she asked.

"Until she dumps me," I responded.

Two of the other gang members who had been approaching gave Tallulah a brief shoulder hug, ignored me, then helped us carry the food to the house.

The outside seemed in somewhat of a state of disrepair. Clearly the exterior was in need of a fresh coat of paint, and at first glance, work needed on the porch and garage roof. Despite that outward appearance, the inside was clean, homey and looked as though the carpet had been recently replaced and the walls painted.

Trigger's mother was not what I expected. Even dressed in clothes that were well worn, this woman could have been mistaken for a model. She couldn't have been a day over forty-five. She was as tall as Tallulah, and though heavier, had a well-proportioned, voluptuous figure that men coveted. She had lovely brown eyes that, at the moment, were piercing holes into my skull with laser precision.

"Mama!" Tallulah greeted. "You look great. How are you?"

"Oh, I'm doing good, child, but you about to get an ass whipping," she said. "I got a bone to pick with you, girl, so tell me who this young man is, so I can get to it."

Tallulah turned back to me and smiled before directing her attention back to Cora. "Mama, this is Grayson. Go easy, okay?"

"It's a pleasure to meet you, Mrs. Brookes," I said, turning on as much charm as I could manage in an otherwise very uncomfortable situation.

"Boy, sit your ass down on that sofa and don't be trying to sweet talk me. I'll get to you in a minute." She directed her attention back to Tallulah, while Jasmine took a seat beside me and smiled. "First of all, why you bringing enough food to feed the whole neighborhood? Second, stop sending extra money in the rent check. You don't even stay here, and a month of your mail barely fill the fryin' pan. And why ain't Tyrone able to reach you these last couple of weeks. You know I worry about you. You trying to raise my blood pressure?"

"Tyrone?" I whispered to Jasmine.

"Trigger's name," Jasmine quietly replied.

"Mama," Tallulah answered, "Trigger's boys might be hungry, too. And I brought lots of paper plates from the restaurant. We can fix a few big plates for Mrs. Thomas and Mrs. Johnson down the street. I know they don't get out much and they might enjoy a nice dinner they don't have to cook." Again, I saw that big smile Tallulah flashed when she was expressing affection for the person she was talking to.

Continuing, she said, "and I already told you that I need to declare this address as my legal residence. It has to appear that I live here, so I have to pay what would be considered a reasonable rent. And I'm sorry I was out of touch. Things have been happening that I had to deal with and I didn't want you involved."

"Come here, girl," Cora said as she wrapped Tallulah in a big hug. "Now tell me about that one over there."

Tallulah looked at me and smiled. "I know you don't know him yet, but Grayson is a good guy. He's been taking really good care of me. I love him, Mama."

I had to smile. I knew how she felt, but hearing her admit it to others sent me over the moon. Just as our eyes met and I was about to return the declaration, I felt another stare drilling me. And, of course, she wasted no time, sticking it to me.

"What on earth does she see in you, boy? You look like you should be dancing in some Chippendales show or something. You treating my girl right? You ought to know I don't approve of no hanky panky less you plannin' on marrying my girl."

Tallulah seemed content to let me squirm. She smiled at me and waggled her eyebrows clearly enjoying my discomfort. Well, stand back, sweetheart, because this right here – it's where I do my best work. Put me in a pressure situation, surrounded by hostiles, where everything is at stake and it's like flipping a switch – I am ON.

I knew Jasmine and Cora simply wanted reassurance that I would love and take care of Tallulah, which is the opposite of what Trigger wanted. I am sure he didn't want me within ten city blocks of her. I knew I had to balance my responses to try an appease everyone in the room. Tricky, but not impossible.

"Mrs. Brookes, Tallulah and I met under unusual and strained circumstances, but I love her. I want to protect and take care of her. But I think we all know that she is independent, strong and won't take crap from anyone. I only stand a chance if she decides I'm worth it, and I plan on doing everything in my power to prove to her I am. If not, we all know she would have no problem kicking my Chippendale ass to the curb."

Cora smiled at me. "Okay then, let's eat."

The rest of the evening went well. Trigger still seemed wary of me, but he seemed to loosen up a little. Jasmine spent the evening talking about school. She was obviously a bright girl with a promising future. Cora was happy to sit back and watch her family interact, while keeping an eye on me. I'm sure she, too, was still a bit wary, but she appeared to relax each time Tallulah looked at me or laid her hand on my arm with affection.

Trigger's guys were invited to join us, but not before plates of food were prepared and distributed by them to a few of the elderly neighbors down the street. I also noticed Tallulah slide an envelope of cash in a kitchen drawer. I knew Cora would not accept it otherwise.

After dinner Tallulah, Trigger and I excused ourselves and went outside. Her van was parked on the side of the garage and covered by a large tarp. T-Bone joined us and proceeded to remove the tarp. The van looked exactly as it did when we left it at the RV park.

"I checked everything," Trigger said. "If you want to get your trailer and bike, we can head over to Tony's, but not until 11:00 tonight. Business happening."

Trigger handed Tallulah a set of keys which she used to open up the van. As promised, everything was pretty much as we left it. Even my large duffle with the equipment Morgan had left me sat on the table. We entered and looked around. I checked inside the duffle and sure enough, everything was still there.

Tallulah exited the van, walked up to Trigger and hugged him. "Thanks," she said, "I owe you. I need to unload our stuff, but then you can take the truck." She handed keys to T-Bone. "Can you pull my truck up, please?" she asked.

Without responding, T-Bone walked to the truck and pulled it into the driveway. We unloaded the bags and boxes from the truck into the back of the van. Tallulah opened one of the boxes, removed a couple of guns and handed them to Trigger who passed them off to T-Bone. They all spoke in hushed tones, but I got the gist of the exchange.

Tallulah separated herself and walked over to me. "Should we take my bike and trailer? If we do, it makes sense to buy another bike. If anything goes down, it might be smart to have two bikes for an escape plan."

I thought about it and decided against it. "Let's not take it. We can move more freely and under the radar without it. I'd also be worried about weather issues and the inability to take anything with us. Will it be okay if we leave it for now?"

"Yeah," she replied, looking a little disappointed. "It'll be fine." She did some final checks on the van then decided we should go. After saying our goodbyes, which included another stern lecture to me from Cora, we took off and headed south.

We had agreed to pick up supplies and regroup in the Walmart parking lot. While in the store, we split up to gather things more quickly. As I was looking for a pack of disposable razors, I looked up at the security mirror hanging from the corner ceiling at the end of the aisle. It was how I saw Tallulah talking on one of the burner phones. It didn't concern me until I asked her to use the phone to reach out to one of my contacts in Denver, and she told me she didn't have a phone on her.

I told her I forgot to grab shaving cream and said I'd meet her at the checkout. When I walked back to where I had seen her talking on the phone, I saw a garbage can not far from where she had been standing. There, sitting just beneath a napkin atop a pile of trash, was a cell phone.

CHAPTER 36

Tallulah

*D*ammit! I didn't want to lie to Grayson, and though technically, I didn't, I also neglected to tell him about the phone call I had placed right before dumping the phone. I just needed to know if Sean was dead or alive before pursuing this. If Sean was really dead, there would be no need. The things I knew about or participated in while with Ian were sensitive topics around Grayson. I couldn't justify much of it and I always felt like a bad person when I spoke about it with Grayson. He always seemed as though he weren't judging my actions from that time in my life, but I know he didn't approve. He may have understood, but he didn't condone.

Sean was a big part of that time. I took comfort in the knowledge that, if Sean were a cop, he could not prove that I had done anything illegal. Because of Ian's attempts to keep me separated from his business, but most especially from Sean, any knowledge or involvement I had was outside of Sean's awareness and presence.

Sean did, however, know things about me that I had hoped died with him. I also suspected that, if he was a cop and had been looking for me, it was possible that he had the knowledge and resources to turn over the wrong rocks and inadvertently leak information that led the Ukrainian mob to find me. Even if Sean didn't die, I had to be sure the secrets he knew about me did. Henry was the only one I had come across that thought Sean was alive and well. The phone call reaching out and asking him to get a message to Sean was my only chance for now.

It did occur to me to call Tommy, as well. While Tommy didn't react at my statements regarding the death of Ian and Sean, he didn't really confirm it either.

He acted a little strange when we talked about it, but I didn't think much of it until now. I decided I needed to get the same word out to Tommy, but it would have to wait. As it is, I've misled Grayson once today, and I needed to handle this carefully.

Grayson was quiet as we unpacked our purchases. I knew we had to proceed as if Sean were not a factor in our plans.

"I should check in with Charlie," I said. "I need to know if anyone's been asking for me."

Grayson said nothing as I dialed Charlie's number. His familiar voice was both a comfort and an irritant, at the same time. "Brodsky Bail Bonds," came the gruff voice.

"Charlie, it's Lou."

Before I could say anything else, he laid into me, as I expected he would. "Where the fuck have you been? I get you're pissed about Joe's meeting, but I haven't heard from you for a lot longer than normal. I got Snake doing double duty, and now Joe's pissed at me and won't even take my calls. You wanna tell me what the hell is wrong with you?"

"Charlie, shut up a minute and listen. I had a situation and I'm dealing with it. I can't take any jobs right now, but I need to know if anybody's been looking for me."

There was a brief pause before he responded. "Are you in some kind of trouble?"

"No exactly. I just need to resolve a problem. Don't worry, it's nothing to do with you."

"Did I ask that? I didn't ask that. The first thing you assume is that I only care about my own ass? Really?"

"Oh, for crying out loud, Charlie," I said, surprised he felt offended by the suggestion. It's not as if that wasn't his usual concern when trouble arose. "I didn't mean anything by it. I'm grateful for your help and I wanted you to know I wouldn't drop shit on your doorstep. I just need a couple more weeks to sort my shit out, and I'll be back on the job again."

"The only one asking about you is Snake. He wanted to know when you were coming back to help out. I'll get someone else to help cover for now, but you know I'd only do this for you. I'll lay off for a couple of weeks if you contact Joe and make it right with him. I don't know what went down that he's so pissed, but I need you to fix it."

I signed. I didn't have the time or inclination to call Joe Sendak, especially after he obviously had set me up for Grayson to find me. While the end result means I should really be thanking him, Joe had no way of knowing that's how it would have turned out, so in his mind, he knowingly threw me under the bus. But, honestly, it was Charlie I had to think about and knowing that relationship was important to him because of Joe's impending retirement, I knew I had to fix this. "Fine."

When I closed the phone and looked up, Grayson was done unpacking and was sitting in the passenger seat that was swiveled to face the interior of the van. He sat patiently and said noting, which at the moment, was unnerving me.

"Charlie said no one has asked about me, but I need to help him fix things with Joe Sendak. I get the feeling It has something to do with that meeting Joe helped you set up to find me."

"I'll take care of it," Grayson said with no emotion. I wanted to say something else to ease the tension, but before I could, he grabbed the cell phone and dialed a number. I was bothered about the distance between us. He must have known about my earlier phone call to Henry and was upset I didn't tell him about it. I knew he was fine with the idea that it would take me time to open up to him completely, but I'm sure he wouldn't accept deception or lies, even if they were by omission. Not in response to a direct question. As I heard him speak to Joe Sendak, I left the van. I needed some air and I had to think about the best way forward.

It was a few minutes before he exited the van and walked over to me. He smiled slightly and gently caressed my arm. "Everything is cool," he said.

"What was his issue?" I asked.

"He was nervous about the possible blowback from setting up that meeting. He heard about the incident at the diner a couple days later, and since it was the same place where he arranged our meeting, he figured one thing had to do with the other. Because you work with Charlie, he's wary of calling him. I told him Charlie didn't know anything about it, and the mess at the diner was unrelated."

"He bought it?"

"Yeah. He'll call Charlie."

"Great. Thanks. Listen, Grayson, we need to talk about something else." Time to bite the bullet.

"Okay."

"We can stick with out plan about laying bait with Dombrowski to flush out anyone else who might be looking for me, but I can't discount the possibility that Sean is alive and he has something to do with all of this. I called Henry, the one who sold us the truck. He thought Sean was alive, so I asked him to get word to him that we need to talk. I told Henry I'd check in every once in a while. If Sean agrees to talk, he'll leave me a way to reach him through Henry."

"Why didn't you tell me? Don't you trust me?" Grayson asked, looking a little hurt.

"Please understand. That time of my life was a period I'm not really proud of. I also have concerns about Sean's real identify and what he knows about me. I'm also a little concerned that what happened between him and Ian that last day had something to do with me. I guess I was hoping to stay ignorant of that. If Sean isn't dead, it may be something I have to deal with, and I wasn't sure how to bring that up with you. I would have told you, but I think I wanted confirmation that Sean was alive before we had that conversation." It sounded lame, even as the words were coming out of my mouth, but it was all I had.

Surprisingly, Grayson didn't seem upset. Instead, he looked at me with a warm expression then wrapped me in a gentle hug. He leaned in and quietly spoke. "Please don't feel like you can't tell me anything. No matter what, I won't judge. All I want is for you to feel and be safe. Don't shut me out. We can deal with Sean if and when we get more information."

"I'm sorry," I spoke into his chest, afraid to lift my head and see a disapproving expression.

"Hey," he said as he lifted my face. "I love you." He kissed me gently and we walked back hand in hand to the van.

The next week we stayed busy. We took out new gym memberships at National Fitness. Their 24-hour, nationwide franchised operations meant being able to use a gym in virtually any part of the country. In the Denver metropolitan area alone, there were 15 locations to choose from. We could move around the area and always have a place to work out and shower.

Next, we found a month-to-month house rental that we could set up for surveillance. It was a small house in an inexpensive area of the city. Since it was surrounded by other homes, we didn't want to risk a shootout, so rather than actually stay there, we set up security cameras and motion sensors to see if anyone came looking.

It turns out Grayson's cover as a security specialist was not fictional. He assessed the area and was able to design a system to maximize coverage by the cameras and motion sensors. We used most of the equipment Morgan had provided, but purchased additional cameras and wi-fi to monitor the house remotely. That was my department. I set up and designed the necessary connections to monitor all activity from our laptop.

We stocked up on supplies of food and water, and because of my design we were able to stealth camp in the city without having to hook up to outside power or water supply. The solar panels, marine batteries, portable generator and specially designed electrical system insured we had sufficient power supply. We stored multiple 7 gallon jugs of water rather than one large water tank, so refilling and cleaning would pose little inconvenience. The water filtration system insured clean drinking and cooking water. I assured Grayson we could stay off-grid for very long periods of time. We constantly moved from street parking to retail lots.

When we spoke to Dombrowski, we were careful to use information that would help us narrow down where the leak might be coming from. We provided the address of the house we rented and Dombrowski made sure to expense the cost from a discretionary fund that only a small group of people had access to. We also opened a private mail box and bank account using one of the aliases the CIA had created for me. Parsons was instructed to access operating funds from their department budget and wire money into the account. Grayson was able to convince Dombrowski not to plant anything with Jared until we were sure the other breadcrumbs we dropped didn't lead anywhere.

After two weeks, Grayson was convinced no one was coming for me. I had opened a small storage unit using the same name as the one on the bank account, then had the storage unit auto debit the monthly fees from that account. I chose a unit which location was visible on the security cameras and was able to hack into their system. We monitored and recorded all activity on all cameras both at the house and the storage place, and nothing out of the ordinary had occurred.

Since we were able to monitor from virtually anywhere in the world, we decided to take a trip away from Denver. We didn't want to go too far in case one of the traps lured someone in, but a quick getaway sounded nice. The weather was getting cooler, but still pleasant enough for hiking during the day with warm clothing, so we drove up to Estes Park.

It was a beautiful few days spent hiking during the day. We decided to spend a night at the infamous Stanley Hotel. We had a romantic dinner and an entire night of love making. It again gave me hope of some kind of normalcy in my life once all the other nonsense was over. If it was ever going to be over.

We reluctantly headed back to Denver and though we had monitored the camera recordings, we decided to review the footage again. I was beginning to worry. It seemed the leak may not have come from inside the CIA, and if that's the case, I had to seriously consider the other possibilities.

CHAPTER 37

Grayson

As we watched the footage from the security cameras that had been recorded over the last couple of days, I noticed a far away look in Tallulah's eyes. It almost seemed as if she wasn't really seeing the images in front of her. I knew she wanted the leak to be from Parsons, and while the lack of activity didn't definitively rule him out, I had a feeling there was more to learn about this situation than I had originally thought.

That was about to be confirmed when I got a call on the encrypted phone. "Yeah."

"I have an update," Dombrowski started. I put the phone on speaker and told him to continue. "I have Jack Rayburn here with me. I just got some intel you should hear."

An unfamiliar voice started speaking. "We've been working on some actionable intel about a Ukrainian group buying arms from a dealer we've been watching in Afghanistan. We were interrogating one of the Ukrainians we picked up and trying to weed out information about the deal. We were following up on a rumor regarding an upcoming sale where the plan was to take out a rival buyer to eliminate the competition for some pretty nice hardware. The Ukrainians were known to hire a group of Panamanian mercs to do their wet work on unfamiliar territory. Turns out, they stopped using these particular guys because they botched a job in the United States. Denver, Colorado, to be exact. I heard about your shootout at the OK Corral and called Dombrowski. Thing is, when we asked more about the Denver incident, we learned the Ukrainians abandoned that pursuit because they figured if there was any valuable research, it was turned over to our government and likely buried. They assume your girl wouldn't know what to do with it, because the research belonged to another scientist. They think she was just a messenger for her father, some Army Colonel, and didn't know what she had."

"You get that?" Dombrowski asked.

"How confident are you about this guy's information?" I asked. It was too much to hope that Tallulah was no longer a target.

"Pretty solid," Jack Rayburn replied. "Some of his other information – the stuff unrelated to your op – turned out to be reliable. We think it's real."

Dombrowski took the phone off speaker and spoke into the handset. "What do you want to do?" he asked.

"Nothing," I answered. "We'll monitor here for another week, but if nothing happens, we can formulate another plan."

"What the hell for?" he practically yelled. "The group that came after her is backing off."

"Because we still don't know who leaked the information, especially about the location of the meeting at the diner. I'm not taking any chances until I'm sure the threat is over, and I won't know that until I find out who fucked us."

"We can open an internal investigation when you get back here."

"No. I need more time. Just give me more time to figure this out. I can't be sure about Tallulah's safety until we know."

"Bring her back here and we can set her up with identity and a small stake to get her relocated."

I looked at Tallulah who was starting to look worried. There was no way that was happening. "Absolutely not. You have to trust me. This is important. Not just to Tallulah, but to the Agency as well. Just because nothing has happened here doesn't mean we can eliminate anyone at this point. I think we can't close the book on this until we know for sure."

Dombrowski took a long pause. "At this point, I don't suppose it would do me any good to order you to do anything. Trainor told me he thought you two are together. I don't want to know. Just check in with me regularly." And he hung up.

She looked at me with a curious expression on her face. "Did you ever find out who set up the electronic trip wire Jared triggered?" she asked.

"No. After Dombrowski and Parsons said it wasn't them, I didn't know how to go about finding out without bringing in more people. I needed someone in the Agency with serious enough skills to trace it back to the source."

"No," she said with a renewed sense of direction. "I'm thinking Sean may have something to do with this. Can we wait and see if he tries to make contact? I don't know that much about him. He said his last name was Barrett, but if he was a copy, that was surely a cover ID."

"I could talk to my FBI contacts to see if they can locate him based on the operation to take down Ian, but without knowing more about the leak, I'd be concerned about putting more information out there. I think it would be better if we wait to see if he contacts you." I didn't like it, but it was the smarter way to go. It would also buy me more time with Tallulah.

Since Ian's home base was in L.A. and would be familiar territory to Sean, we decided to head in that direction. We would monitor the house and storage unit in Denver for one more week, and absent any activity, we'd pack up and leave.

For the next week, everything seemed so normal. Yes, we lived in a van, but as it turns out, it was a growing trend. There was an entire community of people living, working and traveling in converted vans. We occasionally ran into people stealth parking at rest stops and Walmart stores.

Living in the van had the benefit of making our relationship much more intimate. There are few secrets about your personal habits that can me hidden living in cramped quarters. While we had gym memberships which allowed for daily showers and used public restrooms throughout the day, we also had a composting toilet and shower stall for emergencies. I learned she considered coffee a major food group and took it black. And though she ate healthy foods, she never met a cheeseburger she didn't like. She liked laundry mats on Wednesday and grocery stores on Thursday. She constantly worked on a computer program she was writing, and liked watching cute puppy videos on YouTube.

As much time as we spent in the van, I was sure we'd be ready to kill each other soon. Amazingly, the opposite was happening. The more time with her only served to increase her pull on me. It felt as though we hungered for each other constantly.

I used the time to monitor the security cameras, and reading through Vasiliev's research notes. Even though I couldn't make heads or tails of the scientific jargon or mathematical calculations, I focused on other notations that focused on test subjects and other areas of inquiry. I marked sections of the notes that I thought may be significant at some point and could go back to them later. It was tedious work, but it kept me busy while Tallulah did her thing.

After a week, we decided that we needed to pursue other possibilities and heading to the west coast would be the best plan. Besides, Vegas was on the way. I thought it might be fun to camp out at Lake Mead for a few days. The beauty of living out of a self-contained van was the mobility and convenience of moving from one place to another quickly. Between having solar panels, a generator and using the van's alternator, we never ran out of power. I had to be impressed by the design and build of Tallulah's van conversion. Though small, we moved around easily and could park virtually anywhere without being harassed. We stocked up on supplies and started our journey.

Our plan entailed driving toward Vegas at a leisurely pace. We would make frequent stops and find campsites and RV parks along the way. I loved when we went to campsites. We would make a fire and sit together in a folding lounge chair, usually with Tallulah between my legs, leaning back against me, while I held her and we watched the fire. Sometimes we would talk about my family or her experiences traveling with the Colonel, but mostly we just enjoyed the quiet and relaxing with each other. In my life, I had never spent so much time away from the action. There were times I missed it, but I knew there was a way to have a career and a personal life. It just may not be in the CIA.

CHAPTER 38

Tallulah

I t took longer to reach Lake Mead than we had anticipated. With all the stops at campsites, getting supplies along the way and finding the best roadside fruit and vegetable stands, this road trip was turning into an extended vacation. While we spent time working on our own projects, me with my computer programs and Grayson with reviewing research notes, we also spent a significant amount of time just hiking and enjoying quiet moments.

We found a great RV park near the edge of Lake Mead. It had great views and good amenities. We met a nice retired couple who were traveling southeast and had decided to spend a couple days at the lake. They had a larger RV and traveled with their dog, whose name they informed us was pronounced "Fido" but was spelled Phydeaux. It sounded funny until they told us they were originally from the French Quarter of New Orleans.

I knew I was putting it off, having only checked in with Henry once and being told there was no word from Sean. We were leaving tomorrow and after five wonderful days at the lake, it was time to return my focus to resolving this once and for all. I grabbed the burner phone and dialed Henry.

"Nicholas Brothers. Henry speaking."

"Hey, Henry, it's Marsha," I said, making sure to remember which alias I used.

"Marsha! Man, I'm glad you called. Sean called a week ago. He wants you to call him. He said he still has the same number. Do you have it?" Henry sounded excited.

"Well, yeah, I do. Did he say anything else?"

"He called again today and wanted to know if I got the message to you. I told him that you were going to call me and I didn't have a way to reach you. Gotta tell you, he was a little pissed about that. Any chance you can call him soon? If you don't, his head might explode."

"Uh, sure," I replied, worried about his sense of urgency.

I was sitting outside and saw Grayson walking back from the public showers. His hair was wet and he looked so relaxed. He was smiling until he saw my expression and the phone in my hand. He had barely reached me when he asked, "What's wrong?"

"I called Henry. He heard from Sean. I guess I knew deep down he was still alive, but having Henry confirm it still caught me a little off guard."

"Does Sean want to hear from you?" Grayson asked.

"Yeah. In fact, Henry said he seemed anxious for me to call. He still has the same number, which I wouldn't have thought to call. Even if he were still alive, I would have thought he'd have dumped that phone by now. I should call him."

"What's your plan?"

"I guess I just need to find out what happened that day, confirm he's a cop, see what he knows about me and how he knows it, then work my way up to figuring out if he has anything to do with our current dilemma."

Grayson laughed. "Is that all?"

"I'm scared."

As he's proven so often, Grayson would always be there for me, while allowing me to make important decisions and forge my own path. He pulled me into his arms and said, "I'm here. However you need to handle this, I'll be right beside you."

With Grayson standing next to me, I dialed the number I knew belonged to Sean. It barely rang before Sean picked up. "Marsha?"

"Hey, Sean." Suddenly, I didn't have a clue what to say. It didn't matter. Sean started speaking right away.

"I wanted to find you, but I wasn't sure where to start. I thought you might show up at the rally point, but after a day, I knew you weren't coming. Can we meet? I think we need to talk."

"Where are you?" I asked.

"L.A. Where are you?"

"On my way to L.A. We'll be in Vegas tomorrow, then driving to L.A."

"WE?" he asked, sounding angry.

"Yeah, 'we'. I'm with someone now. He and I are driving together and are stopping in Vegas tomorrow."

"Then we definitely need to talk," he said. "I can take the first flight out tomorrow and meet you there. I'll be at the Flamingo. Meet me at the bar that looks like a Jimmy Buffet song. I'll be there by noon." He hung up.

I stared at the phone. I had mixed feelings running through me. It was strange hearing his voice. After thinking he was dead, it was a strange experience to actually speak to him. I was also filled with fear. While I didn't wish him dead, if he had any information about me, it would have died with him. Now I was again faced with the unknown. I really hated that. I also couldn't figure out why it appeared so urgent to see me. Not knowing had me on edge. So much so, that I didn't realize Grayson was just standing there waiting for me to speak. I looked up from my phone at his blank expression, just patiently waiting.

"He wants to meet me tomorrow in Vegas," I said. I waited for his reaction, but he seemed to be holding out for more detail before responding, so I obliged. "He'll be at a bar in the Flamingo around noon. He's flying out from L.A."

"If we leave first thing tomorrow, we can grab breakfast on the way and be in Vegas with time to spare. Are you up for this?"

"Yes. But," I said carefully, "I want to propose something." Grayson waited patiently for me to continue. "I want to meet Sean alone."

"No."

"What do you mean 'no'? I need to get information from him, and he may not be so forthcoming in front of someone he doesn't know."

"I don't know this clown, so I'm not going to trust him. I'll stay back, but I have to keep eyes on you at all times." Grayson had that look on his face. It was a look that said, *I support you, this is not up for negotiation.*

"Please, Grayson, I need you to trust me."

"I do trust you. It's him, I have a problem with."

"I'm telling you," I implored, "Sean won't say anything if you hover and we'll be nowhere closer to finding out how the information leaked. I need to know for sure or I'll be looking over my shoulder for the rest of my life."

That did it. Grayson had a look of utter frustration. "I'll hang back, but I'm sitting in the bar. I need you to promise me you won't leave my sight. If he tries to move the meeting after you get there, I'm stepping in."

"Okay."

Neither of us managed much sleep that night. We were both restless and unable to silence our thoughts about what would happen the next day.

In the morning, we left Lake Mead and, after stopping for a quick breakfast, drove straight through to Las Vegas. When we arrived, we found an RV park with good amenities, access to main roads, near the strip and close to our gym. After checking in and securing the van, we took a cab to the Flamingo. We had about 45 minutes before Sean was set to show up, so we spent that time casing the hotel, studying the hotel map, making sure to identify all possible exits, and getting the layout of the restaurant/bar. I found a table in a quiet part of the restaurant that had the added benefit of being within Grayson's line of site from his seat at the bar.

I kept a cell phone on me which promptly began to ring the minute I sat down.

"Hello?"

"Will you agree to leave the phone line open so I can monitor the conversation?" Grayson asked.

"Uh, no."

"Why not?" Grayson asked. He acted truly perplexed by my refusal, but I knew better. He knew there was no way I would allow that, yet he was concerned enough about this meeting to ask.

"Because Sean's not an idiot. Twenty bucks says he makes you two minutes after walking in. He may not walk out even knowing you're there, but he'll be cautious." Even from across the room, I could see Grayson's irritated expression. He hung up the phone and took a sip of his beer.

I ordered a cherry coke and waited patiently. It wasn't long before I saw a man approaching my table. At first, I didn't recognize him. Then I saw his eyes and immediately knew it was Sean, only this was a different Sean.

The last time I saw him, he was dressed in his usual attire of jeans, a short sleeved t-shirt and gym shoes. His long, sandy blond hair was normally worn loose and fell in shaggy waves. The man approaching me was wearing a charcoal gray pinstripe suit and polished black dress shoes. His hair was still long but pulled back in a tight ponytail. His emerald green eyes were trained on mine with laser focus. When he reached the table, I waited for his greeting, but nothing came. He simply stood there and stared.

"Well, you clean up nice," I said, trying to start the mood off light.

"And you look beautiful, as always." He pulled out a chair and sat. He stared for a moment longer before shaking his head slightly, as if to clear his thoughts. "The asshole at the end of the bar – he yours?"

"Why are you wearing a suit?" I asked.

"So, it's going to be like that." Sean looked over his shoulder at Grayson who had shifted his attention elsewhere. "Look, I know we have a lot to talk about, but I'd prefer we did this somewhere less public. I checked into a room upstairs. We can talk privately up there."

"No. Things have happened since I last saw you and I have a lot of concerns, not the least of which is what your involvement is in all of it. Until I get some answers, I don't think it's wise for me to go anywhere with you?"

"You're afraid of me?"

"No," I said honestly, "just wary of your motives. We never finished the conversation in the hotel room that day and I got the feeling there was a lot left to be said, and not all of it good."

"Fair enough. You want to start?"

I took a deep breath. "Are you a cop?"

"ATF."

"Are you investigating me?" Best to start with the tough questions.

"No. That investigation ended when Ian's body hit the ground. My reports included reference to his girlfriend named Marsha Bradley, who was in Ian's life, but unaware of his dealings. I played down your involvement and since we both know that name is an alias, no one gave you a second thought. As far as the task force is concerned, you were just a bimbo he fucked between deals."

"Thanks."

"I didn't say that's what you were. I'm saying that's what I told the task force."

"What's the task force?"

He paused for the moment before explaining. "A few years ago, there was a significant increase in illegal arm sales. A lot of movement of these arms were being negotiated by a couple of pretty big fish in the game. Ian was one of them. The CIA had intelligence about Ian's operation from a source overseas, so a task force was formed with FBI, DEA, and ATF."

"If this was about arms sales, why DEA?"

"The dealer in New York didn't limit his sales to arms. He moved drugs and women, too. In any event, I was asked to join the task force. I already had an in with some of his lower level guys and was able to work my way up inside. By the time Ian brought me into his circle, you were already with him. But I think this conversation has gotten way ahead of itself."

I was confused by that. "What do you mean?"

"I think introductions should come first, don't you think? Hi. My name is Sean. Sean Mason."

"Sean is your real first name?"

"Yes," he said extending his hand, "nice to meet you. And you are?"

I hesitated. He called me Tallulah the last time I saw him. Now was the time for a show of good faith. I took his hand across the table. "Tallulah Westfield. Nice to meet you, too."

"Yeah. If you were wondering, I already knew that," he said with a smug look on his face.

"How?"

"There's something I should tell you. I wasn't going to, but I think it's time we trust each other. The information I'm about to give you is classified. I could get into serious trouble, but I don't want there to be any secrets between us going forward."

This is one of the many things I was afraid of. He seemed to think we would have some kind of relationship beyond this meeting. As much as I wanted to quash that assumption, I didn't want to do it at a time or in a way that would alienate Sean before I learned more. Given my history with secrets, this was going to be a hard needle to thread.

I wanted patiently for Sean to continue as I thought about the situation. He looked as if he was waiting for me to say something, but gave up and started to explain.

"The head of the task force was an Assistant Director at the FBI that I was pretty well acquainted with named Thomas Cunningham. He was the one that recommended me for the task force. A few agents that worked together on various cases sometimes got together for drinks and Cunningham liked to tell stories that made him seem important. He once told a story of how he had to intervene in an accident investigation because one of the cops was floating some conspiracy theory involving the victim, a military man named Colonel Marshall Westfield.

"The story included rumors about the Colonel raising an adopted daughter who had an IQ in the stratosphere, but was trained in military basics, including weapons, explosives and hand-to-hand. She was supposedly some Rambo incarnate that looked like a Victoria Secret model. The rumor was she dropped out of sight after the Colonel died. I didn't think twice about the story until that incident went down in Oregon. You remember the deal?"

"Yeah. I remember." It was a buy that had a few complications. Even though it ultimately ended well, there were a few tense moments during the exchange. It was one of the few time I went along on a buy and only because the arrangements to hire extra men in Portland fell through and Ian wanted more than the usual number of guns in elevated positions watching over the meet. The location was a logistical nightmare and we ended up having to move around quite a bit during the whole ordeal.

"You started on top of the storage warehouse," Sean continued. "I watched in awe the way you moved from one position to another. You used hand signals to communicate with the other guys, as if you'd been trained in the military. I watched the way you handled your weapon and managed the situation with a practiced ease like it was no big deal. No one is that cool under pressure like that. I never did buy that story you told Ian about how you were so scared and nervous that you might shoot yourself in the foot.

"I had my handler run your alias and, surprise, nothing came up. Marsha Bradley didn't exist before 2015. On a hunch, I looked into Tallulah Westfield, but the odd thing is, while the ID was real, I couldn't find any pictures. Except an old passport photo taken when you were nine. The eyes in the photo. That's what gave you away. When I tried to pull up the photo again later, the file was sealed.

"A couple weeks ago, Cunningham was arrested and indicted on a number of charges, but the long and short of it was, he was the inside man for quite a few criminal heavy hitters. He had a significant balance in several offshore bank accounts. It's still an ongoing investigation which is why it's classified. We're finding more of the people he was connected to and the resources he manipulated. It's why I was pulled from my last assignment and sent back to L.A."

While this was helpful information, I thought we were getting off track. Still, I had one burning question I wanted the answer to. "Why did Ian try to stab you?" I asked.

"You saw that?" Sean seemed surprised. "I thought you took off when the first shots were fired."

"I saw you guys go behind the shipping containers and thought you might still need cover to get away, so I stayed. But then I saw Ian pull a knife. Next thing I know, there's gunfire and the two of you of you go down. That's when I ran. When the news reported four suspects dead, I assumed you were one of them."

"Ian caught me in the arm. I hit the deck when one of the shots ricocheted off the container I was standing next to and I just stayed down. The fourth guy was Mick." Mick was another one of Ian's guys but wasn't suppose to be at the meeting that day.

"Where was Mick?"

"Hiding. He came out after Ian went down. Apparently, his instructions were that if Ian failed to kill me, Mick was to finish the job. FBI sniper took him out."

"So why did Ian try to kill you?" *This ought to be good.*

"He thought something was going on between you and me. He asked me if I fucked you in the hotel room. He tried to stab me when I told him I didn't fuck you, but I was in love with you."

Wow. Didn't see that one coming. "Why did you say that?"

He looked at me questioningly, almost as if to imply I should know the answer. "Because I did. I do."

Double Wow. REALLY didn't see that one coming. "Sean. I can't – you don't – it's not." I didn't know where to go with this.

"Look, Marsh-" he stopped for a beat. "Can I call you Tallulah?"

"Actually, friends call me 'Lou'."

"Lou. I know you're with the asshole sitting at the bar and my guess is his eyes are burning holes in my back right now. But I know you weren't in love with Ian. I don't care about whatever you've been doing since Ian died. I think we'd be good together and I've waited a long time to tell you that. I felt it then and I know it now. If we were able to finish our conversation that day, I would have been completely honest with you. I know if you give me a chance, you'd see how good things can be between us. I just want that chance."

Now was the time to put a stop to this. Information or not, I couldn't let this continue. It would be falsely giving him hope for something that would never happen. "There's a lot that's been going on, and I know you say you don't care, but I've been running around for the last couple of months with a bullseye on my back. Somebody has been taking shots at me. I've been dodging bullets – figuratively and literally."

"So, it's true. I heard about a shootout at a restaurant in Denver. Your name was mentioned in the same sentence with Homeland Security. Were you involved?"

"Yes, but that threat is mostly over. It had to do with information the Colonel had left for me to find before he died. I turned it over and I'm told those that were after me are no longer interested since I don't have the intel. My ongoing problem is that the location of that meeting was somehow leaked to the ones who tried to take me out. I may be safe for now, but I have to know how the information got out to be absolutely sure there no longer is a threat."

Sean looked guilty for the first time since sitting down. "That would be me."

I felt like I just got smacked across the face. "COME AGAIN?" I realized my voice had gone up an octave and ten decibels. Grayson started to rise to head in my direction, but a subtle shake of my head told him to stand down for now. He reluctantly complied, and I lowered my voice. "Explain."

"After Ian died, I got sent to a new assignment in New York using the same cover to infiltrate a rival arms dealer's organization. I had to move fast to maintain the story that I was looking for a new boss after Ian died. It didn't leave me any time to try and find you. I called my friend Danny in the FBI Cyber Crimes Division. He reran his search on your name and alias and came up empty. I told him to keep watch and if he ever did find any information to tag it with an-"

"Electronic trip wire," I finished for him. *Shit.*

"Yeah. With my new assignment, I knew I wouldn't be able to get to you, but I wanted to make sure no one else was looking. Unfortunately, by the time Danny set it up and put it in place, I was back in deep cover in New York. Then someone tripped the wire. He tried to cover his tracks and even made an attempt to back trace the trigger, but Danny was able to discover he was CIA. Danny couldn't reach me, so he pulled all the alerts and left word with Cunningham. It wasn't until after Cunningham was arrested that we learned he fed your name to some Ukrainian mobster who had put out word that you may have information he wanted."

"Are you fucking kidding me right now?" I couldn't believe this.

"I wish I were. Anyway, I learned all of this after I got back from New York and found out about Cunningham's arrest. I started looking for you. Danny told me the information Cunningham passed on to the Ukrainians included confirmation that the CIA was also looking, too. I heard some bureaucrat named Parsons had inside information about you, so that's how it tracked to you. As far as I know, since the fiasco in Denver, no one is looking for you anymore."

"I appreciate your honesty and telling me things that could get you into trouble. The sense of relief is a little overwhelming right now. But the truth is, for all that you've done for me, I can't be with you. You were right that I wasn't in love with Ian. But I am in love now. He's the one I want to be with."

Sean's expression morphed into anger. "Does he know who you are?"

"Of course."

"No. I mean REALLY know, and I'm not referring to Tallulah Westfield."

Panic suddenly set in. "What are you talking about?"

He pinned me with an intense gaze. "You know exactly what I'm talking about. I started to tell you about it that day in the hotel. I can't prove it, but you know I know. Question is, does he?"

"I don't know what you're talking about."

Despite my adamant denial, Sean decided to put all his cards on the table. He laid out everything he believed he knew about my true identity and how he reached those conclusions. With each passing minute and each spoken word, my heart sunk further and further. He was right that there was no proof to what he was claiming to know, but in truth, he connected the dots pretty well.

"I don't care about your past or your secrets. I just want you," he said. "No one else needs to know and if we're together I would never betray that."

"Are you threatening me? Implying that if we aren't together, your betrayal is on the table?" I could hear my voice getting tighter.

"Don't put words in my mouth. But if your man loves you, it shouldn't matter, right? You should consider whether your feelings are real if you're still keeping secrets."

"Setting aside the fact that my personal life is none of your fucking business, you can't prove anything."

"I don't have to prove it. He just needs to know the story for doubt to fester. I just want you to see that real love means we don't have to hide who we are."

I had reached my limit. As much as I liked Sean when he worked for Ian, the man in front of me now was different. He was determined to have what he wanted. But so was I. And the man I wanted was currently sitting at the bar, looking like he was about to leap out of his seat and run across the room.

"Sean, I appreciate everything you did for me. The information you've given me was provided at great risk to you and your career, so don't think I'm not grateful. I truly am."

"Whose issuing threats now?"

"That's not a threat. You think you know something based on a hunch. You have no proof. If lording questionable information over me is the only way to win my affection, do you really want it? That guy at the bar? He loves me. You're free to think he's an asshole, but I love him. Please let it go. We both know what happened and why and it's time to move on. Please."

CHAPTER 39

Grayson

I t was killing me. Just killing me. Watching the interaction between Tallulah and Sean was harder than I thought. Her changes in expression as the conversation went on felt like torture. She went from small smiles to confusion to anger and back.

It finally reached a point where I thought I couldn't take it any longer. She had already waved me off once, and I almost didn't adhere to her wishes. But just as I was about to chuck her plan, march over there and carry her out, if necessary, she stood from the table. She walked around to Sean, bent down and planted a kiss on his cheek. She straightened and walked out of the bar.

I dropped some cash on the bar and followed her out. I was tempted to turn and see if he was watching her leave, but I wasn't sure I could refrain from starting a fight if I didn't like the way he looked at her, so I chose not to glance in his direction. I knew he had clocked my presence the minute he walked in, so I had no concern about leaving with Tallulah. He seemed unconcerned about my presence at the bar and chose to speak with her despite it.

I saw Tallulah heading from the main entrance to the hotel and caught up with her just as she reached the outside air. I took her hand in mine and we walked silently down the strip. After a few minutes, I hailed a cab and we headed back to the RV park. In total silence. I knew that no matter what was said, she needed time to process it all before conveying it to me. At least I hoped she planned to convey it to me. I had exercised all the patience and understanding I was capable of, but that well was not bottomless and was on the verge of being completely exhausted.

When we got back in the van, rather than open it up, she stood outside and leaned against the door. In the time we had spent together, especially in such closed quarters, I had come to read her very well. I knew when she was tired, sad, happy, excited, anxious and a host of other emotions we had experienced together. Her expression today left me wondering. I couldn't get a read on her feelings at this moment and that worried me.

After what felt like an eternity, she looked into my eyes. "I think we're in the clear," she said. There was a small casino next to the park and Tallulah led me there. The bar in the center of the casino floor was not very crowded, but the distraction of the slot machines and other gambling activity would drown out any attempts to hear our conversation. We ordered two beers after which, she gave me the rundown of her conversation with Sean. She didn't seem as relieved as I would think she'd be, given the revelation that no one else would come looking for her.

"What are you not telling me?" I asked, knowing there was more to this story.

"Sean wanted me to give him a chance to be with him. He said he was in love with me and that is why Ian tried to kill him."

"What did you tell him?"

She looked in my eyes and smiled. "I told him it wouldn't happen because I'm in love with you."

"Good. What now?"

"He's going back to LA, I think. I know you have to report to Dombrowski, but I have to ask you to do something for me."

"Anything."

"I don't want to tell anyone about my connection to Ian and Sean. No one knows about it and I want to keep it that way."

"If I tell Dombrowski we couldn't find the source of the leak and we've given up the search, he'll probably leave it alone. He might still open an investigation, but without the information that connects everything, he won't find anything. I'm okay with leaving it like that." I know how conflicted she was about that time in her life, and I didn't want to cause her any more grief about the decisions she made at a time she was scared and alone. If those choices were wrong, she'd struggle to live with them, but that was for her to work out and me to support. Everyone else be damned.

With all that out in the open and my sense that we had achieved closure, she still seemed unsatisfied with the result, as if there was still a nagging issue that had yet to be resolved.

As much as I didn't want to, I had to ask. "Is there anything else?"

"Can we leave it for later? I was hoping we could play tourist for a while. I'd like to do some gambling and see a couple of shows. I've never seen any big Las Vegas productions before. I heard some of them are really good and before we leave, I'd really love to catch one."

Something was definitely bothering her. She was almost desperate to change the subject and distract me from pushing the issue. I knew her meeting with Sean shook her a bit and perhaps, this was her way of regaining her equilibrium through distraction. All things considered, I was being patient, understanding and maybe even a little overly indulgent, but that streak would end soon, if I wasn't satisfied all issues were resolved. Nonetheless, I'd grant her this time to process everything and decompress from the events and revelations of the last few weeks.

"Sure," I said. "How about we take a room at the hotel next door. We can spend the rest of the day indulging in each other and room service, and I'll have the concierge find us tickets to a good show. What to you say?"

She smiled. That big smile that causes grown men to blush.

We grabbed a few things from the van, did checks on the equipment and supplies, then headed to the hotel. Once in the room, I called Dombrowski and informed him that we were abandoning our search and heading back to Washington in a week. He was not happy about the delay in getting back, but he had bigger fish to fry and let me know he'd be dealing with me when I got back.

For the next five days, we became the typical tourists. Aside from daily checks on the van, we spent that time wandering around, participating in all the hotel gimmicks, swimming in the pool and of course, gambling. At the end, we were up about forty-five hundred dollars, largely due to a lucky run at the craps table. We took all our meals at hotel buffets and room service. We worked off those calories with daily visits to the gym and nightly visits to heaven. The one place I knew there were no secrets between us lived in the moments when we held each other. Even on nights when the sex between us came hard, fast and raw, it was still the manifestation of a kind of love I hadn't known until we met.

Tallulah seemed to really be enjoying that time, but there always seemed to be an underlying worry in her eyes. She tried heard to mask it, and seemed especially grateful when our time was spent in dark theaters watching some crazy Cirque de Soleil show. After a week of indulgence, the time had come. We had just arrived back at our room. I was armed with a plan for raising the issue about what else was unresolved with Sean. I exited the bathroom to find Tallulah sitting on the bed with her head down. *Uh oh.*

"There is something else I need to tell you, but I can't seem to get it out," Tallulah said quietly. "I don't think it matters now, but I know I should let my secrets go, no matter what you do."

I needed to reassure her. "If you're afraid to tell me because you think I won't love you, you're wrong. Nothing you tell me will change the way I feel." She had to know that. She had a dozen aliases, traveled with arms dealers, utilized the services of wheelmen, gang bangers and money launderers. To say nothing of the fact that she killed two men, albeit in self-defense, and practically right in front of me. How could anything else change my feelings when I loved her in spite of all that? Then it hit me.

"Don't tell me. Not yet."

"What?" She looked at me as if I had lost my mind. Maybe I had.

"I'm all in. I love you and I'm willing to bet big. Let's just roll the dice. After that, we can lay all the cards on the table."

"I know we're in Vegas, but what's with all the gambling metaphors and what the hell are you saying?"

"Marry me," I blurted. After the words left my mouth, I waited for the panic to set in. Nothing. Just an overwhelming feeling of happiness. Yes. This was the answer. I would have asked her eventually, anyway, so why not now. Prove to her that no secret could tear us apart by making that commitment to her before she told me everything, knowing there was more to come.

"You're insane."

"Well, okay. Not the answer I was looking for. Perhaps I didn't do it right. I'm inexperienced in the art of romance. Let's try this again." I got down on one knee in front of her and took her hands in mine. "I love you. No matter what our future holds, we're going to face it together. Whatever secrets are yet to be revealed, it doesn't matter. I will always love you. Will you marry me?"

"Yes." And there was that smile.

CHAPTER 40

Tallulah

I woke up feeling a little warm. I realized it was because Grayson had wrapped himself around me, legs and arms tangled up and intermixed with sheets and pillows strewn about. Last night had been incredible. After accepting his marriage proposal, not another word was said. There was no need. Our connection felt so strong, words were superfluous.

Just as I tried to untangle myself from Grayson's hold, his eyes opened and he smiled. With a quick peck on the cheek, he got up and headed to the bathroom. I laid back and stared at the ceiling. I was getting married today. I still couldn't believe it, but as long as it was happening, I was going to hang on with both hands. The man I love wants to marry me and I plan to embrace his love and our life together.

Yes, there was more I had to tell Grayson, but I made a promise to myself that as soon as the wedding was over, I would tell him everything. He was taking a leap of faith by asking to marry me before I gave him the last of my secrets. I owed it to him to take the same leap of faith and trust that he could accept anything I told him, as long as it was the truth. That faith would hold us together.

After we showered and dressed, we sat down for a leisurely breakfast in the hotel. We agreed to check on the van, then go our separate ways to prepare for our wedding.

"Where are you headed first?" he asked.

"I need to find a dress and shoes. I should probably also get my hair trimmed. What about you?"

"I think I'll buy a new suit," he said looking down at his casual attire. "I saw a barber shop a few blocks over, so I was planning on getting a shave and a haircut. Why don't we plan on meeting back at the room at 2:00? That gives us a few hours. I called a chapel that can handle everything, and they have an opening at 3:00. How's that sound?"

"Great." He was smiling and holding my hand across the table. As happy as I was, there was still a dark cloud hanging over us. I decided to address the elephant in the room. "I want you to know that as soon as the ceremony is over, we'll talk and I'll tell you everything."

"As long as I know you'll trust me with your secrets, it doesn't matter when you tell me."

I couldn't help but be amazed and not just a little bit grateful that I had found the one man that I could trust in this way. I vowed that before we started our life together, there would be no more secrets between us. Then something else occurred to me.

"What about your family?" I asked. "Won't they be upset that you got married without telling them?"

"Actually, I was hoping you'd consider stopping in Indiana to meet them. I'll call ahead and warn them. But honestly, I think they'd be happy to know I had a girlfriend, to say nothing of the celebration that awaits when they found out I married her."

"Besides," Grayson continued, "they already had the big, fancy weddings for my two older sisters. The whole ordeal in both cases left everyone stressed, tired and poor. I think they'll be relieved that we eloped."

I wasn't sure that was true, but it made me feel better that he didn't think his family would hate me for our impulsive decision to take the plunge without them present.

We parted ways at the front of the hotel. Grayson started off on foot, and I grabbed a cab. The concierge had given me the name of popular dress shop and made an appointment at the hotel salon for 12:30.

It took a while to find the right dress. I knew I didn't want a traditional wedding dress and I said as much to Grayson. All that fancy shmancy stuff just didn't appeal to me. Instead I settled for a silk dress in beige with matching pumps. The only pair of red lace underthings I owned was a big hit with Grayson, so I decided to get a new set of matching panties and bra in white lace.

When I arrived back at the hotel, I dropped my purchases off in the room and left a note for Grayson on top the pile that simply read "Don't Peek!". I took a quick shower and ran downstairs. At the hotel salon, they trimmed my hair, washed, blow dried and used a curling iron to put in a few soft waves. I had also purchased a gold barrett for my hair that they used to pull it back. I didn't really wear makeup, but a young girl at the salon, told me she could apply just a little in a very subtle way, just to enhance my features. She masterfully did exactly what I had asked and I was back in our room right on time.

I walked in just as Grayson was zipping up his pants. The matching suit jacket in charcoal gray lay on the bed and his shirt collar was still open. He looked incredible.

"Don't move," I said. "And don't say anything until I get dressed. I want to look nice for you."

"You are already beauti-"

"-No. Don't. Wait until I'm ready."

Grayson laughed. "I have to go downstairs and confirm some arrangements anyway. Can you be ready in 15 minutes?"

"Yes."

Grayson slipped on his shoes, grabbed his tie and jacket, stuffed things in various pockets and left the room without another word. As soon as the door shut I started running around like a mad woman. Despite my nerves and worry, I managed to get dressed with a minute to spare. When Grayson walked in the room, I was ready and standing by the bed, hoping beyond hope that he wouldn't be disappointed. In the back of my mind, I had seen pictures and movies where the bride looked like a princess. I never aspired to be that, but I thought some men might expect their bride to look that way on their wedding day.

"Holy Fuck!"

Okay, that reaction could go either way.

Grayson stood in the room and stared at me. It was about to get uncomfortable when he finally spoke again. "You look stunning." He walked toward me and, for the second time, knelt in front of me. He pulled out a box from his pocket, opened it and held it up to me. A beautiful solitaire diamond on simple white gold band glistened from inside. "Will you marry me?" he asked.

"Yes. But didn't we do this part already?" I asked, a little confused.

He removed the ring from the box and slipped it on the ring finger of my left hand. "I didn't do it right," he explained. "I forgot the ring. Maggie told me I could have blown it because I didn't propose with a ring."

"You called Maggie?"

"Yup. I had to tell her. She's a little pissed she wasn't invited, but since no one else was either, she calmed down. I just need to let her know when we plan to be in Indiana because she promised to make the trip, too."

He stood up and removed another box and opened it. "I hope you don't mind," he said as he showed me the contents. "I figured we needed wedding rings, so I got a matching pair of plain bands that matched your engagement ring."

The rings were plain but beautiful. "I'm glad you thought of it. I honestly didn't even think about rings."

Grayson took my hands and looked deeply into my eyes for a long moment. "I love you."

"I love you, too."

"One more thing," he said. "I got you a small wedding present. I want you to have it before we go." He grabbed a box on the bed I had not noticed until now. It was a simple white box with a blue bow on it. I opened the box and had to check my emotions lest I burst into tears. Lying there in white tissue paper was a salt and pepper shaker set. They were a beautiful set in silver. That he understood the symbolism and what it meant to me touched me deeply. I wrapped my arms around him. "Thank you."

"You're welcome." He reluctantly released me then gestured toward the front door. "Shall we?"

At the chapel, Grayson took care of everything. It took a while to go through all the paperwork and I wasn't sure what the deluxe package included, but Grayson insisted we have it. While the couple in front of us had ten or twelve guests in attendance, when we entered for our ceremony, the room was empty. Except for the minister and his lovely wife in the purple muumuu, no one else was there. I was sad and relieved at the same time. I didn't like being the center of attention, but somehow the empty room only served as a reminder of how solitary a life I had lived and that all these changes in my life would be quite an adjustment.

As we stood before the minister and listened to his speech about love, commitment and fidelity, a thousand other thoughts were racing through my head. When I looked over at Grayson, I felt a little calmer, but not much. I knew everything was changing, but I decided to welcome the change.

At the moment of our vows, I turned and handed my bouquet of flowers to the minister's wife then held Grayson's hands. The look of love in his eyes was so intense, I barely heard the words the minister asked Grayson to repeat. It wasn't until he began to speak, that I took notice of the richness in his voice and the command and promise with which he was making his vow.

"I, Grayson Daniels, take you, Tallulah Jane Westfield-"

A familiar voice rang out from the back of the chapel and interrupted the moment.

"That bitch in front of you may be who you agree to take, buddy, but that sure as hell *ain't* who you're getting."

I knew it was Sean without turning to look, but I couldn't bring myself to acknowledge it. I finally lost the battle with all the emotion I was trying to hold in that day. Something that almost never happens happened. I started to cry. Unable to process, all I could mutter was "I'm so sorry."

CHAPTER 41

Grayson

"What the fuck is happening right now?" I asked as calmly as I could manage.

I didn't have to confirm it with Tallulah to know that the interruption came from Sean. The man she met with in the restaurant was wearing a suit, his long blond hair pulled back. While I hadn't gotten a good look at his face then or now, I new it was him. The guy who just turned and left the chapel had long shaggy hair, tats on his arms and dressed more like he was headed for a Grateful Dead concert than a corporate office. I saw enough in his features, size and movement to know it was Sean. Now the question was why.

Before I could lose my shit, the minister stepped aside and took his wife by the arm. "You obviously need a moment. We'll be waiting in the reception area. Our next appointment is in 10 minutes, so if you want to continue the ceremony, you should let us know right away." With that, they exited the room.

I stood there trying to decipher what Sean's comment meant. He must have known I knew Tallulah's identity and that "Marsha" was just one of her aliases. I know she had something else to reveal, but what unnerved me was the possibility that Sean knew about it before I did.

I looked at Tallulah's face and my heart dropped to my stomach. What had started as a single tear leaving a wet path down her cheek had turned into a torrential flood. I grabbed a box of Kleenex sitting in the first row of pews and held it out for her. She grabbed a few and started wiping her face.

"We should leave," she said through her sniffles.

"We'll go back to the hotel and talk. Just tell me one thing. What does Sean know that I don't?"

There was a long pause before she spoke. "My name."

"I don't understand," I said completely baffled.

"My name is Tatiana Vasiliev. The scientist, Pavel Vasiliev, was my father."

I don't remember exactly how we got back to the hotel or up to our room. I just remember that the trip was silent, each lost in our own thoughts, with our wedding rings burning a hole in my pocket. I was having a hard time wrapping my brain around this revelation. How was it possible and who else knew? I had promised to love and protect her no matter her secret. Only now, I felt torn. Loving her would never change for me, but my ability to look past this may have. I couldn't understand how she would tell Sean this information, but be so reluctant to confide in me. That was the question that needed to be addressed.

We stayed locked in our room for the next 12 hours. At the end of it, I knew what I needed to, but I was left with a decision. Did anything between us change? She was emotionally drained and physically exhausted. I held her in my arms and when we woke a few hours later, I knew I still loved her, but this difficult journey was far from over. There were still things that needed to be done to protect her. Whether we ended up together at the end of it would remain to be seen. For now, we had work to do.

*** To be continued in Book 2: The Secrets We Reveal. ****

Please visit my website to subscribe to the mailing list that will give you updates on release of Book 2 and other upcoming titles.

https://lipsky-ent.com/joni